The Social Code

Sadie Hayes

 St. Martin's Griffin ☙ New York

THE SOCIAL CODE. Copyright © 2013 by Palindrome, LLC. All rights reserved. Printed in the United States of America. For information, address St. Martin's Press, 175 Fifth Avenue, New York, N.Y. 10010.

www.stmartins.com

Design by Anna Gorovoy

Library of Congress Cataloging-in-Publication Data

Hayes, Sadie.
   The social code / Sadie Hayes.
      p. cm.
   ISBN 978-1-250-03565-3 (trade paperback)
   ISBN 978-1-250-03564-6 (e-book)
 1. Universities and colleges—Fiction.   2. New business enterprises—Fiction.
3. Brothers and sisters—Fiction.   4. Twins—Fiction.   5. Social classes—Fiction.
6. Orphans—Fiction.   I. Title.
   PZ7.H3148727Nex 2013
   [Fic]—dc23

                                                        2013018115

St. Martin's Griffin books may be purchased for educational, business, or promotional use. For information on bulk purchases, please contact Macmillan Corporate and Premium Sales Department at 1-800-221-7945, extension 5442, or write specialmarkets@macmillan.com.

A different version of this book was originally published as a serialized e-book under the title *The Start-Up* in winter 2011–2012.

First Edition: September 2013

10 9 8 7 6 5 4 3 2 1

This book is dedicated to:

Ron Conway, John Doerr, Heidi Roizen, Roger McNamee, Guy Kawasaki, Mary Meeker, Jack Dorsey, Tina Seelig, Tim Draper, Michael Dearing, Bill Gurley, and Brendan Fitzgerald Wallace.

Thanks to all for being an inspiration. And, thanks especially for having a combined four million Twitter followers. #SocialCode @DigitalSadie

Acknowledgments

Writers write because they know something about words, but in this case there aren't enough to properly thank Dan Kessler and Panio Gianopoulos for their vision and their trust: Santa Monica brainstorms will be memories I forever cherish, and ones I imagine I'll one day categorize as pivotal. Thank you to Carey Albertine for her support, her energy, and her endless supply of practical wisdom. The admiration I feel for you three and the charge you're leading is beyond measure. And of course, a special thanks to Jennifer Weis and the St. Martin's Press team, and to our evangelist Susie Finesman for bringing it all together.

The last thing Adam and Amelia Dory expected was to become the richest family in the world. Having come from nothing, the eighteen-year-old twins were happy just to have a chance to escape the legacy of foster homes and small-town drift. Now here they were, attending Stanford University on scholarships, with bright, happy futures ahead of them.

It was the kind of thing you heard at graduation ceremonies, all heartfelt and misty-eyed, while a marching band played "Pomp and Circumstance." What you didn't hear about, though, were all the details that came with it: the envy, betrayal, theft, broken laws, backstabbing, misdirection, and seduction. This was Silicon Valley, a place where unbelievable fortunes were made—money that put Wall Street and Hollywood to shame— and for every twenty-two-year-old billionaire parking his Porsche in front of his mansion, there were hundreds of people scheming how to take it away from him.

Starting out back then, Adam and Amelia knew none of this.

If you were to ask them, years later, if they still would have gone through with it, you might have gotten a surprising answer. That is, if you could find them. . . .

Part I

1

The Prisoner's Dilemma, v. 2.0

If Amelia Dory had come to class, none of this would have happened.

But instead, Amelia had spent the night at the Gates computer lab writing code, noticing that it was morning only when the sun began to rise. By the time her twin brother Adam's alarm went off at 9:38 A.M. (the exact optimal time to brush-teeth-grab-bagel-and-make-it-to-class), he had a text message from her time-stamped 7:14 A.M. saying that she was skipping PoliSci to sleep after another "accidental all-nighter." After first feeling frustrated, Adam turned his sister's absence into a positive: Rather than sitting in the front row with Amelia to make sure she paid attention, Adam entered the lecture hall and took a seat in the back row, where he could check out the girls in the class.

If Amelia had come to class, Adam wouldn't have sat in the back row; he wouldn't have been noticed by the professor or embarrassed by those girls; he wouldn't have replied to that text message; he wouldn't have gone to that party; he and Amelia wouldn't have gotten into trouble; they wouldn't have started the company; and the company wouldn't have made them household names, because the company never would have been.

But, as it was, Amelia *didn't* come to class.

Political Science wasn't hard for Adam. He'd never been out of the country, so the international part was a little hard to grasp, but the idea that everyone wanted more power and that this often caused conflict was particularly familiar.

A cute brunette in a short plaid skirt took a seat in front of Adam. He'd never seen her before, but she was just right in that hot-but-not-too-hot-to-talk-to-him kind of way. He took a deep breath and was leaning forward to say something when she stood up and waved to . . . Patty Hawkins. Fuck. Abort mission.

Patty Hawkins was Amelia's wealthy and preppy roommate. Adam wasn't sure if Patty knew who he was, but he was certain that any girl who was saving her a seat in class was not the kind of girl who would give him a moment's notice.

Professor Marsh, a legendary professor who was rumored to have once been a CIA spy, cleared his throat to begin the lecture. Adam slouched in his seat and settled in, peering at the cute brunette in front of him. Reading her g-chat conversation over her shoulder, he learned that last night at the Sigma Chi Derby Party the girl cheated on her boyfriend, Rob, with his best friend, Mitch. Of course, Adam didn't know any of those people.

"Mr. Dory? Mr. Dory!"

Adam looked up. One hundred pairs of his fellow students' eyes darted between him and a very angry political science professor. Why would Mitch do that to Rob? How could Rob not see them leave the party together? Was he cheating on her, too? While Adam's head was swimming with strangers' gossip, Professor Marsh continued to glare.

"Mr. Dory, I'm glad you could join us this morning. As you seem to be so riveted by today's discussion, I was wondering if you might help me out. I described the Cold War's arms race as the classic prisoner's dilemma. Do you mind explaining the concept of the prisoner's dilemma to the class?"

Adam swallowed nervously. "Well, I . . ."

"Yes?"

He took a deep breath. "The prisoner's dilemma . . . has to do with trust and cooperation. Let's say you have a boyfriend and girlfriend named . . . Ralph and Bridget. They love each other, but one night at a frat party Bridget hooks up with Ralph's best friend, Mike."

"A frat party?" Professor Marsh raised an eyebrow.

"Sure," Adam replied nervously. "Like the Sigma Chi Derby Party." The class broke out into laughter and some even applauded. Adam felt encouraged. "So, Bridget cheats on her boyfriend, Ralph, with his best friend, Mike. The next day, they are both scared out of their minds of getting caught. Before they have a chance to talk to each other, they each run into Ralph. Bridget doesn't know if Mike told Ralph, and Mike doesn't know if Bridget told Ralph. If *Mike* told Ralph what happened, it'll make Bridget look like a slut. But if *Bridget* told Ralph, then it will make Mike look like a bad friend. Of course, if they *both* keep their mouths shut, then neither of them looks bad . . . but they can't trust the other one not to tell."

Professor Marsh smiled. "And why can't they trust each other?"

"Because they're both cheaters. They know what the other person is capable of. That's the point of the hookup—I mean the prisoner's dilemma. Even though the two should cooperate to win, they can't trust each other, so they both get caught."

One hundred pairs of eyes turned anxiously to Professor

Marsh, who paused before saying anything. An imposing old man with broad shoulders and a shock of white hair, his calm willingness to humiliate students made him one of the more infamous professors at Stanford. Everyone expected Adam Dory to get torn apart in front of the class, but Professor Marsh only nodded. "That's correct, Mr. Dory. A very . . . titillating example, but a very good one."

Professor Marsh held up his hand and stared at Adam for a moment before continuing. "Additionally, for your extraordinary disrespect earlier, I'd like three hundred words on what you'd rather be doing with your life than sitting in my political science class."

"Ooooohhhhh . . . burned!" a lone voice belted from the corner of the lecture hall. Everyone laughed.

Adam's satisfaction quickly gave way to embarrassment. The cute brunette turned around and shot Adam an I'm-going-to-kill-you look; he avoided eye contact with her by pulling out his iPhone, only to be greeted by an urgent text message.

"Call me ASAP. Need u to bartend party tonight in Atherton. Call me within 5 minutes or someone else gets the gig. Sheryl."

Saved by the bell, class ended and Adam bolted out of the lecture hall to avoid the brunette and call Sheryl back. Just as the phone started ringing he felt a hand grab his arm.

"What the hell is wrong with you?" Patty said. "You like reading over other people's shoulders?"

Adam froze, hoping that by not moving he would turn invisible. At the same moment, a woman's voice answered on the phone: "Hello?"

"Patty, I didn't mean to . . ." Adam stammered, not quite sure how to defend himself. He looked at his phone and held a finger to signal to Patty that he needed a minute. "Hello? This is Adam Dory. I'm calling back about the bartending gig?"

This only infuriated Patty more, and she ripped the phone from Adam's hand, slamming her manicured finger onto the screen to end the call. Adam glanced around, looking for an escape route. "Hey, that was a really important—"

"Listen," Patty interrupted. "I get that you've probably never hooked up with a girl and are seriously uncool, but what kind of game are you trying to pull? Do you think by spying on a girl's g-chat conversations you'll somehow figure out a way to get with her?" Patty was fuming.

"I was trying to . . ." Adam wanted to die. And he wanted to call Sheryl back about the party tonight before someone else got the slot.

"You should know your place, Adam Dory. My friends— Rebecca included—are way out of your league."

Adam had no idea who Rebecca was, but he knew that Patty was right. Stanford had students who were legitimate big deals. Of the seven hundred female faces in his freshman class, it was impossible to figure out which ones had cured disease, participated in the Olympics, or had fathers who ruled their respective countries. But they were around, and knowing they were his new peers made Adam feel at once important and very, very small.

"Ugh, you're such a lost cause. Such a geek. No wonder you don't have any friends." Patty tossed Adam his phone and headed back inside to console her friend. Adam took a deep breath as he noticed Patty rejoining a crying Rebecca: All things considered, that could have been worse.

Desperate to get back to Sheryl before it was too late, Adam hurried outside and sat his bag under a palm tree as he called Sheryl again.

"Hello?"

"Hi, this is Adam Dory again. I'm so sorry about that. Is the spot still open?"

"Yes, I still need someone. The guy that was supposed to be here got food poisoning and Brett from Bartend-U said you were good."

Adam felt his cheeks blush at the compliment from Brett, the trainer in the bartending class he'd taken to earn extra cash. "That's great. I had plans tonight, but I think I can move them around." By "plans" he meant dinner with Amelia at the dining hall, but he wanted Sheryl to think he was important.

"Okay, great. But listen: This is a very important client; we've got 376 guests coming. I can pay you double your usual, and tips should be good, but you've got to be in top shape."

"Yeah, sure thing," Adam said, doing his best to play it cool. "Where do I go?"

"I'll e-mail you the address. Park at the elementary school down the street."

"I don't have a car."

She paused. "Then how do you intend to get there?"

"I'll ride my bike." Adam felt his image being ruined.

"Fine. Just be here by five. And make sure no one sees you biking."

"Will do, Sheryl. See you at five."

So much for tonight's homework, Adam thought. He sent Amelia a text: *"Gotta cancel dinner 2night—just got gig in Atherton. They're paying double! Will steal fancy dessert for you. ☺"*

2

The Stanford Freshman Roommate Policy in Action

Across campus, Amelia Dory was sound asleep at the desk in her dorm room when her roommate, Patty, entered, loudly chattering on her cell phone.

"Oh my God, did you *see* her? She was so drunk and throwing herself all over Darren Landry. And I'm sorry, but that skirt was totally not the right size. I mean, if you're going to gain your freshman fifteen, at least try to hide it. *So* embarrassing. I am so, *so* glad we decided to go DG. Can you imagine if we'd had to pledge with her? Anyway, are you going to the SAE party tonight? I've got a family friend's graduation party but definitely want to stop by after. No, it should be fun. It's for T.J. Bristol. Yeah, I know. He's super hot. I think of him like a brother but could def set you up. I *know* graduation is in three weeks. I guess his dad's going to be out of town for it so they're throwing him a party early. Anyway, just a lot of Atherton families, but it will be a fun pre-party to SAE. Fab! See you tonight, love! Kisses!

"Oh my God, were you asleep?" Patty turned to see Amelia for the first time. "Oh my God, Ameel, I am so, so sorry!"

Patty Hawkins was tall and fit. She'd been a swimmer most of her life but quit her senior year of high school; she told her parents it was because she didn't want the pressure of being a college athlete, but really she'd read an article about how excessive exposure to chlorine could irreversibly destroy a woman's hair follicles. Still, she had broad shoulders and, though slim, commanded a lot of space. Her blond hair fell to the middle of her back and her tanned face was always made up with mascara and pink lip gloss.

"No, no, I needed to get up," Amelia answered groggily, trying to piece together when she'd fallen asleep last night. She looked down to see that she was still in her clothes from the day before and hazily remembered that she'd left Gates computer lab well after dawn to go to bed, but had an idea about how to fix her program on the way home and rushed to her laptop, evidently falling asleep here before she made it into her pj's. "What time is it anyway?"

"Is this what happens when I don't come home at night? I swear to God, Amelia, if it weren't for me you'd do nothing but code and sleep at your desk!" Patty teased, with a twinge of judgment.

Amelia was her roommate's antithesis. Together, they were an impeccable example of Stanford University's policy of pairing freshman roommates of different backgrounds. Where Patty's parents were trustees of the university, Amelia and her twin brother, Adam, were college kids on scholarships. While they both often stayed out all night, Patty was passed out at frat parties, while Amelia lost track of time in the computer science lab. Where Patty obsessively worked out at the campus gym to burn off her vodka-cranberry-lemonade cocktails, Amelia's exercise consisted of walking to and from class; she'd tasted a beer once.

Nevertheless, the two girls were friendly with each other. They'd accommodated each other's quirks and had never had an argument. Both knew they probably wouldn't see each other after this year, when Patty would move into the Delta Gamma sorority house and Amelia would stay in the dorms.

"Ugh. Adam'll get me through PoliSci, but I think my English professor is going to fail me," Amelia moaned, gathering her school bag and jacket and searching for her keys.

"Don't get me started on your weirdo brother. He spent PoliSci creeping on my friend. He was reading her g-chat conversations!"

"Well, I'm sure he didn't . . ." Amelia trailed off. She had a habit of defending Adam no matter what her brother's actions were, but at this moment she didn't feel like incurring the wrath of Patty Hawkins.

"Now Rob knows that Rebecca may or may not have hooked up with Mitch."

"I really think my English professor is going to fail me." Amelia wanted desperately to change the subject.

"Please, Amelia. You are, like, the smartest person at this school. You couldn't fail if you tried." Patty slipped into her silk bathrobe and shower shoes. "But, my God, Amelia, at least change clothes!"

"You're right, you're right." Amelia laughed. "Oh, I'm just so close on this one code sequence. It's completely taking over my life. Maybe I should just go to the lab and work it out so it's off my mind."

"You sound totally exhausted." Patty stood in the corner of her room, fumbling in her sock drawer. Her hand found the small orange bottle of pills that her childhood doctor still prescribed to help her stay focused in school. "Here, take one of these if you want to get your stuff done quickly." She placed the bottle on Amelia's desk. "I'm sleeping at my parents' house tonight but I'll see you tomorrow," Patty said as she left the room for the shower. "Good luck with your coding!"

Amelia changed into a clean pair of denim shorts and a plaid shirt and slipped on three-dollar rubber flip-flops from Walgreens. She was five feet six inches tall, but her slight frame made her seem much smaller, as did the fact that her shoulders sloped forward from hours in front of the computer. Her straight blond hair was always pulled into a ponytail, which unintentionally accentuated her high cheekbones. She wore plastic-framed glasses over her green eyes and occasionally slathered on ChapStick when she met with a professor.

Amelia put the bottle of pills back on Patty's side of the room. As she was leaving, she checked her cell phone and saw her brother's text message. Quickly, she typed, *"No worries . . . gonna be a long night at the computer lab. I'll stop by your room tomorrow to collect my dessert. Have fun!"*

3

Macallan, Champagne, and Two Maraschino Cherries

Adam tried to play it cool as he punched in the code to the front gate of the Bristol estate, but he could hear his heart beating in his head. The family changed the code every day for security purposes, Sheryl had told him, so there was no use trying to remember it after tonight. She'd told him the family was an "important client," which he understood as code for "rich." As the gate swung open he realized what "rich" actually meant.

The gate opened onto a circular drive that approached a sweeping three-story white mansion delicately draped with wisteria in full bloom. Two large sycamore trees provided shade over an eight-car garage. The circular drive enclosed a lawn that had been mowed to create a careful crisscrossing pattern on the grass, and a manicured rose garden lined the fence separating the house from the neighboring estate. Adam took a deep breath and, per Sheryl's instructions, headed toward the back entrance next to the garage, resisting the urge to peek inside to discover what automobiles were housed within it.

These people make serious money, Adam thought to himself.

The hour of preparation flew by as Adam filled crystal glasses with smoked almonds and blue-cheese-stuffed olives. Sheryl gave him a starched white uniform and was kind enough to help him with his bow tie.

Once he passed her inspection, she led him out the back kitchen door to his station for the evening. He audibly gasped when he saw the Bristols' backyard. It started at the edge of a rose-enclosed patio adjoining the house and held a massive white tent that glittered with thousands of white Christmas-tree lights. Twenty round tables were draped with white table-cloths and showcased elaborate flower arrangements at their centers. At each table, ten places were set with three forks, two wineglasses, and multiple porcelain plates. The tables surrounded a large wooden dance floor, where jazz music was coming from a DJ stand. A swimming pool glittered behind the DJ, and behind it sat a mini version of the white mansion, which Adam realized must be the pool house.

"You have thirty minutes to figure out how to act like this is normal." Sheryl elbowed him with a smile.

The bar was set up on the patio, stocked entirely with top-shelf liquor. Beneath the bar, hidden by a white tablecloth, were cases of additional bottles. A nearby table was stacked with shining crystal glasses, organized by type, from martini glasses to bulbous red wineglasses to delicate champagne flutes.

"You'll run out of liquor and glasses quickly. Enrique is your barback, so make sure you let him know when you're running low. Just keep pouring, and keep the drinks stiff. Fine to take tips, but put them away immediately—we don't want anyone to feel pressured."

Guests started arriving at six o'clock, and by six-thirty Adam had sent Enrique away with three cases of empty Grey Goose bottles. For all the glamour of the setting, he was struck by the casual attire of the party's attendees. There wasn't a suit in the crowd; the men were dressed mostly in dark denim or khakis, and most weren't even wearing sports coats. Far from the elaborate cocktail dresses he'd expected, the women donned sundresses or white denim and sandals. College-aged guys and girls mingled naturally with their parents, who didn't seem to mind the cocktail glasses they all had in hand.

"What type of scotch have you got back there, bud?" asked a tanned gentleman with curly white hair and a sideways grin. He leaned his elbow on the bar and popped a handful of almonds into his mouth.

"Macallan, sir."

"How old?"

"I'm sorry, sir?"

"How old is the Macallan?"

"Um, I . . ." Adam had no idea. He quickly reached for the bottle, hoping it would provide an answer. "It's, um . . ."

The gentleman took the bottle from him and looked at the label. "Ten," he said as he showed Adam where the label indicated the year. "Bristol's a cheap son of a bitch. I bet he's got a bottle of twenty-five in the kitchen for himself." He winked at Adam. "I'll take a glass anyway. Got to get through this party somehow."

"Absolutely, sir." Adam nodded and reached for a tumbler.

"Know your scotch if you're going to serve this crowd," the gentleman advised. "And your white wine. Get those two right and you'll have everyone eating out of your hand." He lifted his glass to Adam as he walked away.

Adam turned to face a tall slender girl with long blond curls twisted into a side ponytail. She was wearing a pink dress that hung delicately from her shoulders to her midthighs, revealing knockout legs accentuated by strappy gold heels. She was smiling warmly at him. "He always complains about these things, but deep down he loves them," she said.

Adam was speechless. A girl this pretty had never spoken to him before. He started to say something but couldn't find his voice. The girl stuck out her hand.

"I'm Lisa."

He shook her hand.

"Adam. Nice to meet you. Can I get you anything to drink?"

"That'd be great. How about a vodka lemonade?"

"Sure thing. Coming right up."

"So, what do you think so far?"

"I'm sorry?"

"About the party. What do you think?"

"It's incredible. I mean, the place is gorgeous. And you just know all these people must have done extraordinary things to be so . . . financially successful."

She paused and looked at him with her head tilted to the side, thinking about his comment.

"Cherry?" he asked.

"Two, please."

He dropped two maraschino cherries into her drink and handed the glass to her. She nodded and turned to walk away, just as Patty walked up to the bar.

"Oh my God. Adam Dory? Do I have to file a restraining order against you?"

"Patty, I'm sorry. I didn't mean to . . ." Adam started blushing. Just as he mustered the courage to have a conversation with the prettiest girl at the party, Patty had to show up.

"Well, bartender, have you stalked me and my friends enough to know my favorite drink?" Patty was clearly already drunk, and she smirked at Adam as she looped her arm around Lisa's shoulders. "Adam, I'd like a . . ." Patty paused, swaying a little on her heels and thinking hard before blurting out her order. "Vodka cranberry lemonade, please."

Lisa turned to Adam. "You know Patty?"

Patty butted in. "*Adam* is the twin brother of *Amelia,* my roommate."

"You're at Stanford?" Lisa turned to face Adam, a surprised expression on her face.

"Yeah, I'm a freshman."

"Oh, wow. I mean, that's great. Congratulations. I didn't realize . . ." She stopped herself, afraid she might say something rude. "I'm starting there in the fall. I'll be a freshman."

"You are?" Adam said this a bit too quickly, and he scrambled to hide his enthusiasm. "That's cool." He shrugged.

Lisa smiled. "We'll have to be friends."

Patty laughed and shook her head. "I think you two will be in very different social circles. No offense, Adam, but the only time I see you at parties is when people pay you to wait on them."

Adam felt his jaw clench. Right when Lisa was starting to acknowledge him as an equal, Patty had put him back in his place.

Lisa blushed as she turned to Adam. "Sorry, she's too drunk. Come on, Patty, let's go sit down." With a flick of her wrist, Patty downed most of her cocktail.

Adam swallowed hard and attempted a smile. "Don't worry about it. Have a great summer!"

"Thanks, Adam. I'm going to take her back before she does something to embarrass herself."

Adam watched Lisa guide Patty to the center table as the DJ got on the microphone to announce dinner. The first course was served, then the second. Waiters served wine at the tables, giving Adam a break, save the occasional request for a cocktail.

After the dinner plates were cleared, a man in his fifties

approached the DJ booth and took the microphone. He was tall and handsome and would have been imposing were it not for his charismatic smile, which Adam could sense even from the bar in the back. The man, who was apparently Mr. Bristol, asked for the crowd's attention.

"Ladies and gentlemen, I can't tell you how glad I am to have you all here tonight to celebrate the extraordinary accomplishments of my son. T.J., will you please stand up?"

From the center table where Patty and Lisa were seated, T.J., a thirty-years-younger image of his father, stood with a proud smile.

"When T.J. was a little boy, he was absolutely determined to be a professional soccer player. He followed the European teams religiously and spent hours and hours in the backyard practicing his pass. Though he didn't make it on that track, he always applies that same rigorous determination to everything he does. So I didn't have the slightest doubt about his continuing our family's legacy at Stanford when he applied four years ago. Since then—"

His ringing phone stopped him short and his face went white as he reached into his pocket and looked at the screen. "I'm so sorry," he said into the microphone as he gestured to his wife. "I've got to take this. Lori?"

Lori, Ted's striking blonde wife, hurried from her chair with a martini in hand as Mr. Bristol hurried off stage, speaking into his phone. "Well, always something exciting around here!" She giggled into the microphone as she glanced around at all the guests. "Why don't we have another song? DJ? Something special for our graduate!"

The guests started chatting again, all of them giddily wondering what Mr. Bristol's call was about. He was one of Silicon Valley's most prominent investors, so it must have been important if he was getting a call at seven o'clock on a Friday night. But Adam's eyes fell on T.J., who still stood in the middle of the floor, looking blankly at the space where his father had just been. His jaw was slack and his face pale, his striking blue eyes crisp with what, at first, Adam thought were tears, until he noticed T.J.'s jaw tighten and his eyes reengage with their surroundings in calm determination and contempt. He turned back to his table, full of good-looking peers, clapped his hands, and shouted, "Shots, guys?" There was applause from his comrades. "Waiter, twelve tequila shots, pronto!"

The waiters hustled to get dessert to the tables and the DJ turned up the music, encouraging people to start moving away from their crème brûlée and onto the dance floor. The inebriated crowd was in full swing when the DJ cut off the music and Mr. Bristol got back on the microphone, grinning from ear to ear. "Friends, can I beg you for your attention one more time. We're bringing around bubbly." Sure enough, the waiters were all passing out flutes of freshly poured champagne on silver platters. "I'd like to share some exciting news. Everyone have a glass? Ready? The London papers just published that the Aleister Corporation has officially announced their acquisition of Gibly . . . for three-point-eight billion!"

The entire room roared. A man near the bar grabbed an unopened bottle of champagne, shook it, popped the cork, and sprayed it all over the people in the crowd, who laughed delightedly.

Mr. Bristol went on. "It's the largest acquisition of its kind in history and one that will take us to new international prominence. Not to mention, between us here tonight, we've got about two of the three-point-eight billion reasons to celebrate. I couldn't be happier that you're all here for this monumental occasion. To Gibly!"

"To Gibly!" the crowd responded.

Adam couldn't believe it. People at this party—people he was serving—had just made hundreds of millions of dollars. The waiters were rushing around the dance floor, filling up champagne glasses as the partygoers toasted over and over, cheering their accomplishment. Adam searched for Patty but couldn't find her—she'd probably passed out somewhere. He scanned the crowd for Lisa and noticed her standing off to the side of the patio with T.J. The two were deep in conversation, and she was holding his hand.

Adam felt his heart race with jealousy.

How could he have been so stupid to think a girl like that would ever be interested in a guy like him? Patty was right; the only reason he'd talked to Lisa was because she needed a drink. That they would be peers at Stanford didn't mean anything. She was in a different league, a league that included rich, attractive, older guys like T.J. He quickly looked away, but not before Lisa glanced up and caught him looking at her.

To Adam's horror, Lisa walked toward him, pulling T.J. by the hand to the bar.

"Adam, can you please make T.J. a very strong Manhattan? I'm going to go find Patty and make sure she's still alive."

"Sure thing," Adam said as he reached for the whiskey. Lisa smiled at him in gratitude, but he refused to smile back as she walked off to find Patty, leaving him with his new nemesis.

"What a fucking night, huh?" T.J. said to no one in particular, his elbow perched on the bar as he looked out across the room.

"There seems to be a lot to celebrate," Adam responded coolly.

"For sure. Gibly was a huge acquisition. One of the biggest Silicon Valley's ever seen."

Despite his instinctive dislike of T.J., Adam couldn't hide his interest. "What is it?"

"What is Gibly? Have you been living under a rock? Gibly is what makes your phone almost magical. It's the most important software platform of the century. You know how you can speak into your iPhone and it'll translate it into a text message? That's Gibly software. Or how you can use the NFC chip inside your phone to pay for things now, instead of using a credit card? Gibly. Or how your phone will send you an automated update any time your favorite store is having a sale? All Gibly."

"Wow. I guess I never really thought about the software behind all those things. Your dad developed that?"

T.J. laughed. "No, fucking smart-ass software engineers developed it. Dad invested in it. He gave them a few million two years ago in exchange for half of the company so they could afford to eat while they spent twenty-four hours a day coding."

"So, he just made two billion dollars off of three million?"

"Yep. Welcome to venture capital."

"But he didn't actually do anything other than give them money?"

"Well . . ." T.J. said, straightening up, clearly offended. "He advised them. And shit, he saw their potential. If he hadn't stepped in, these guys would never have gotten off the ground. They would have closed shop and gone to work as linemen in some computer programming factory and the world would never have had this software. VCs make a lot of money, sure, but they make it all possible."

"I wasn't criticizing," Adam said quickly. "It's amazing. Must be really cool to be a venture capitalist."

"Of course it's cool," T.J. said, turning to face him. "It's the best fucking gig on the planet."

Adam handed T.J. his Manhattan. T.J. took it with a nod. "No one knows what you need better than your sister, huh?" he said.

"Sorry?"

"My sister, Lisa. She can always tell when I need a drink."

Adam couldn't hide his surprise or delight. "Lisa's your sister?"

"Yes. Put your tongue back in your mouth."

"Oh, I—"

"Whatever. She's hot. I get it." T.J. gestured toward his drink. "Don't you want one, too?"

"I'm pretty sure I'm not allowed," Adam said, grinning. His whole night had changed. Maybe he had a chance with Lisa after all.

"And *I'm* pretty sure I'm the one who's paying you, and, therefore, I get to say what's allowed. Pour yourself something."

Adam hesitated. He glanced around to see if Sheryl was nearby. "Come on," T.J. said. "Surely they don't expect you to make it through these parties sober. Besides, how will you know how good a job you're doing if you never taste your creations? This Manhattan is terrible."

"You have a point," Adam said. He reached for the shaker to pour himself a Manhattan and refill T.J.'s half-empty glass.

"So, what do you think of Stanford? Lisa said you're a freshman."

Adam nodded. "It's great. I mean, the classes are a little boring, but I like California a lot."

"Where are you from?"

"Indiana."

"Yeah, California's a little different, I imagine." T.J. paused. "So, do you know what you want to major in?"

"No idea. My twin sister is this big computer science geek, has it all figured out. But me, no clue."

T.J. perked up. "What area of computer science is she in?"

"I'm not sure what you'd call it. She's just always tinkering, coming up with little programs and iPhone apps. She's obsessed.

Spends twenty-four hours in the lab without stopping, forgets to eat and everything. She's a machine."

"And she's a freshman at Stanford, too?"

"Yep. She's Patty Hawkins's roommate, actually."

"Oh, Jesus. No wonder she hides out in the computer lab."

Adam laughed. The whiskey was settling in. He was feeling more relaxed.

"What's your major?" he asked.

"I'm MS&E. Management science and engineering. It's half engineering and half business classes. Great major. Super tough, but solid. And I did minors in econ and French."

"Wow!" Adam was impressed. Now that T.J. wasn't dating Lisa, he had nothing but admiration for this intelligent, charming guy in front of him. "You must have declared early to get all that in."

"Yeah, I always knew it was what I wanted to do. I think it's important to have a plan and to stay diverse. MS&E gave me a good setup for business school, econ a more academic study, and French some diversity that throws people. No one ever expects a guy like me to know anything about Balzac." He smiled. "You really ought to figure out a plan for yourself. Figure out what you really want to be."

Adam thought back to what Professor Marsh had said that morning and sighed. "I've been hearing that a lot lately."

T.J. paused, then said, "I could help, you know. Sometimes it's helpful to have someone who's been through it to bounce ideas off of."

"You'd do that for me?"

"Absolutely. Why not? Cheers." T.J. clinked his glass against Adam's. "How about a refill?"

Adam's spirits were high with this affirmation from T.J. and the whiskey as he cheerfully mixed another Manhattan.

"So, do you still play soccer?"

"What?"

"Your dad said—during his toast he said you used to be really into soccer."

T.J.'s jaw clenched a little but he responded coolly. "No, soccer ended up not being the right sport for me. It was a little too . . . cooperative. I've found I prefer individual competition."

"Oh." Adam was worried he'd said something wrong.

T.J. chuckled. "Dad's been pretty wrapped up in this Gibly stuff. Guess he's missed the past, oh, ten years." Then with a big forced smile he added, "What do you say we get out of here, Adam? Go have some real fun?"

Adam looked at his watch. He'd made a deal with Sheryl that he could leave at nine-thirty so he could work on his homework problem set, and it was now past ten. He briefly wondered when he would get to that problem set, then brushed the thought aside. "Sounds good. Where to?"

The Nerd Lab Bender

Back on campus, Amelia didn't notice her own bloodshot eyes or cramped hands. She was on a roll. It was approaching one o'clock in the morning and she'd been in the Gates Computer Science Building since before noon. She'd gone through three shifts of teaching assistants, graduate students who hung out in the computer lab in case undergrads had any glitches and made sure people from outside the university didn't sneak in to try to poach ideas. While most of the campus was dead at this hour, the real action in the Gates Building had only just started; around eight o'clock, programmers had filed in with Chinese take-out and set up shop for the evening, and right now the energy was palpable, with twenty-odd engineers typing away at their computer screens.

The Gates Building had been donated to Stanford by Bill Gates himself, and, for someone like Amelia, it was heaven. The warm, blue glow of large-screen PCs lit up the long rooms, and eager computer scientists perched on ergonomic chairs coding away around the clock. Gates had designed the building with engineers in mind. Vending machines were stocked with ramen noodles and Hot Pockets in addition to the standard candy bars and potato chips, and the fridge was filled with a free supply of Red Bull. Bathrooms were equipped with showers, in case students didn't want to go back to their dorm rooms to freshen up, and the lounges were equipped with Xboxes and Wii sets for taking a break. But the real energy was in the computer rooms. The mixture of adrenaline, creativity, and anticipation was hard to describe. Everyone in the room was on the cusp of something groundbreaking. The guy next to you might be creating the next Facebook or Groupon, or maybe even Google. People came in and out, but most of them stayed for long stretches—fifteen and twenty hours at a time—the excitement of a new idea outweighing physical exhaustion.

Even though there wasn't much chatter, there was camaraderie among the engineers. When you finished running a major program, it was normal to throw your arms in the air and yell "I am awesome!" and everyone would wildly applaud and respond "You ARE awesome!" On the occasional instance when someone's computer crashed and they lost their work, the whole room felt the devastation. Those were the worst possible moments for an engineer. It wasn't just the fact that countless hours were for nothing, but that you had to retrace your steps, take a break from the momentum you were building for the next thing, and go back and reprogram something from the past. At moments like those, no call was necessary to alert the room about what was going on at your station; the person next to you would realize it and send an instant message to everyone in the room. Then everyone would stop, gather around the computer scientist in crisis, and repeat the mantra "If your computer never crashes, you're not working hard enough. Or you're an idiot."

Everyone would then pat you on the back and you'd laugh and sigh and get back to work.

It was in this room that Amelia felt, for the first time in her life, really at home. The sound of tapping computer keys and the sight of line after line of zeroes and ones and Courier typeface up and down the screen and the steady heat and buzz of computers running were all familiar and good. Her favorite computer station was in the far left corner, at the end of the table, number eighteen. The front and right side of the desk were enclosed in a cubicle divider, but the left side was open to a floor-to-ceiling window that looked down from the third floor to the street below and across to a popular campus café.

Whenever she got stuck on her code, Amelia would gaze out the window and people-watch. She liked to observe how they behaved, how they interacted. She'd watch how walkers bumped into each other because they were looking down at their phones, punching text messages or trying to surf the Web. She'd note the annoyance of a girl waiting for someone at the café across the street, checking her watch incessantly, or the nervous twitch of a student dressed awkwardly in a suit, interviewing for a job at a table inside.

And every Friday at one o'clock, she'd stop to watch a Chinese couple that met every week for lunch, always at the same table. He was slim and tall, always dressed in khakis and a polo shirt. The woman was petite, with long black hair, always carrying a pretty purse and wearing oversized sunglasses that she never removed. Amelia felt close to the couple, having watched them through various phases of joy and argument (they'd been arguing a lot lately), and gained a certain comfort in the steadiness of their routine. Today he'd brought her flowers and she'd hugged him with delight, but when she received a call midway through lunch, she'd left him sitting alone with the flowers at the table.

That was almost twelve hours ago, before Amelia had made her breakthrough on this code. She'd taken an iPhone application class during her first quarter at Stanford and had been addicted to programming little games and shortcuts ever since. But this was the first time she'd tried to create a program that was totally original.

Amelia paused. It was the end of her marathon programming session, when weariness ordinarily overtook her, but instead she was filled with a surge of energy. It came all at once, like a sudden break of sunlight in a cloudy sky, the awareness of just what she was trying to accomplish. To create something out of nothing, to forge a path through the frontier of Silicon Valley that nobody before had even considered.

It's the new things that change the world.

"Hey, Amelia?" George, a junior, popped his head over her cubicle.

"Just a sec, George." Amelia didn't look up as she typed furiously, squinting at the screen in front of her.

George waited for several minutes while Amelia finished a line of code. When he saw she was slowing down, he went on. "I'm going to go grab a slice of pizza and wondered if I can get you anything?"

George was tall and pudgy, with a mop of curly blond hair and wire-frame glasses. He almost always wore brown corduroys and a Google t-shirt he'd gotten for free during his internship there last summer. He'd been hugely kind to Amelia since she'd arrived on campus, showing her where everything in the lab was, and even inviting her as a date to his Psi Phi fraternity mixer.

"George, I'm almost there! Ahh! I think I've got it!"

"What? What have you got? Let's see!" George hurried around to stand behind her chair.

At 1:34 in the morning, with George standing over her shoulder, Amelia held her breath and pressed the "Enter" key to run the program from beginning to end to check it for bugs. At 1:37, the "ACTION COMPLETED" message popped onto her screen, indicating that no bugs were detected. She plugged her phone into the computer, logged into TestFlight, and downloaded the program.

By 1:53, Amelia and George were both holding their breath. Amelia cradled her iPhone in one hand as her other hand hovered above the button on her new program.

Amelia thought about the past year and all the changes she and Adam had experienced. They grew up together in Indiana and were everything to each other. They had never met their parents, didn't even know anything about them. For as long as they could remember, they had been "juvenile dependents," cared for by the state. Their only family, their real family, was each other. They bounced around foster homes and formed fleeting friendships, but they always returned to one truth: They were twins, and they were inseparable.

They called themselves the Dorii, the plural of their last name that they'd made up during a pact that they'd always stick together.

The Dorii's loyalty for each other got them through the most difficult times. Together, the Dorii survived loneliness, they withstood brutal teachers and social workers, and they ignored the harsh reality of their world.

The Dorii even survived the one time they were separated, when Amelia did something wrong and was sent to a juvenile detention center. The two never talked about the time Amelia went to jail.

A year ago, when they applied to college, despite the odds and expense, they agreed that they would only go if they were both admitted. They would never separate again. Now they were here, and Amelia was free to do nothing but code and code all day long, indulging in her one true passion, free from the responsibilities and fears of their old life.

At last, Amelia built up the nerve to press the button on her iPhone. It was an ambitious and risky experiment, almost doomed to fail . . . but it didn't. It worked perfectly. Amelia had a way of beating the odds, always.

Like a kid on Christmas, Amelia squealed with delight, throwing her arms around George in an ecstatic hug, not noticing how much it made him blush.

"It works, George! Oh, it works!"

"Say it, Amelia!"

"Oh, I can't, George. It's not that big of a deal."

George turned to the room and yelled, "Hey, guys, Amelia is awesome!"

The whole room turned to look at her, and she felt her face turn red but couldn't hide her smile. "Amelia, you're awesome!" they all cheered.

George lowered his voice, hoping to have a moment alone in a very public place.

"Amelia, this is really huge. What you figured out with this . . . What you got the iPhone to do . . . I think it can become something big."

"I'm so relieved, George! I knew there was a way to do it, and it's been bugging me for, like, an entire week."

"An entire week?" George was dumbfounded. "You mean you started this a week ago?"

"Well, yeah. I started it on Sunday. What is today? Friday? Yeah, a week."

George looked at her in astonishment. "Amelia, there are Ph.D. students who couldn't cross-correlate such different waveforms if they spent an entire year on it. You seriously did it in a week?"

"That's not true. It wasn't that complicated. You just had to figure out how to—"

"Create a carrier signal at alternating frequencies, and then run a modulation algorithm that coordinates those frequencies with cell tower proxies—that is incredibly complicated, Amelia. You're not just awesome, you're, like, the next Sergey and Larry."

Amelia shrugged, embarrassed by the comparison to the Google founders, Stanford graduates who were revered as gods around campus. "I just made an iPhone application, George. I didn't invent Google."

"Whatever you did, it's incredible."

"I'm just glad it worked." Amelia smiled. "I'm also *exhausted*. I'm going to go home and go to bed!"

"Do you want some pizza first? Let me grab my jacket."

"Don't worry about it, George. I'm super tired. Just need to get to bed."

"At least let me walk you home?" George gave Amelia a suave, charming smile—or at least his best effort—as he slung his backpack over his shoulder.

"I've got my bike. Thanks, though! I'll see you around." With a wave, Amelia left George standing in the computer lab.

Amelia practically skipped down the stairs and out of the Gates Building; she could barely contain her excitement over having just finished her project. She unlocked her bike and pulled out her cell phone to text Adam the good news.

Back in the dorm, she scooted past a group of dorm mates playing Ping-Pong and drinking from a keg in the lobby. She grabbed her shower caddy and headed down the hall to the bathroom. She stood under the hot water and breathed in the smell of her orange-ginger shampoo. She let herself stay in the shower for a good twenty minutes, treating herself after a job well done. Then she patted herself dry and pulled on her pajamas—a pair of sweatpants and a cozy t-shirt—and smiled at herself in the mirror as she brushed her teeth. Today was a great day, the kind of day Stanford had promised to make possible, and she felt deeply grateful.

It was 3:20 in the morning when she finally shut off the light and crawled into bed, whispering "Thank you" to no one in particular. Closing her eyes, she drifted off to sleep.

Amelia awoke with a start as the door flew open and Patty stumbled in.

Amelia held up a hand to shield her eyes from the hallway light filling the room. She blinked with confusion.

"Ameeeelia!" Patty groaned drunkenly. "Amelia, I am in soooo much trou-ble," she said, accentuating every syllable.

Amelia sighed as she pulled her legs out from under the covers and sat up on her bed. Patty shut the door with unintentional force. She stumbled toward Amelia's bed and climbed on top of the covers, letting her head fall against the pillow.

"Can I get you—?"

"No. No. No," Patty mumbled, staring up at the ceiling. "I don't need anything. I'm just in . . . I'm in so much trouble, Amelia. I really, really did a really not-good thing. Like, a really not-good thing."

"What happened? What's the matter?"

"I hooked up with . . ." Patty took a deep breath and sighed. "I hooked up with . . . Chad."

"Who's Chad?" Amelia asked.

"I mean, I didn't really hook up with him. We, like, well, we made out a lot and did . . . other stuff. A *lot* of other stuff. But we didn't have sex."

Having never kissed anyone, Amelia knew Patty had more experience with boys than she did, but she didn't know what sorts of things were defined as "hooking up." Patty's confession to her was a little startling and very embarrassing.

"Oh, Amelia. He is sooo hot, and his lips are sooo soft, and his hands are sooo strong, and he is soooo . . ."

"What?"

"He's soooo Shandi's fiancé."

"Who's Shandi?"

"Shandi?" Patty sat up and stared at Amelia. "My sister!" she shouted, and then fell back on to the pillow with a groan.

"Oh, wow," Amelia said under her breath, but Patty picked up on it.

"I know! Aaaand Shandi's coming home next week, and we're having a big family dinner to welcome her home, and I just hooked up with her *fiancé*. Oh, Amelia. This is not good."

Amelia took a deep breath and switched into solution mode. "Well, let's think about this rationally."

Patty giggled. "Yes, let's do. Let's think about this ra-tion-al-ly."

"Where did it happen?"

"At T.J. Bristol's party. Oh! Your brother was there, by the way. I think he has a crush on my friend Lisa."

"What? Adam was . . . Okay, that's not the point. Did anyone see you with Chad?"

"No. Absolutely not."

"Are you sure?"

"Absolutely not."

"Where did it happen?"

"It's all a little fuzzy, Amelia. I mean, we had tequila shots, and then there was some announcement, and everyone was cheering, and I went to the bathroom, and Chad was there. Where did he come from? I'm not sure how he got there, but he was there when I came out, and then we were outside, and then we were in a car. Wait . . . How did we get in a car? Ohhhh . . ."

Patty groaned again. "I need to go to sleep." She rolled over and shut her eyes right as her phone beeped, indicating a text message. "Will you get that?" she mumbled to Amelia before drifting off into a heavy snoring slumber.

Amelia picked up Patty's pink-bejeweled iPhone and tapped the text message that had just come through.

"*FYI. More where this came from. You are such a naughty girl.*"

The message was from T.J. Bristol and came with a video attachment. Amelia looked at Patty, who was dead asleep, then back at the phone before tapping to open the attachment. A twenty-second video clip played, showing a guy and a girl—oh, God, it was Patty—on top of each other, aggressively making out, in the front seat of a Lamborghini. The guy in the video pulled off Patty's shirt and the clip cut out.

Amelia felt her jaw drop as she looked at her sleeping roommate. Not good, indeed. She tucked the phone next to the pillow and gently removed Patty's shoes, bracelets, and earrings and pulled a blanket over her. She brought the trash can next to the bed in case Patty woke and threw up, and filled a glass of water to place on the dresser. Then she turned out the light and crawled into Patty's bed, exhausted.

Information Gathering

The bright California sun streamed through the window and woke Amelia early. She got out of bed to head to the hall bathroom and, when she opened the door, found Adam passed out in the hallway. He was cradling something in his arms, like a teddy bear. It was a Tupperware container full of the dessert he'd promised Amelia.

She didn't know whether to laugh or scold him as she shook him awake.

"Wha . . . ?" he said as he blinked open his eyes. "Ohhhh . . ." He moaned and put his head back down on the floor. "Do you want some cake?"

"Adam, what on earth? Did you sleep here all night?" Amelia couldn't conceal a smile at her brother's rough-and-tumble state. His dirty-blond hair was shaggy across his forehead, his dark green eyes puffy and a little bloodshot.

"Umm . . ." Adam looked at her but didn't make any attempt to lift his head from the floor. "I must have. Oh, wow. I do *not* feel well."

"Come on, let's get you out of the hallway." Amelia giggled as she helped him into her room. "Quiet, though. Patty's sleeping."

Adam took a deep breath, shook his head and blinked his eyes, and snapped back to life, crawling up from the floor and into Amelia's room. "Man, have I got a lot to tell you. I've had a total breakthrough, Amelia."

"Me too! You won't believe what I did at the computer lab last night."

"Why is Patty sleeping in your bed?" he whispered, noticing that Patty was still clad in the dress she'd been wearing the night before.

"Long story," Amelia said as she walked over to her computer. "Come here; let me show you—"

"What time did she get home?" Adam was still stuck on Patty. "Amelia, you would not believe this party. I have never seen so much booze. And all the kids were drinking with their parents like it was totally natural. But here's the thing, Amelia, these millionaires—no, billionaires—they're smart, they're super smart. But you know what? They're no smarter than you. And I realized last night, Amelia, that you could program something and we could get a venture capitalist to invest. We could be one of them, Amelia. We could start a tech or Internet or computer or whatever company and be freakin' millionaires."

Amelia looked up from her computer. "What are you talking about? Why on earth would we start a company?"

"To make money, Amelia! And get out of the shit life we've been living. Why should we be on scholarships, riding our bikes around because we can't afford a car, when you've got all the brains—probably more brains—than any of the guys that are making billions off of deals like Gibly?"

"What's Gibly?"

"It's the software behind mobile payments, like for the

iPhone. Gibly makes buying stuff with your phone easy; that's why they do the voice-to-text software, so you can just speak and buy. Last night, Gibly was sold to some company in England for, like, three-point-eight *billion* dollars and all these guys at this party made crazy money off of it."

"That doesn't sound so complicated. Why did someone pay so much for it?" Amelia went back to her computer and started typing something.

"Exactly! It's not that complicated." Adam's hangover was replaced by excitement as he leaned against his sister's desk. "It's not that complicated *for someone like you.* You could do something like that in your sleep, and we could build it into a company and make a killing and never have to worry about anything again."

"Adam." Amelia stopped typing and took a long look at her brother. "Money causes problems. The pursuit of money causes problems, and I don't like the way you're thinking."

"But . . ."

"I don't want to hear it," she snapped. Adam looked at his sister, stunned. "We haven't had the best luck, Adam. The way you're speaking, the way you sound . . . You sound like . . ." She trailed off. "This type of thinking has gotten us into trouble before."

Amelia turned back to her computer and lowered her voice so as not to wake Patty. "In our new life, I program because it's the one thing in the world I absolutely love doing. It's interesting and inspiring and occasionally creates something that makes the world an easier place to live in. Money ruins everything. It will ruin our lives."

"Don't be selfish."

"I'm sorry?"

"You're being selfish, Amelia. You have talents that you can share with the world. Sitting in a lab by yourself, creating programs that could help people but don't because you're too stuck on not exposing them, is selfish."

"I didn't say—"

"And not using your talents to help us get out of where we are—I mean, I would do it for you, Amelia. In a second. If I had your talent, and I knew it could help us, I wouldn't hesitate."

"I did try to use my talents to help us once, Adam, and it didn't exactly turn out well," Amelia snapped back.

"That was totally different. *This* is totally different. This is setting up a legitimate company that legitimately helps people and makes money—lots of money—in a totally legitimate way."

Amelia had tuned her brother out and was busy looking at her computer. "That company was called Gibly, right?"

"From the party? Yeah, Gibly."

Amelia was typing furiously, her brow furrowed in confusion.

"What is it?" Adam asked. "What's wrong?"

"This is a little sketchy," Amelia said to her computer screen, then typed some more.

Adam was staring at his sister, his face a mixture of nervousness and excitement. "What do you mean by 'sketchy'?"

"Adam, if this is right—I mean, if I'm in the right place . . . Yes, I'm definitely in the right place. Adam, Gibly's tracking their users' information in a major way."

"What do you mean? What does that matter?"

"I mean, they've put tags on all their users, and there are, like, one hundred million of them. And they're not only tracking all the Web sites they go to, they're using GPS to track users' locations at every moment. Come look at this."

Adam walked over to Amelia's side of the computer screen, where she'd pulled up a database with lines of information.

"How'd you do that?" Adam asked.

"I went into their platform."

"You mean you hacked in?"

"I'm just peeking in. Here, let's find you. Give me your phone. Everyone's phone has a unique number."

Adam handed Amelia his phone. With a swipe she unlocked the screen and found the UDID, the string of letters and numbers that told the world "This is Adam Dory's iPhone." Amelia turned back to her computer and did a quick search, but then shook her head.

"Either I entered the number incorrectly or you were at a place called Hanky Panky in Redwood City at two A.M."

Adam's face turned beet red as Amelia looked up at him. "I . . . I," he started.

Amelia giggled. "Oh my God! You were at a strip club?!"

"I went with T.J. and his friends! It was T.J.'s graduation party, and he was helping me think through all this. Whatever. The point is, that's totally right and totally weird. Why would anyone want to know where I was all the time?"

"How did you put it a moment ago? To make money? Adam, can you imagine how powerful you'd be if you had tabs on where one hundred million people were at any given moment? If you had that information, you could sell it for, like, three-point-eight billion or so."

"But who would want that? I mean, who would care where I was at any given moment?"

"Beats me. What company did you say acquired it?"

"An English company. Alletto Company or Alice or A . . . Alice-Ter? Yeah, the Aleister Corporation."

Amelia went back to typing. "Aleister is just a holding company. It looks like they own a grocery store chain and an auto manufacturer and a few other random companies in the U.K. and Europe. Why would they buy a technology company?"

Adam waited while his sister continued to search for the answer.

"Here's a Wall Street analyst report that says they're trying to diversify. That everyone's getting into technology now. I guess that's true. But why would you spend three-point-eight *billion* to get into a new industry?"

She typed some more. Adam could see the excitement on his sister's face, and he loved it.

"Whoa!"

"What?" Adam couldn't stand it. "What is it?"

"Aleister! These Aleister guys have been collecting ten-million-dollar payments from something called VIPER every week for the past . . . year."

"No way. How did you find that out?"

"I hacked—I peeked into their company accounts," Amelia said nonchalantly.

Adam looked at her, jaw dropped. "You're ridiculous. You know that, right?"

Amelia rolled her eyes. "Just look at this." She pointed to the accounts. "Ten million every week for a year—that's, like, half a billion dollars. Who do you think VIPER is?"

Adam looked at his sister. "I'm guessing it's someone interested in knowing the whereabouts of about one hundred million people."

Adam and Amelia exchanged a meaningful glance, recognizing the danger of what they'd just discovered.

"Okay, let's not get too excited. I'm sure there's a good reason," Amelia said.

"Yeah," Adam said. "They just announced the sale. I bet all of this will come out in the papers soon enough, right?"

"Yeah, totally," Amelia said, glancing nervously back at her computer.

"Come on." Adam patted her on the back. "Let's go get some food. I need something greasy to get me through this hangover."

"Okay." Amelia snapped back into focus. "I'm dying for a dining hall waffle."

The twins grabbed their stuff and carefully closed the door so as not to wake Patty, who hadn't moved throughout their whole conversation.

When she heard the door click shut and knew they were gone, Patty rolled over and picked up her phone. She had woken up before Amelia, and in a hungover stupor saw T.J.'s blackmail text message. She lay awake, simultaneously paralyzed by guilt and scheming to figure out how to stop T.J. from telling Shandi. Patty tapped the iPhone to compose a note to herself: "Gibly storing information / TJ and Adam at Hanky Panky / VIPER monthly payments to Aleister." She wasn't yet sure exactly how, but she had a feeling information like that would come in handy.

6

The Rules of the Game

"What time is it?" the girl in T.J.'s bed asked groggily as she stretched her arms above her head in a yawn.

"Eleven-fifteen." T.J. stood at the full-length mirror next to the door of his fraternity room, the collar on his crisply ironed white shirt popped as he straightened an Hermès tie around his neck. He'd been up since eight o'clock studying the latest trends in Internet investing. He'd read that day's *Wall Street Journal*, Tech-Crunch, and Yahoo! Finance, and searched thirty Silicon Valley companies he'd been following on LexisNexis to make sure he was up to speed on any headlines that involved them. He'd showered, shaved, gelled his hair, and put on his favorite navy suit, one he'd had custom made last summer during an investment banking internship in Hong Kong. It looked great, he thought, but the navy made it more casual, like he wasn't trying too hard.

"Eleven-fifteen? Oh my God, why are we awake? We just went to bed, like, four hours ago."

"Six, actually. Five if you take out the hour we were hooking up before you passed out."

"Oops." She giggled. "Why don't you come back to bed so I can finish what I started?"

He turned to face her. She'd tossed away the covers and was propped fully naked on her side, pushing her enormous breasts forward in a pose she'd probably seen in a magazine that told her it was irresistible. Her bleached blond hair was a mess and her eyeliner was smeared. She had a nice body but was overly tanned and he typically liked girls with thinner faces than her round cheeks allowed.

"Can't," he said as he turned back to the mirror to finish tying his tie. "Have a really important meeting downtown."

"More important than me?" She pouted coyly.

"Listen, I don't have time to take you home, but I left forty dollars and the number for a cab company next to your purse. They're usually here in ten minutes."

She let out a sigh, realizing she wasn't going to get him to come back to bed, and searched the sheets for her underwear.

"Do you have shorts or something I can borrow so I don't have to walk out in my dress and heels from last night?"

"When would I get them back from you?"

She stopped searching and looked at him. He was still looking in the mirror. She rolled her eyes and said sarcastically, "Um, I don't know. The next time I see you?"

He finally turned and crossed the room back to his desk. "I really don't know when that will be. I've got a ton going on. There's a back door if you turn left out of my room; that takes you to the outside stairs. Just tell the cabbie to meet you in the back and no one will see you."

The girl's mouth fell open as she sat naked on his bed. "Oh my God, you're actually serious."

He didn't respond.

"Oh my God," she repeated, now covering her chest with the

sheet while she hurriedly collected her clothes, feeling her cheeks burn and hot tears start to well.

T.J. was putting his things into a laptop case and running through a mental checklist of what he needed to bring. He really didn't have time to deal with drama from a girl whose name he only knew because he'd searched her purse while she was sleeping and found a Santa Clara University ID card. She was a sophomore, apparently, and had been the most attractive girl at the bar he'd gone to after the party last night. She was an easy score—he ordered her a shot of Patrón and she was completely impressed. Three more and they were making out on the dance floor, his hand up her skirt for all to see. They were half undressed by the time the cab pulled up to his frat house, with that freshman Adam passed out in the front seat. He told the cabbie to take Adam back to his dorm and gave him an extra tip.

To defray her disappointment, he said, "Don't get so stressed. It's only sex. We used protection. It was fun." Having collected all his things, he turned to face her and smiled a warm, charismatic grin. He touched her cheek. "It was really wonderful meeting you, Sandy. You're beautiful, and I had a really good time getting to know you."

She blushed uncontrollably, sniffled, and nodded, but couldn't bring herself to say anything. He held her gaze for a moment, then turned away. "Will you lock the door on your way out? Thanks so much, babe."

His BMW 3 Series Sedan beeped as he unlocked it and climbed inside. He loved this car, mostly because he'd had to earn it himself. His parents were adamant about not raising spoiled rich kids, so when he and Lisa had turned sixteen, they'd only been willing to buy each of them a "reasonable" car—a Volvo or Subaru or Saab—something safe and high quality, but nothing "brand-y." So, he'd worked hard during summer internships in finance, first in New York and then Hong Kong, and then invested his earnings into funds he researched with a family friend who was a senior partner at Goldman Sachs. His investments had performed exceptionally well (beginner's luck, he'd told everyone, though he was in fact incredibly proud), and he'd used the proceeds to upgrade his Subaru Outback to a BMW with all the highest-end features: built-in Bluetooth and navigation system, Bose speakers, and satellite radio. He'd been resentful of his parents' frugality at first. It was hard being the only kid in high school without a nice car, and he thought the decision was incredibly hypocritical given the eight collector's sports cars his father had in their garage at home. But, in retrospect, they were right. The satisfaction of knowing he'd gotten this car and its amenities on his own made him feel a lot better than if they'd been handed to him.

As he drove toward University Café, where he was meeting Roger Fenway, T.J. felt his heart racing with excitement. Roger was the founder and CEO of Kadence, a music content generator that he'd sold to Apple for a billion dollars in the late nineties. He'd since become an angel investor, giving money to early-stage start-ups he thought were promising, and growing his wealth in the process (more than a dozen of the companies he'd invested in had done as well or even better than Kadence).

T.J. had never met Roger—he was notorious for shunning the Atherton social scene—but knew through the gossip chain that Roger was starting an incubator on Sand Hill Road, the golden mile for the top venture capital firms *in the world.* Roger was eagerly selecting promising young talent and grooming them with money and advice to start new companies.

T.J. was determined to become one of Roger's investments, and this was the meeting that was going to seal the deal.

The Secret Sauce

Roger patted the trunk of his Tesla Roadster affectionately as he clicked the door locked and headed toward University Café. He loved this car. Finally, smart engineering, smoking-hot design, and environmental consciousness had fused into a vehicle he could be totally psyched about driving. He'd met Elon Musk, the founder of Tesla Motors, years ago at a Cool Product Expo, and they'd bonded over the Grateful Dead. When Elon called him a year later asking him to invest in his new company, it had been a no-brainer.

"Never turn down a Dead Head" was Roger's only strict investment thesis.

Roger was meeting T.J. Bristol, the son of Ted Bristol, an old friend from the early days of Kadence. Ted had been an early investor and a great advisor, especially during the sale. He was smart as a tack and had helped Roger structure the deal so that Kadence's users didn't get screwed when Apple took over. They were pretty different socially—Ted was an icon of the Silicon Valley social elite, where Roger happily avoided any event where flip-flops and shorts were not socially acceptable—but he liked Ted well enough and was always happy to talk to a kid interested in entrepreneurship.

Roger chuckled as he spotted the kid that must surely be Ted's son through the window. T.J. was decked out in a fancy suit, carrying an expensive leather briefcase, and typing something frantically on his phone. He didn't notice as Roger walked up to the table.

"T.J.?" Roger, wearing khaki shorts, a Hawaiian-print Tommy Bahama button-down, and Rainbow brand flip-flops, stuck out his hand.

T.J. took a moment to process the character in front of him, and then leapt up from his chair. "Mr. Fenway! Hello! T.J. Bristol. It's really wonderful to meet you, sir. I'm sorry I—"

"No sweat. I try to keep a low profile." Roger smiled casually and took a seat.

T.J. grinned. His father had told him Roger was "chill," but he hadn't expected someone quite so . . . casual.

"So, T.J., what's on your mind?" Roger said, leaning back in his chair and smiling to the waitress to let her know they'd order whenever she was ready. He glanced at the television hanging on the wall behind her: Animal Planet. Excellent. Last month, Roger had complained to the owner of University Café that the only thing they ever played on the television was CNBC, which, in his opinion, created a hostile atmosphere. There was nothing more depressing than the exaggerated reality of the twenty-four-hour news cycle, he'd explained, and cafés like this one ought to inspire the entrepreneurs of Silicon Valley to be more innovative, not more mired in the what-could-go-wrong scenarios pitched by newscasters. The owner had laughed and promised to test other channels. Roger had suggested Cartoon Network, but Animal Planet wasn't a bad compromise.

"Well," T.J. said, "I'll get straight to the point. I heard you were setting up an incubator, and I'd like to get involved."

So, that's what this was about. Roger chuckled and smiled. "I am starting an incubator! It's going to be fantastic. I'm such a believer in positive energy, and I think there's nothing better than getting a lot of really smart, ambitious, creative minds together in one space and seeing what happens."

"I agree. Completely. And I'd really like to be part of it."

"Awesome. What do you want to do?" Roger asked as he directed his attention to the waitress, who had approached the table. "I'll take the turkey avocado panini and a—what kind of beers do you have on draft?"

"Fat Tire, Budweiser, Stella—"

"Fat Tire. Perfect. T.J., what are you having?"

"I'll have the grilled chicken Caesar salad, dressing on the side. And sparkling water, please."

Roger nodded (what had become of college kids these days, ordering dressing on the side and sparkling water?) and smiled at the waitress. "Thank you, my dear," he said, before turning back to T.J. "Where were we?"

"You were asking what I'd like to do at your incubator," T.J. said, "and I was going to say that I'm open to hear where you think my skills would be most useful." T.J. hadn't expected this to be so easy. It was like Roger was asking him to write his own job description.

"Well, what are your skills?" Roger sat back in his chair and tried to stay focused on T.J., though he was secretly watching the television screen behind his head, where a lion was stalking a herd of elephants somewhere in Africa.

"I'm very strong both quantitatively and qualitatively." T.J. had rehearsed his answer in front of the mirror this morning.

"I've done two investment banking internships, in New York and in Hong Kong, but I've supplemented that rigorous quantitative analysis with minors in economics and French, which have given me an opportunity to explore softer skills."

The camera panned in on a baby elephant. Uh-oh.

"The economics degree gave you softer skills?" Roger lifted his eyebrows.

"Well, compared to the rigor of hard-core investment models, economics is awfully theoretical and fuzzy."

Roger nodded; perhaps that was true. He'd never studied much of either.

T.J. waited for him to say something, but Roger had turned to the waitress, who was holding their lunch.

"So," T.J. said, trying to refocus his lunch partner. "I think I could fit in anywhere."

Roger took a bite of his sandwich, and chewed carefully. "Do you want to be an entrepreneur?"

"More than anything," T.J. said. "In the long term, I want to be a venture capitalist, but I think the best way to be a good investor in start-ups is to start something of your own, you know? Besides, after two summers working in huge companies with difficult bosses, I really think I'm better off working for myself."

The lion was getting close, hiding behind a bush.

"Sure," Roger offered. "Working for yourself is great. Set your own hours, make the decisions. It can be a lot of pressure, though," Roger said, half listening as he looked past T.J.'s head to the television.

T.J. laughed. "Oh, I think I can handle the pressure. I had a project last summer where I had forty-eight hours to finish a one-hundred-fifty-page pitch deck for a critical client meeting. I literally slept for four hours over two days—didn't leave the office, didn't shower, had all my meals delivered to my desk—but it went off without a hitch."

The TV cut off right as the lion was closing in on the herd, snapping Roger back to the conversation. He decided to egg the kid on. "What's a pitch deck?"

Roger glanced at the waitress, then at the television, indicating she ought to turn it back on, which she did, as T.J. continued. "A pitch deck is something you make in PowerPoint, then print out and bind and give to clients. It explains the costs and benefits of a deal. So, there are a ton of charts and graphs explaining everything."

"So, you came up with one hundred fifty pages of charts and graphs in forty-eight hours?" The adult elephants saw the lion and started to charge, the mother placing herself between the lion and the baby, but—it cut out again. Dammit!

"Oh, no. I checked the spelling and the alignment and made sure there weren't any typos. The charts and everything are pretty standard for the company and just have to be updated and pasted into the deck."

"Ah." Roger beckoned to the waitress. "What's going on with the television?"

"I'm not sure, Mr. Fenway. Let me check to see why it keeps cutting out."

"Thanks, love." Roger smiled and looked back at T.J. "Here's the thing, T.J. I think there are a lot of people who think they want to be entrepreneurs, but they don't really. I mean, starting a company is tough. You have to put your life and reputation into your idea, to live and breathe it all the time. And no matter how great you think your idea is when you start out, you question it sometimes. It can be easy to get sidelined by people who tell you it's impossible."

T.J. smiled. He'd heard this before. "I totally understand

that. I think growing up in Silicon Valley has given me a great perspective on the commitment it takes. And having been through two corporate internships, I know I have the motivation to stick with it."

Roger nodded. This kid was obviously bright and polished, but he didn't have the spark. It wasn't his fault—most kids didn't. "So, what's your idea?"

"My idea?"

"Yeah. You want to join the incubator, so what business idea are you working on?" The TV flickered back to life. Now the lion was devouring the baby elephant. The rest of the herd had vanished.

"Well, I don't actually have an idea yet. I think that's what's so great about the incubator. It gives you time to really think about an idea."

Roger chuckled at this. "Oh, I don't know that sitting around in an office on Sand Hill Road is going to suddenly inspire an idea!" Again! The TV cut out. What was going on? Roger sat forward in his chair and looked around the room. Was anyone else seeing this? A girl at a table in the corner was holding—was that a remote? No, it was her phone, but she was pointing it at the television. What was she doing? "Excuse me a second, T.J."

Roger stood up and walked over to the girl. "Excuse me, miss?"

The girl, a pretty young thing who was obviously shy, looked up anxiously from her computer at the man standing over her.

"May I ask you a question, Miss . . . ?"

"Oh . . . uh, Dory. Amelia Dory," she said, not used to being approached by strangers.

"Well, Miss Dory, may I ask you a question? What were you just doing with your phone?"

Amelia blushed from behind her glasses. "Oh, I—I'm so sorry. Were you watching?"

"I was," Roger said. "And I completely missed the slaughter because someone kept turning off the TV."

"I'm so sorry, I didn't realize anyone was watching and I—well, I just really hate those programs. I mean, the baby elephants are always so helpless. But I can't keep from watching them. They just totally suck you in."

"So, you stole the television remote?"

"No, I . . ." Amelia paused. "Well, I used my phone."

Roger smiled. "And how, exactly, did you use your phone to turn off the television?"

Amelia blushed. "I actually . . . Well, I wrote a little program linking the phone signals with television and radio frequencies, so I can control them with my iPhone. It's like an eye. The program is, I mean, in that it can see other devices and access their frequencies."

Roger looked carefully at her for a moment, studying her face, her demeanor, the shyly proud excitement in her voice as she admitted her invention. This girl had it.

"No one's done that before. It's like your iPhone sends out a ripple in still water." Roger reached out his hand. "I'm Roger. Roger Fenway. I think your invention is very clever. Do you have a minute?"

Roger sat down in the chair across from her. "Actually, I'm working on a paper. I missed class the other day and have this new assignment and I—"

Roger interrupted. "I promise I'll let you get back to your assignment, but first I want to make you an offer. I'm starting an incubator on Sand Hill Road and I'm looking for smart people like you to come and use their skills to start companies. I'll put the money in."

Amelia's jaw clenched and she looked back toward her computer. The conversation earlier with Adam was still fresh, and she was still upset.

"Was it something I said?"

"No. I'm just . . . I'm not interested."

Roger paused, mouth still open. He'd never been rejected so abruptly. "Do you mind if I ask why not?"

"I don't want to start a company. I like programming. I love programming. And I have no interest in making money off of it."

Roger leaned back and smiled broadly. Oh, she was *so* it. She was the real deal. "Trust me, I completely understand why you feel that way, but if you approach it the right way, you can have both," Roger said.

"No, I'm sorry. I'm really not interested. And I have to get back to this paper."

"Well, Amelia, I admire your conviction and your invention." Roger took out a pen. "And I'm giving you my contact information in case you change your mind."

"Hey," she protested as he scribbled onto the inside cover of her notebook, which was sitting open on the table.

"Take care, Amelia."

Roger returned to the table with T.J. "Sorry about that," he said.

"Not to worry," T.J. said.

Roger pulled two fresh twenties from his wallet and put them on the table, a sum that was fifteen dollars more than the cost of his meal. "I don't want to take up your whole afternoon, T.J. It was great meeting you, and congratulations again on graduation. Have a blast with the rest of your senior year."

"Thanks. Should I also . . . about the incubator . . ."

"Oh yeah, I'll let you know how it's going. It doesn't sound like it's going to be very useful for you at this point, but if you come up with an idea, be sure and get in touch."

T.J. didn't understand what had happened. He thought he'd gotten a job, and now Roger was leaving and implying that there wasn't a spot for him. He scrambled to think of a way to get Roger to sit back down, but he was waving to the waitress.

"See you around, T.J." Roger reached out his hand and T.J. instinctively shook it.

"Yeah, see you around. I'll . . . I'll e-mail you with an idea."

"Sure thing, buddy." And Roger was out the door.

8

Sunny Afternoons in Atherton

According to the Google Maps app on his phone, it would take Adam an hour and ten minutes to walk from campus to Atherton, where his bike was still parked at the elementary school down the street from the Bristol house. This was not an area meant for walking. Everyone had luxury cars that transported them neatly from home garage to office garage, so sidewalks weren't in demand. Adam trudged along the asphalt shoulder, listening to Arcade Fire through his phone, sweating from the scorching-hot day. Why hadn't he left earlier this morning before it got so damn hot?

He was still frustrated with Amelia and her resistance to his idea about the company. He was looking down at the pavement, deep in thought, when he sensed a car cruising alongside him. Startled, he looked through the rolled-down window of a Lexus hybrid SUV and pulled out his earphones.

"Hey, Adam! Do you need a ride?" It took his eyes a moment to adjust as he peered through the window at—could it be?

"Lisa! Hi! Uh, yeah, a ride would be awesome." She stopped the car and he climbed into the passenger seat. "I'm just going down to pick up my bike. I left it at the elementary school the other night after the party."

"Oh, sure. No problem."

Lisa looked even more beautiful than she had at the party. She'd obviously just come from the pool. She was wearing tiny white shorts and a pink halter top that had turned dark from the still-wet bikini top underneath. Her hair was damp and clipped back in a sloppy bun.

"Sorry." She smiled self-consciously, noticing him looking at her. "I just came from the pool. I'm a total mess."

"No, not at all. I mean, don't apologize. You look . . . great."

Lisa blushed and smiled without opening her mouth as she pulled the car up to the bike rack in the school parking lot. "That it?"

"Yeah." Adam started to thank her, but he didn't want this moment to end.

She didn't either. "Want to come have a glass of lemonade or something? It's so hot out there. You'll burn up if you try biking all the way back to Stanford in this heat."

Adam smiled. "That would be awesome."

Adam hopped out of the car, put his bike into the back of the SUV, and they drove back to the Bristol house.

Lisa pulled a pitcher of lemonade out of the fridge and poured them both large glasses.

"I'm just going to run up and take off my wet bathing suit. Make yourself at home," Lisa said, as she pointed to the living room.

Adam watched her skip up the stairs, her shorts accentuating the perfect roundness of her butt. *Focus,* he told himself, trying not to think about her changing upstairs.

He walked into the living room and studied the bookshelf. Family photos in polished silver frames balanced out rows of color-coded antique books. Adam looked at the smiling faces—T.J., Lisa, and their parents, all tan and gorgeous. In one photo they were dressed in black-tie attire in front of a castle somewhere, in another they were bundled in ski jackets on top of a snowy mountain, and in another they were in bathing suits on a yacht in front of a white cliff (Greece, maybe?).

"Want to see more?" Lisa had crept up behind him. She smelled like lilies, and he noticed she'd put on lip gloss, which shimmered pink against her tan skin.

Adam blushed. "Yeah, I'd love to."

Lisa pulled a stack of albums off one of the shelves and led Adam over to a big white sofa next to the window. When she opened the first album, her face lit up. "Look at these. From the Beijing Olympics. We were in the front row for the opening ceremonies. And here—afterward we met the president of China at this super-fancy dinner on some swanky rooftop where they launched fireworks while we all drank champagne. It was so much fun."

She turned the page. "And these are from Christmas. The year we rented that beautiful Swiss chalet in Chamonix. You could ski straight out the back door onto the mountain and, afterward, end up at the most ridiculous après ski parties."

Adam was enthralled with the pictures. He couldn't believe she'd been to all these places. But he was even more enthralled with Lisa's smiling face as she looked at the photographs. He was watching her—a strand of hair had fallen tenderly down the side of her face—when she opened a second album and, for a split second, her cheeks went pale. Quickly, she flipped to the next page.

"Here!" She pointed to a picture of her younger self on top of an elephant. "We rode elephants in India. T.J. was terrified and refused to do it." She giggled. "Oh, he'd die if he knew I told you that!"

Adam smiled. "At least you're not showing me his baby pictures. I bet those are really incriminating."

She giggled again. "Oh, they definitely are!" She opened a third album. "Look at this one." She pointed to a picture of T.J. as a toddler, naked, sitting in a diaper covered in brown goo, crying with a look of pure anguish on his baby face.

"Oh my God, that's not his—"

"Ha ha, no. It's chocolate pudding. Apparently he got upset while his nanny, Odelia, was making it, and he splashed the whole bowl all over himself."

Adam smiled. "How about your baby pictures? I bet you were really cute."

Lisa got quiet and looked down at her purple polished toes. "Those aren't out. I mean, there aren't many." She hesitated. "There aren't many pictures of me when I was a baby."

Adam grimaced. It was going so well and now he'd upset her! "Oh, that's cool. I didn't mean to—"

"No, don't apologize. It's not your fault. I just don't really like the earlier memories, that's all."

"Is that why you skipped the page before?"

Lisa looked up at him, her eyes peering deeply into his, as though she was searching for a sign that she could trust him. He could lose himself completely in those eyes.

"Yeah, it is," Lisa said. She fiddled with the corner of the second album and then, as if deciding that Adam was someone she could open up to, turned back to the page she'd skipped.

The photo on the page showed a smiling toddler, pudgy with a head of blond curls, holding the hand of a younger Mrs. Bristol, who was grinning as she led the girl up to the front door of the house they were now in. The door was covered by balloons and a sign with a painted clown and the words WELCOME, LISA! WE LOVE YOU!

"I don't understand," Adam said.

"I was—I mean, I *am*—adopted," Lisa said quietly.

Instinctively, Adam reached for her hand. "There's nothing wrong with that, Lisa." He wanted to hug her, to hold her and press her head against his chest and kiss away her tears.

"I know. It's just—well, I think I always feel guilty, like I don't really deserve any of this. Like I'm an outsider." She looked up at him. Her eyes were brimming with tears, but she smiled through them. "I don't know that I've ever admitted that to anyone."

Adam smiled warmly back, his gaze meeting hers. "I think it makes you deserve it even more. And I think it makes you even more incredible."

Lisa blushed and forced a laugh to try to lighten the mood. "I can't believe I told you all that. I just met you last night. I don't know what it is about you. I guess I just really feel like I can trust you."

Adam's heart was beating so fast he worried she'd hear it. "You can."

She smiled back at him and squeezed his hand, which still rested on hers.

Just then they heard the back door open, and Maria, the housemaid, called out from the kitchen. "Miss Lisa, are you home?"

Lisa stood up as she called back. "Yes, Maria, I'm in here," she said, and then turned to Adam. "Can I drive you back to campus?"

"No, no, I can bike back. I think I'm ready to brave the weather now."

9

Poached Salmon with a Hint of Blackmail

Every Sunday for as long as she could remember, Patty's family had gathered for the Hawkins family dinner. The dinner was mandatory for any Hawkins within a fifty-mile radius, and often included close family friends.

Tonight's dinner was going to be awkward, and there was no way around that. Patty's sister Shandi was home from college; Shandi's fiancé, Chad, was joining the dinner; and Patty could still feel Chad's hands on her body. So, yeah. Awkward. Mrs. Hawkins had texted Patty earlier to let her know that she'd invited T.J. Bristol to make up for the fact that they'd been out of town for his graduation party, and did she want to text him about sharing a ride from campus? *No, thank you, Mom,* she thought. *I don't share rides with people trying to blackmail me.*

The dinner was going to be so awkward, in fact, that Patty was trying to think of it as a sitcom she was watching, rather than one she was a part of. *Don't get emotional,* she told herself as she drove her red-and-white-striped MINI Cooper convertible from campus to Atherton. *Just be an observer, like they teach you in yoga.*

She got to the house at six o'clock and snuck in through the kitchen door, giving a big hug to Felicia, the Puerto Rican cook who had been with the family since Patty was in preschool.

"Everybody here?" she asked Felicia as she poured herself a glass of pinot grigio. She immediately took two huge gulps.

"Mr. Hawkins and Miss Shandi are in the living room. Mrs. Hawkins is still upstairs getting ready, yeah, yeah, yeah." Felicia waved her hand as if to say, "You know Mrs. Hawkins is *always* upstairs getting ready." She went back to furiously mixing sugar in a bowl.

"What are you making?" Patty asked, stalling in order to finish her wine.

"Ice cream. Vanilla mint with a touch of lavender."

Patty reached out her finger to take a taste, but Felicia batted it away. "No, no, no! It's for the baby shower your mother is hosting on Wednesday for Mrs. Jacobson."

Patty gave Felicia a pouty face until she conceded. "I'll save you a bowl and put it in the freezer. But don't tell your mother. And get in and say hello to your sister already."

Patty nodded, satisfied, and downed her wine. "Thanks, Felicia," she said as she skipped through the swinging door to the living room.

"Hello, family!" she exclaimed with sarcastic enthusiasm as she entered the room. Mr. Hawkins and Shandi were deep in conversation, seated on plush armchairs in front of an antique coffee table. When Patty entered the room, they both looked up. Mr. Hawkins smiled and got up from his chair, embracing his younger daughter and kissing her on the forehead. "Hello, my dear! You're looking lovely!"

Shandi remained seated, propped on her left hip, her slim legs crossed at the ankles, a champagne flute elegantly suspended between three fingers. She looked like she was posing for an oil painting. She was wearing a simple purple silk slip dress and gold sandals with turquoise stones at the toe strap; her long brown hair fell in gentle curls down the front of her shoulders, and her three-and-a-half-carat princess-cut engagement ring sparkled obnoxiously atop the thin finger that could barely support its weight. Shandi smiled politely at her younger sister and held out her right hand. "Hello, my dear," she said to Patty, who reluctantly obliged her beckoning, taking the hand and kissing her still-sitting sister on the cheek. The way her sister pretended to be some proper society princess from a Jane Austen novel made Patty want to gag.

"Hi, Shandi. Welcome back."

"Thanks, love. You look . . ." She struggled to come up with an adjective. "Tan."

"Can I get you a drink, Patty?" her father offered as she took a seat on the sofa facing the two armchairs.

"Yes, please," Patty responded, as though the thought of having a drink (or having had one already) hadn't crossed her mind. "Is there any pinot grigio open?"

"Coming right up."

The doorbell rang and Patty heard Felicia open it for T.J., who sauntered into the living room grinning and carrying a bouquet of white roses.

"Hello, ladies!" he said jovially to the Hawkins sisters. "How is everyone this evening?" He walked over to Shandi, protesting as she started to stand up, and leaned down to kiss her on either cheek. "Aren't you looking lovelier than ever?" Shandi blushed. As much as she wrote him off as an asshole, the part of her that had had an enormous crush on him from fifth through ninth grade couldn't help smile whenever he gave her a compliment.

T.J. crossed to the sofa and plopped down next to Patty. "Mind if I join you?"

Patty rolled her eyes. "Of course not, T.J." He stared straight at Patty and smiled coyly, as if inviting her to start the charade.

"So," he asked, "where's Chad?"

Not picking up on where he'd directed the question, Shandi answered. "He's at a business school mixer but should be here any minute. I can't wait for you two to meet."

As if on cue, the doorbell rang again and Mr. Hawkins, who was walking back from the kitchen, welcomed his future son-in-law.

"Look who I found," he announced to the room as he brought Patty her glass of white wine.

Shandi stood up from her chair and let Chad rush over to embrace her in his strong arms, kissing her gently on the lips. "My beautiful bride-to-be. Man, have I missed you."

They stayed for a moment in that sickeningly perfect embrace. Patty watched them, and T.J. watched Patty.

Finally, Chad crossed to the sofa and stuck out his hand to T.J. "You must be T.J. I'm Chad. Great to meet you."

With a sly grin, T.J. returned the firm handshake. "It's great to meet you, Chad. I've heard so much about you. And . . ." T.J. glanced at Patty. "I've seen so many photos, I feel like I practically know you already."

Chad nodded politely. He didn't care to fraternize with so many people who were younger than him. An unfortunate ramification of marrying someone four years your junior was that you didn't always get along with her friends.

As if he had delayed the inevitable long enough, Chad finally turned to Patty, who remained seated. Walking across the room, he lifted his hand into a high five. "What's going on, little sis?" She furrowed her brow, cocked her head to one side, and looked up at him just long enough for them both, and T.J., to notice, but not long enough for anyone else to pick up on the exchange. She grabbed hold of his hand to help her stand up from the sofa and smiled. "I'm great, Chad. It's really swell to see you. I'm also starving. What does everyone say to forcing Mom downstairs so we can eat?"

"I'm coming, I'm coming," Mrs. Hawkins called from the stairs, which she was hopping down in a cute Lilly Pulitzer sundress and sandals, her hair perfectly coiffed and her makeup impeccable. "Felicia, can you go ahead and start serving the salads?"

The first course went smoothly enough. T.J. and Patty sat on one side of the table, facing Shandi and Chad, and Mr. and Mrs. Hawkins sat at either end. Shandi dominated the conversation, going on and on about Yale—she was staying an extra year to finish a master's degree in art history—and about the latest parties in New York at the Frick and the New York Athletic Club and you-just-wouldn't-believe-how-sophisticated-New-York-parties-are-compared-to-California-ones. Gross.

Patty watched T.J. politely nod as Shandi continued, but she could feel him waiting to say something and was terrified of what that something was.

As Felicia served the main course—poached salmon with dill-cucumber sauce, Israeli couscous, and grilled asparagus—T.J. saw his opportunity. "So, tell me about the wedding planning," he said.

Mrs. Hawkins was delighted. This was her favorite topic of conversation.

"Well, it's going to be in Maui. I wanted the Glen Ridge

Vineyard in Napa Valley—have you been there? It's stunning and very difficult to book. It was listed in *Vogue* last year as one of the top twenty-five most beautiful places in the world to get married." Mrs. Hawkins shrugged. "But our Shandi wanted Maui, so Hawaii it is."

"Patty, are you a bridesmaid?" asked T.J.

Shandi answered for her. "Of course; she's my maid of honor, but I'm having nine other bridesmaids."

"You must be very excited to watch your sister marry Chad, Patty." T.J. turned to her. "I've never been best man, but I've heard it's tremendously special to watch two people you care so much about give their vows to each other from the front row."

Mrs. Hawkins was touched. "Well aren't you sweet, T.J.!"

T.J. smiled gleefully and took a bite of his salmon. Patty took another gulp of wine.

"You know what would be really cool?" T.J. said. The table all turned to him. Patty cringed. "Remember in the royal wedding, when William drove Kate off in that classic sports car? You should do that. Dad has this great 1968 Lamborghini that would be perfect."

T.J. paused and grinned at Patty.

"I don't know if you got a chance to check out the collection at my party the other night, but this Lamborghini is something else. It's navy—oh, it would suit you so well, Shandi—and I'm sure if you promised to take care of it, Dad would let you drive it, Chad."

"T.J. Bristol," Mrs. Hawkins said, her eyes bright with if-only-I-were-thirty-years-younger affection. "You are too much. That is a lovely idea. Don't you think, Shandi?"

"That's really sweet of you to offer, T.J., I'll definitely think about it. I mean, we'll think about it." She turned to Chad, who was midbite, and squeezed his hand affectionately.

There was nothing that bored Mr. Hawkins so much as wedding talk, and he used the pause to switch the conversation. "How long has your father been collecting those sports cars, T.J.?"

"Oh, I think he bought his first one after the Kadence sale. His celebration present to himself."

Mr. Hawkins smiled. That deal had been huge. It had set a new bar for Silicon Valley wealth. "Well, he certainly deserved it. My, what a deal that was. I only put fifty thousand dollars in and the return was enough to cover both these girls' college tuition, plus some. Wish I'd taken your father's advice and put in more. He's truly a visionary."

T.J. was focusing on his food, but he looked up politely at Mr. Hawkins, his affability somewhat diminished. "He got lucky, that's for sure."

"Luck doesn't build the kind of reputation your father's got. He fucking gets it; he sees where things are headed."

T.J. looked down at his plate and mumbled just loudly enough for Patty to hear, "Here we go again."

Mr. Hawkins was on a roll. "I remember him talking about changes in music, practically forecasting the whole demise of the recording industry. We all thought he was nuts. I wouldn't even have put in fifty thousand dollars if it weren't for the fact that I wanted to keep him on as a client." Mr. Hawkins chuckled. "Now, when your dad offers me a deal, I don't think twice. I mean, Gibly? Didn't even hesitate. I don't get it, I don't get why it sold for so much, but if Ted Bristol tells me something's going to be big, I know it's going to be big. I put in a ton of money, and now look: It's like Christmas around here, all thanks to your dad."

T.J. finally looked up and forced a smile. "Perhaps he'll have a new sports car for you two to try out," he said, looking at Patty.

Felicia, God bless her, interrupted to clear the plates, and the conversation devolved into gossip at the tennis club.

As Patty ate her crème brûlée, she smiled. She'd just figured out a strategy for persuading T.J. to get rid of the tape.

10

Deuce

After dessert, Mr. Hawkins asked if anyone wanted to join him in the movie room to preview a new documentary on the drug wars in Mexico. Like most homes in Atherton, the Hawkinses' house had a room in the basement with fifteen reclining theater seats, a massive projector screen, and a surround-sound stereo for watching films. Mr. Hawkins's latest hobby was an investment in Franklin Media, a socially conscious film production company. The investment made him no money, but getting early DVDs of upcoming releases made him feel cool and hip.

"As riveting as that sounds, I think Chad and I will head back to his place," Shandi said. Chad shrugged his shoulders to his future father-in-law. "She makes the calls," he said.

T.J. claimed he needed to get back to campus, and Patty declined on the basis of schoolwork. "I'll walk you out," she told T.J. Then, so that only he could hear, she added, "We need to talk."

T.J.'s grin returned as he followed her outside to the patio, where she pulled out a chair from a round wrought-iron dining table. "Sit down," she said as she took the seat opposite him.

He followed her instructions, pushing the chair back and leaning with his hands crossed behind his head and his right ankle crossed over his left knee. "Miss Hawkins, you are really something. Quite a performer."

"Where did you get it? Who taped it?"

"You sweet little naïf," he said. He loved this and she hated him for it. "Do you really think my father would leave all those sports cars in a garage without a full security system?"

"Fuck," Patty said. She shook her head as she realized her stupidity. Of course there were security cameras in the garage.

"Don't worry, no one knows except me and a security guard. He had quite a good time watching you, by the way. Or, I guess I should say that no one else knows *yet*."

"Why are you doing this? I've never done anything to you."

"That's not the point, Patty. The point is power."

"What?"

"The point is to accumulate power," T.J. said slowly, as though he were giving a lecture to a child. "I have something on you now, and therefore if I ever need something from you, you have a reason to give it to me."

"How clever of you. And what do you think I might one day be able to provide?"

"I don't know; you're a popular girl. Maybe there's a sorority sister I want to meet or a rumor I need to start. I think you could prove very handy, Patty."

"What if I told you I had something that could help you deal with your daddy issues?"

T.J.'s smile evaporated and he glared at her. He uncrossed his hands from behind his head and said with contempt, "What are you talking about?"

Now it was Patty's turn to smile. "Your daddy issues, T.J.

You know, your inferiority complex? Your hurt feelings that Ted never makes time for you, even answers phone calls during your graduation toast? The fact that you'll never, ever, no matter what you do, live up to him in this town?"

T.J.'s jaw was clenched and his lips pursed. "You have no right to—"

"Oh, T.J., I have every right to. You started this game, not me." Patty's mischievous smile acknowledged that she knew she'd struck a chord. The power had shifted in her favor.

T.J.'s anger was mounting, his chest expanding with every breath. "What have you got?"

"Not so fast, my friend. Conditions first."

T.J. nodded with forced patience. "Okay, what are your conditions, bearing in mind they're dependent on the quality of your information?"

"Oh, trust me, it's quality. Conditions are: In front of me, you physically destroy the tape in full, including any copies that may have been produced by you or the security guard, and erase all digital evidence entirely."

"And in exchange?"

"I give you information that will halt the Gibly deal and destroy your father's reputation."

"How on earth would you have that information?"

"I have my sources."

"And why would you want to halt the Gibly deal? You just heard how much your family has invested in it."

"I think the information is going to come out regardless. The difference is, I can give it to you now and give you a head start to tell your father and be a heroic son, or at least a powerful one. As much fun as it is to have me wrapped around your finger, I bet having Ted on your leash would suit you even more."

T.J. considered this carefully. As annoying as it was, she was right. He wanted this. He wanted his father to respect him one way or another.

"Okay," he said. "I'll destroy the tapes. There's only one hard copy. I'll mail it to you and you can do whatever you want with it. And the digital version is on my laptop in my car. We can erase it after you tell me what you've got."

Patty's thin lips spread into a satisfied smile. "Very good," she said, sticking out her hand to shake on it.

T.J. thought the handshake a little unnecessary but did it anyway. "Okay, spill."

"So." Patty sat up in her chair. "It turns out Gibly is stealing people's information. Well, not really *stealing* it, but apparently when you download any of the applications onto your phone, it installs a code that tracks everything you do on your phone, including all the Web sites you visit and, through your GPS, everywhere you go."

"Lots of software tracks where you go. How do you think Google knows what ads to feed you? It drops cookies and follows where you go. You're going to have to do a little better than that, Patty."

"Yes, but Google doesn't keep a database that records everywhere you've been and everything you've seen, organizing it by the unique ID number on the back of your phone."

"Gibly does that?"

"Yep! Did you seriously take Adam Dory to a strip club after your party?"

"How did you know that?" T.J. sat forward in his chair. "No way."

"And that's not all. Apparently Aleister has been receiving massive payments from some random bank account for the past year for an unspecified service."

"You mean . . ." He started to put it together. "There's no way they'd be selling that information."

"Three-point-eight billion says they are," Patty shot back, pleased with her wit.

"Patty, this is massive. I mean, that's a huge fucking deal. You better be right about this. How did you find all this out?"

"Adam Dory was in my room the other day blabbing on about starting a company and told his sister, my roommate, about Gibly, and she hacked into the site and found the database. Then she hacked into Aleister's bank accounts and found the secret deposits."

"But that's . . . how is that possible? Gibly may be the most sophisticated software on the planet. There's no way some freshman could hack in."

"She's a total nerd. Like, *beyond* nerd. Imagine if a computer and an iPhone had a baby—that's Amelia."

"And she and her brother told you about it?"

"They thought I was asleep."

T.J. laughed. "You little bitch. You're even more of a troublemaker than I gave you credit for."

Patty smiled, knowing this was a compliment.

"All right, my dear, let's go destroy those tapes. Are you in charge of your own trust fund?"

Even though Patty didn't have full access to her trust fund until she turned twenty-five, she had assumed investment decision rights on her eighteenth birthday.

"As of last year, yeah."

"Lucky you don't have my asshole father. Mine is out of reach until I turn forty or get married. If I were you, I'd call tomorrow and make sure whatever portion of your money is invested in Gibly gets sold, pronto."

She knew nothing about investing and usually just signed

whatever her father sent her and let him handle it. She made a mental note to go back and check what she'd signed to make sure none of it had gone to Gibly.

"Thanks, T.J. I actually hadn't thought of that."

"No worries." He stuck out his hand. "I think we'll make a good team, you and I."

11

Family Decisions

While Patty dressed up on Sundays for three-course family dinners prepared by the live-in cook, the Dorii put on sweatpants and snuck food out of the dining hall for their Sunday movie night tradition. They were working through AMC's list of the top one hundred films of all time.

Amelia plopped down on the mattress Adam had set up as a couch in his dorm room and pulled her tray of dining hall chow mein onto her lap. Adam's assigned freshman roommate, an aspiring nuclear physicist from the Ukraine who spoke broken English and had a penchant for heavy metal music, had had a mental breakdown in the fall and never came back after winter break. Adam considered saying something, but it was so convenient having a double dorm room all to himself that he eventually decided just to wait and see if the university figured it out. They hadn't, or had chosen not to do anything about it, so he'd pulled the mattress off his roommate's bed and made a makeshift sofa, on which he now joined his sister.

"What are we watching tonight?" Amelia asked between bites of greasy Chinese noodles.

"The Godfather: Part II," he answered as he inserted the disc into Amelia's laptop, which she'd brought over with a cable to connect to a thirty-six-inch monitor Adam had "borrowed" from the Gates Building.

Amelia scrunched her nose in disapproval. She'd hated *The Godfather: Part I,* with all its violence and betrayal, and had hoped they could remove the sequel from their list of must-sees. But Adam couldn't wait to see the next one. He was totally enthralled by the strength of loyalty and the strategy of the family.

"I know, I know. I didn't complain about *Casablanca* week, though," he said as he punched his sister lovingly on the arm.

Amelia rolled her eyes. "Fine, fine."

It didn't matter anyway. Thirty minutes in, she was sound asleep, half a bite of chocolate pudding still left on her spoon.

When he realized she was sleeping, Adam laughed, moved the tray from her lap, and gently placed a pillow behind her head. He was deeply engrossed in the movie when an e-mail notification popped up on Amelia's screen. The mail icon bounced up and down in the corner, its cheerfulness the antithesis of the drama unfolding onscreen.

Adam leaned forward to click the icon so it would stop bouncing, but when he saw the subject line and sender—"Nice Meeting You!" from Roger Fenway—his interest was piqued. He paused the movie and opened the e-mail.

Dear Amelia,

You'll have to forgive my tactics, but I called a few friends at Stanford and got them to track down your e-mail address (luckily there are only two women named Amelia in your freshman class, and the other is from France). I wanted to follow up with you about your awesome invention.

As I mentioned, I'm launching an incubator for start-up companies, and I'd love to have you join. I know you're antibusiness, and I totally get that. Trust me, I was completely antibusiness when I started out. But I think together we could create something that allows you to do even more of what you love to do, and have a lot of fun doing it.

I'm including my contact information just in case you scratched it out of your notebook. I've also attached a PDF that provides more detail about the incubator. Please give it some thought and let me know if you have any questions or want to talk more.

All the best,
Roger

Roger Fenway
Fenway Ventures, LLC
2800 Sand Hill Rd.
Palo Alto, CA 94025
(650) 326-9251
roger@fenwayventures.com

Adam's jaw dropped. What was this e-mail, and why hadn't Amelia told him about Roger Fenway? He quickly googled Fenway Ventures and got over sixty thousand articles mentioning Roger Fenway, the second of which was a Wikipedia entry.

"Shit—this guy's got a Wikipedia page?" Adam whispered to himself. He clicked it open.

Roger Fenway (born June 12, 1958) is a Canadian-American serial entrepreneur and angel investor. In 1988, Roger founded Ultra Effects, a digital motion graphics software that revolutionized the postproduction process of filmmaking. After he sold Ultra Effects to Aldus in 1993 (it was then acquired by Adobe in 1994), he founded Micromedia, a pioneer in desktop publishing most known for products such as Flash and Final Cut. Roger continued his passion for marrying technology with creativity by starting a pet project known as Kadence, a technology that allowed musicians to create, edit, and aggregate music digitally. With the expansion of the Internet, Fenway took Kadence online and created the first online music aggregator. In 2000, he sold Kadence to Apple for an estimated $1.8 billion, and then in 2005 he sold Micromedia to rival Adobe for $3.4 billion. Roger Fenway is firmly established in Silicon Valley lore as the digital media pioneer, and is warmly credited as the father of iTunes, the grandfather of Final Cut Pro, and the uncle of online gaming.

Today, Fenway lives in Woodside, California, and acts as an angel investor to small companies in Silicon Valley. Around Silicon Valley, Fenway is known for his laid-back aesthetic, notoriously wearing flip-flops to high-profile meetings, and his obsession with the Grateful Dead. His wife, Margaret, passed away in 2009 from breast cancer; Roger Fenway is a major contributor and spokesperson for several breast cancer prevention organizations.

Adam didn't need to read more. Almost two billion dollars? In 2000? And another three-and-a-half billion dollars five years later? And this guy was e-mailing *Amelia*? How had she not told him about this? Why was Roger implying that she'd turned him down?

"Are you reading my e-mails?" Amelia's voice sounded groggy, and she called out from the sofa without lifting her head or opening her eyes.

"As a matter of fact, I am, Amelia," Adam said sternly, "and I'd like to understand why you failed to mention your meeting with Roger Fenway."

Amelia popped one eye open and saw her brother, totally alert and looking cross, staring at her from her computer. She sat up. "I didn't think it was worth mentioning. Why are you bringing this up? How did you know about that?"

"He e-mailed you, Amelia. Do you have any idea who this guy is? He has his own Wikipedia page."

"He does? What does it say?"

"That he's fucking loaded, Amelia. And super successful."

Amelia rolled her eyes. "Give me the computer." She grabbed it and read the e-mail and the Wikipedia page. "So what? Like I told him, I'm not interested in starting a company."

"But, Amelia—"

"No. End of discussion."

Adam was getting annoyed, and he was not about to give up. He snatched the laptop from her and opened the attachment Roger had sent with the e-mail. Maybe there was something in there that could hook her.

She glared at him as he read, her arms crossed against her chest. Her brother was irritatingly persistent, but he had never been any match for her stubbornness.

"Listen to this, Amelia." Adam read from the description: "'As part of the Fenway incubator, participants will receive office space on Sand Hill Road, a living stipend, and mentorship from Roger Fenway and his staff. Should participants still be enrolled in college, Fenway Ventures will also pay for education expenses, including university tuition. Equity rights to the company will be negotiated at the time of incorporation on the basis of money invested in the venture itself.'" Adam looked up from the computer. "Free tuition, Amelia! This is incredible!"

Amelia rolled her eyes. "We're on *scho-lar-ship*, Adam. We don't pay tuition anyway."

"But we wouldn't have to *be* on scholarship. We could be making it ourselves. Just you and me, not dependent on anyone."

"Except Roger Fenway! And some corporate ideology about what makes good software. I'm not doing it, Adam. Give it a rest."

Amelia grabbed her computer back and started to shut it down. "I'm tired. If you won't be offended, I'd like to go home and go to bed."

Adam looked at his sister, whose eyes were pleading with him, and, with a sigh, saw for the first time how much she hated the idea. That didn't mean he was going to give up, but he realized he wasn't going to get anywhere by pushing tonight. He reached out and gave her a hug. "Of course. I still think you should give this some more thought, but I didn't mean to pressure you."

Amelia felt tears start to well up and was glad her head was resting on Adam's shoulder so he couldn't see them. The only thing that came close to her conviction about the purity of computer programming was her love for her brother. She'd never imagined that the two might come into conflict.

12

The Art of the Deal

T.J. knocked lightly and cracked open the door of his father's home office enough to stick his head in. "Hey Dad, do you have a—" T.J. stopped short when he saw his father was on the phone.

Ted motioned his son to come in and have a seat, signaling with his hand that the call would only take a minute.

"Totally agree, Stuart. . . . The tax lawyers have been great. . . . Mitch is sharp as hell. . . . They've actually expedited the sale, should be closed in three weeks. Apparently it usually takes two months for the U.K. government to approve corporate transactions like this; I guess they're a bit desperate for the tax revenue. Poor old England. Must be difficult to be dependent upon your former colonies. . . . Yes, I'll be in London the week after next to make sure everything's running smoothly and do a few press appearances. . . . I know I'm missing graduation, but T.J.'s being a real sport about it." Ted winked at his son. "Yes, yes, talk soon."

"Whew!" Ted turned to T.J. as he set the phone back in its cradle. There were deep bags under his eyes, but they still sparkled with excitement and adrenaline. He radiated an energy that said "I am Master of the Universe."

"What can I do for you, son?"

T.J. sat up in his chair, his hands folded carefully in his lap. "Well, Dad, I was hoping you could help me get a job with Roger Fenway's incubator."

"Didn't you meet with him last week? How did that go?"

"It was fine. I mean, I presented my credentials well, but I don't think he understands how useful I could be, in terms of adding business insight to the engineering geeks he brings in."

"Roger's a smart guy, I'm sure he knows what he's doing."

T.J. ignored the sting of this rebuff. "Well, it would help me a lot if you'd call him."

Ted cocked his head and studied his son. T.J. stared back unflinchingly. Finally he said, "T.J., I'm not going to get you this job. I got you the meeting, which is more than most kids your age get, but that's where it stops. You have to get things yourself. Not just because it's fair and meritocratic, but also because it will be more satisfying to you in the end than if I get it for you. You're twenty-two, T.J. It's time for you to start taking responsibility for your own success."

T.J. had been expecting this. "I see it a little differently. I think I'm twenty-two now, and it's time for us to be more of a team. You do something for me, I do something for you."

Ted's face folded into a mocking half-grin, and his right eyebrow rose. "Okay, T.J.," he said with amused patience. "What, exactly, are you going to do for me?"

T.J. smiled and said calmly, "I have some information that I think you'll find valuable. About Gibly."

Still amused, as though he were playing Go Fish with a four-year-old, Ted humored his son. "And what information is that, T.J.?"

"Did you know that someone hacked into Gibly last week?"

"Not possible. The security is the best on the planet." Ted didn't flinch or show an ounce of concern.

Neither did T.J. "They hacked into the user database. The one where Gibly stores the Web activity and physical movements of each unique user."

Ted didn't respond right away. It was a very loud silence.

"What are you talking about, T.J.? Gibly doesn't do that."

"Want to bet?"

At first Ted was irritated by his son's presumptuousness. T.J. clearly didn't have a clue what he was talking about, claiming that someone could hack into the ironclad Gibly. But T.J.'s comment about the database made him pause. What exactly did his kid know? Ted punched a number on speed dial and put the phone on speaker.

"Hello?" a man's voice, thick with an Indian accent, answered.

Still looking at his son, Ted said into the phone, "Amit, this is Ted. How are you doing today?"

Amit, the lead programmer for Gibly, sounded distracted. "Mr. Bristol! I'm—I'm fine, sir," he muttered. "What can I do for you, sir?"

"Just have a quick question for you, Amit," Ted said, his voice dripping with sarcasm. "Did someone hack into Gibly last week?"

Amit was silent on the other end. Ted and T.J. could hear commotion in the background, the voices of programmers yelling at one another in panicked voices. T.J. grinned. Ted blinked, listening intently for some reassurance to come out of the speaker, then looked down at the phone. "Amit? Amit, did you hear me?"

"Yes, sir. I heard you. We're working on it. We've been up for the past four nights and, well, we're—we'll figure out who it was, sir, and we'll get it patched."

Ted stared at the phone, motionless, his eyes darting as his panic increased.

"Sir?" This time Amit was unnerved by the silence. "Everything . . . everything will be okay, sir. The whole team is working on it."

"How could you not have told me this?" His disbelief had given way to anger. "What the fuck! Do you not realize that we're about to close a deal? That this whole thing could fucking fall apart if . . ." He trailed off; it was too much to process. "I'm coming down there. Right now." Ted hung up the phone so hard it almost fell off the desk, and then he stood up. He reached for his briefcase.

T.J. remained seated, hands still neatly folded in his lap. "Would it help if I told you who did it?"

Ted stopped and looked at his son. He'd almost forgotten he was sitting there. His voice was shaking. "Yes, T.J. That would be helpful."

"Will you get me the job at Fenway?"

Ted swallowed hard and tried to keep his voice steady. "Yes, T.J. I'll call in a favor with Roger and get you a place at Fenway."

T.J. smiled. "Thank you. Her name is Amelia Dory. She's a freshman at Stanford."

"How the hell could a freshman at Stanford hack into the most sophisticated . . ." Ted started to speak but the smug look on his son's face stopped him. He knew T.J. was telling the truth.

Ted pulled out a notebook and said her name as he wrote it down. "Amelia Dory. You have no idea what you've gotten yourself into."

13

Lady and the Tramp

By the grace of God, Adam had been able to convince his RA to let him borrow her car for the evening. It was a 1999 Toyota Camry, which wasn't exactly a match for Lisa's Lexus SUV, but at least he didn't have to show up for his date on a bike.

Adam had sent Lisa a Facebook message asking if she wanted to have dinner at Salamanca Tapas Bar downtown. He'd never been on a real date or, for that matter, to a real restaurant in Palo Alto, but he'd gotten a Groupon for 60 percent off weekday dining at Salamanca, and hoped that, even if it wasn't quite as fancy as she was used to, it might be acceptable to Lisa. To his relief, she had agreed.

He'd pulled out his nicest pair of khakis and the button-down shirt he'd bought for his Stanford interview. The shirt was light blue, and he wasn't sure it totally matched the pants, but he thought the color accentuated his eyes and he figured his legs would be under the table during dinner anyway. He showered and shaved, stole hair gel from one of the cubbies in the hall bathroom, and looked at himself, satisfied, in the mirror.

Until he realized he didn't have proper shoes. What shoes did you wear with khakis? He slipped on his Converse sneakers. They didn't look too bad, and maybe she would think he was edgy?

He arrived at the restaurant fifteen minutes early. When Lisa came through the door, looking like an angel in white jeans, heels, and a light blue silk halter top, Adam smiled and stood up to greet his date. Lisa smiled back and gave him an unexpected hug. "We match!" she said, noticing their shirt colors, and he blushed.

The hostess sat them at a small candlelit table. Adam panicked when he opened the menu; he didn't see a single thing that he could pronounce. Why hadn't he looked beforehand to figure out what to order? At the bottom of the menu, there were a few "traditional Spanish rice dishes" listed. Okay, that sounded safe. Done. He closed the menu. "Look okay?" He smiled at Lisa.

"Yes! I love this place. I did a summer program in Madrid last year and absolutely fell in love with Spanish food."

Adam smiled widely. *Phew!*

The waiter approached and Lisa spoke with him in flawless Spanish, giggling lightly at something he said. Adam smiled, allowing the glory of being out with such a beautiful, intelligent girl to make him feel like the luckiest guy alive.

The waiter turned to Adam. "And for you, sir?"

"I'll have the pay-ella," Adam said.

The waiter gave a knowing glance at Lisa and corrected Adam's pronunciation. "The pi-yay-yah?"

Adam's face turned beet red. "Uh, yes. Yes, the pi-yay-yah."

The waiter smiled at his improvement. Lisa reassured him. "Don't worry; the Spaniards love making complicated words so they can mock us for mispronouncing them."

Adam was grateful for her humility.

The dinner passed quickly, conversation never ceasing as Adam and Lisa talked about Stanford and Palo Alto and her favorite trips around the world. They talked about their favorite TV shows and ice cream flavors and laughed at each other's favorite jokes. The paella, it turned out, was delicious, and Lisa insisted they order the house-made flan so Adam could try it.

But when it came time to pay the bill, Adam confronted a new dilemma: how to slip the waiter the Groupon without Lisa seeing. To his relief, she excused herself to use the restroom and Adam hurriedly beckoned the waiter over.

"I have to get the manager to approve it," he explained. "I'll be right back." He walked away just as Lisa returned to the table. *Just in time,* he thought.

But then the manager came over to their table, holding the Groupon. Adam felt his hands sweat. "Sir, this coupon—" The manager stopped when he noticed Lisa. "Lisa! Lisa, my dear, how are you?"

"Sergio! It's so lovely to see you!" Lisa responded with a smile.

"How was everything tonight?"

Lisa grinned. "Oh, it was all wonderful, Sergio. This is Adam." She gestured to Adam, who reached out his hand to shake Sergio's and started to stand up.

"No, no, don't stand up. A friend of Lisa's is a friend of mine. Marco, don't worry about that bill; the meal is on me."

Adam couldn't hide his surprise. "Oh, thank you so much," he stammered.

Lisa smiled. "Thanks, Sergio. I can't wait to tell Dad how wonderful everything was."

"Yes, please do! I'll leave you two to it. Have a lovely evening."

When he'd left the table, Lisa turned back to Adam. "Sorry about that. My dad owns the property and loaned Sergio the money to open the restaurant."

"No, I'm sorry. I bet you've been here a thousand times. I didn't mean to bring you somewhere your father invested in!"

"Honestly, Adam, it's hard to find a place in this town that Dad isn't somehow involved with. And I love this place. I would eat here every single night—if it meant hanging out with you." She blushed. That came out a little too quickly and she worried it sounded too aggressive.

But Adam just smiled, his heart pounding, at a loss for words.

14

Blank Check

Ted's head was spinning as he walked into University Café. He'd had hundreds—maybe thousands—of meetings here, but never one like this. He'd used T.J.'s student directory log-in to find Amelia Dory's phone number and had called her on the way to meet Amit, asking her to meet him at University Café as soon as possible to discuss what she'd found out about Gibly. To his surprise, she'd happily obliged and agreed to meet that evening.

In the meantime, he'd gone to Gibly headquarters and found Amit and the team in a state of panic. Everyone was typing away at computers, trying to figure out how someone had broken into the system. They could see that there had been a security breach but had no way of locating an IP address for the person who had done it. Ted didn't tell them he knew the answer.

When he asked him about the database, Amit confessed that the hacker had found everything. In the early days of Gibly, this database was temporary, built to make sure the software functioned properly. But when this temporary database proved to be the company's most valuable asset, Ted Bristol had instructed Amit to integrate it into Gibly's entire back-end infrastructure. Most temporary databases typically don't last through one hundred million users, but most temporary databases aren't as thorough as Gibly's.

As someone who started companies for a living, Ted Bristol followed one very important maxim: Know Your Exit. It's pointless to start a company if it can't be acquired, merged, or IPO'd. Silicon Valley is a graveyard of start-ups without homes, its landscape littered with naïve entrepreneurs and hapless venture capitalists whose ideas lacked real value.

That's why the database was so important—*the database* was the product being sold for $3.8 billion. Before he started Gibly, a representative of the Aleister Corporation approached Ted. This young British woman with piercing eyes was no older than T.J., but she certainly knew how to play the game. She told Ted Bristol that Aleister was undergoing a renaissance, and they would pay anything to make the company a major player in the tech space.

"Ted Bristol, you're the man to do it," she told him. "If you're up for the challenge. Aleister will pay a lot of money for a database like this." Ted already had enough money to retire early. He didn't retire, though, because it was never about the money. It was about winning, about going beyond where those before you had gone. If he could build a company for Aleister, he would be able to end his career as one of the most successful and clever venture capitalists Silicon Valley had ever seen. Ted Bristol would be in textbooks. His Wikipedia page would have more sections than anybody else's.

Ted glanced around University Café. That someone besides Ted and Amit and Gibly's acquirers now knew about the tracking made Ted more than a little nervous. The legal battles the database would stir up notwithstanding, if anyone found out that an eighteen-year-old had hacked into Gibly, the deal would be off and his reputation would be finished.

He had to shut her up somehow. Ted's career grand finale was on the line.

Sitting at the corner table where Amelia had said she'd be was a slender teenager with a long blond ponytail and glasses. She tapped her foot anxiously, watching the television over the bar. Upon seeing her, Ted let out a sigh of relief. There was no way this fidgety little girl—she couldn't weigh more than 110 pounds—would be the threat that brought him down. He felt his confidence coming back for the first time since his conversation with T.J.

"Amelia?" he asked as he walked up to the table, sticking out his hand. "Ted Bristol. Thank you for meeting me on such short notice."

Amelia jumped, startled, when he said her name. "Oh, hi, Mr. Bristol. Yes, of course. No problem. I really want to—"

Ted put his hand up to cut her off. "We have all night," he said as he sat down across from her and motioned for the waiter. "Have you eaten dinner? Would you like to order anything? I'm going to have a little something."

"Oh, sure." Amelia hadn't expected such an offer; she had thought she was in trouble.

Ted ordered eggplant Parmesan. Flustered, Amelia said she'd have the same.

"Do you want wine?" he asked her.

Amelia was stunned. Didn't he know she was eighteen? "No thanks," she answered quickly. "I'll just have a Coke."

"Suit yourself." Ted smiled. "I'll take a glass of the cab. Thanks, Martin." He always made a point to pay attention to waiters' nametags and address them personally.

"So, Amelia," he said, crossing his hands on the table. "Do you mind telling me a little about what you found on Gibly?"

"Well, first I want to say I'm sorry for breaking in. I really didn't mean to."

"No need to apologize. On the contrary, you've helped us realize a flaw in our security, which our team is addressing as we speak." He was buttering her up, making her feel comfortable.

Amelia let out a sigh of relief. "Oh, that's great. How did you find out, though?"

"Not important, Amelia. What is important is that I understand what you saw once you were in." Ted smiled again.

Amelia didn't exactly think how he found out was "not important"—she was certain she'd covered all her tracks—but for now she knew that making sure Ted knew what was going on with the Web site was more important.

"Well, I found the database where Gibly is storing all of its users' information. Billions and billions of cells recording the Web movements and physical locations of every person using Gibly. It's insane. I mean, that's, like, totally unethical, if not illegal, right? It's a complete infraction of users' privacy."

Ted kept the same neutral smile as the waiter delivered his wine. "Well, yes, I suppose it would be, if it existed. Did you see anything else?"

"Well, then I started thinking that maybe that was why the company had sold for so much. I mean, it's illegal, but that kind of information would also be insanely valuable to everyone from advertisers to terrorists. So, I tracked Aleister's accounts." She stopped, not sure she should have admitted that.

"It's okay, Amelia. I'm not going to tell anyone."

Reassured, she went on. "So, I tracked Aleister, and they've been receiving ten-million-dollar payments every month from someone named VIPER."

Ted took a moment to consider this, but quickly chose to ignore it. What Aleister did was not his problem. His problem was the possibility of this being discovered and his reputation being destroyed.

He took a sip of his wine. "Amelia, I want to reassure you that the database was temporary, just something the engineering team did to make sure that the applications we were putting out were working on different browsers and in different network areas. Last week, when you got into the system, the team was actually disabling everything. In fact, that might be why you were able to get in; the security wall was probably compromised when they were reprogramming. Because of you, though, we're repatching that, too."

Amelia stared at Ted. That didn't make sense, and he knew it as well as she did.

The food arrived and Ted picked up his fork and knife to cut a piece of eggplant. "I want you to know that it's all being taken care of. Okay? But I need a favor from you."

He casually took a bite of his eggplant. "I need you to promise me that you won't say anything about this. To anyone."

Amelia looked down at her food. She poked at the eggplant with her fork.

"And to thank you for your discretion," he went on, "I want to offer you a payment of ten thousand dollars."

Amelia put her fork down. She was no longer hungry. "You want to pay me?"

"Consider it a consulting fee for helping us increase our security. Your getting in has saved us a lot of potential trouble down the road; we'll be much stronger now with the new security patches."

"I don't think . . . I don't want your money." She felt her voice growing more assertive. "Your programmers can't just disable the database. Recording private information is in Gibly's core code. It looks like that's what it was built for in the first place! Everything else—the speech-to-text, the near-field communication, the payment systems—are just add-ons. It would take an entire team six months, maybe more, to undo all of that."

Ted felt his anxiety rising. The deal was closing in three weeks; six months was five months and one week too long to save his reputation.

"Amelia, I can assure you we'll do what needs to be done and all your concerns will be addressed down the line. But right now the deal has to go through. I can't have anything delay it." He reached into his briefcase. "I brought a contract. Just sign it, and I'll write you a check right now for twenty-five thousand dollars. Twenty-five thousand just for doing nothing."

To her surprise, Amelia felt calm and confident. "I'm not signing anything," she said.

Ted decided to try a new tactic. "What if I brought you onto the team? I can guarantee you a job. Do you have a summer job yet? I've got an entire portfolio of companies. You can have your pick of any of them. I'll help make you the next Mark Zuckerberg."

Amelia couldn't help but laugh. "No offense, but I don't want to start a company, Mr. Bristol."

"What do you want, then, Amelia?"

"I don't want to be exploited, and I don't think Gibly's users do, either. The Internet should be a free and open place. Your company steals users' private information without their permission. It's irresponsible. It's immoral." The passion in her voice surprised even Amelia.

Ted looked at her carefully. This girl, this tiny little thing, was actually serious. "One hundred thousand," he told her.

But Amelia didn't flinch. "I don't want your money."

"Do you know how much money one hundred thousand dollars is, Amelia? It would take you and your brother a very long way."

"How do you know about my brother?" Amelia asked.

"I know more than you think, Amelia. A lot more." His expression hardened. "I'm telling you right now, you want to take this offer. After this, things only get worse."

Amelia couldn't believe she was being threatened. "I'm not afraid of you, Mr. Bristol."

Ted took a deep breath. "Listen, go home and talk it over with your brother. I'll call you in the morning and you can tell me your decision then. Once we're in agreement, I'll wire the money to you immediately—and we can discuss any job you might want. I can make your life incredibly easy, Amelia. All you have to do is sign the contract."

Amelia stood up from her chair and put on her jacket. "Thank you so much for dinner, Mr. Bristol, but I can assure you, you're wasting your time."

She walked out with her head high. As the café door closed, Ted slammed his fist onto the table. "Dammit!" The whole restaurant turned to stare, but he didn't care. He threw a fifty-dollar bill onto the table and stormed out.

15

Part of Something Real

Amelia's head was spinning as she got onto her bike and headed back to campus. University Avenue, where the café was, turned into Palm Drive, the majestic entrance to Stanford University. One hundred sixty-six palm trees lined the road that led to the main quad, the magnificent Spanish fortress that composed the original university and sat at the base of the foothills, providing a gorgeous view up into the mountainous skyline. No matter how many times she biked this road, its beauty never failed to make Amelia pause. Tonight was no different, and she felt her heart slow as she looked down the stretch, noticed the breeze in her hair, and watched as the sun set behind the mountains and turned the tiled roof of the main quad a majestic red. Over the past year this place had become a part of her, and she a part of it, and it demanded that she live according to what she knew was right. She owed it to all the minds that had worked on the campus to pioneer a new world of technology. She knew what she had to do.

With calm determination, Amelia raced back to her dorm room, opened her laptop, and created a secure, untraceable e-mail address. She then logged into TechCrunch, the popular technology blog, and looked up an e-mail address for the editorial staff. TechCrunch was known for its stances on freedom of information and user protection, and Amelia knew they'd faithfully handle the information she was about to give them.

SUBJECT: Privacy Invasion at Gibly
STATUS: URGENT
TO: The Editor

I'm writing to inform you of a serious issue with the Gibly platform. I've discovered that the company records each user's personal data. Gibly has been monitoring our movements and purchases and has even recorded our conversations and text messages. A large database containing all of this and more, listed by unique user ID, is housed in the company's servers. Moreover, I have reason to believe it's this database, and not belief in the marketability of the company's applications, that is driving the sale of Gibly to the Aleister Corporation.

I have attached the directions that got me to the database in order to prove my logic; however, I've put a security algorithm on the pathway, so the direction will only work for the next hour. If you need more time, reply to this e-mail and I will reconstruct a new pathway. I'm writing to you as someone deeply concerned with the ramifications such a violation of user trust could have on future Internet applications, for I fear that if the Gibly deal goes through without major changes to Gibly's programming infrastructure, user security will be irreversibly compromised.

She attached the directions, reread the paragraphs, and stared at the "Send" button. Her finger hesitated on the mouse and she felt her heart racing. She wasn't saying that she wanted to take Gibly on, she was just encouraging someone else to look into it, right? That was all she had to do; just send the e-mail, and her part was finished. She took a deep breath, closed her eyes, and clicked "Send."

Ted let out a grunt as he pushed the bench press forward. Six. Seven. Eight. Rest.

When he'd gotten home from University Café he'd tried to work, but it had been a fruitless effort. He was too distracted. He'd come down to his home gym to relieve some stress. The large room had tiled floors and seven pieces of gym equipment, plus a stretching area with a mirror and the Pilates junk his wife was obsessed with.

Working out was helping. The more he exercised, the more he became convinced Amelia would come around to see things his way. One hundred thousand dollars for a scholarship kid from foster homes in Indiana? That was like winning the lottery; no sane person would turn it down. Everything would be fine.

He got up from the bench and moved to the treadmill, pointing the remote to turn on the flat-screen television on the wall as he dialed the treadmill up to a healthy running pace. He began trotting and smiled at a clever Volkswagen advertisement. *What a great rebranding campaign that company pulled off,* he thought.

When the commercial break ended, a news anchor for CNBC appeared.

"Folks, we've got breaking news. Internet accusations claim that Gibly, the Silicon Valley company in the process of finalizing its sale to the Aleister Corporation for three-point-eight billion dollars, has spent the past several years stealing users' private information. Everything from your whereabouts to your purchases to your ATM PIN have been tracked. We're going now to our tech correspondent Christian Johnson for the latest. Christian, what can you tell us about these stunning allegations?"

Ted pulled the emergency stop brake on the treadmill and stared at the television, though he could no longer hear a word they were saying. Just then, his cell phone and the house phone started to ring. He took a deep breath and composed himself. That little nerd didn't know what was about to hit her.

16

Homeless

Adam raced up the stairs of the Gates Building, clenching a letter tightly in his hand, his head whirring with panic. He'd only been in this building twice before; once when Amelia had fainted—she'd been holed up coding something and had forgotten to eat for more than twenty-four hours and Adam's name had been first on her speed dial—and another time to smuggle out the old monitor he kept assuring Amelia he would return any day now.

He didn't like the building. It was too sterile and clean and the blue light and the just-barely-audible buzz of all the computers made him anxious. Plus, all the people there were such dweebs. Not that he was the emperor of cool, but at least he knew where he fell short; these people had created an environment where social weirdness was totally acceptable. Like, it was fine to stare at a machine and not shower for three days, because the guy next to you hadn't either. It wasn't fine; it was weird.

But he knew Amelia would be there and he had to talk to her about the letter he'd just gotten.

He found her on the third floor, at a cubicle near the window, wearing headphones and deeply engrossed in whatever she was typing.

He walked up behind her and shook her shoulder.

"Amelia, we've gotta talk."

"Just a sec." She hardly acknowledged him, still absorbed in whatever was on her computer.

He pulled off her headphones a little too forcefully. "No. Now!"

"Geez, Adam. What is it?"

"They're taking away our scholarships."

"What are you talking about?"

He threw the letter down in front of her. "Our scholarships: our tuition money, our room and board, our monthly stipend. They're taking it away. All of it. The letter says the university is cutting back on aid next year and we no longer qualify. Do you think they found out?"

"They couldn't have. . . . When I turned eighteen my records were sealed."

"How else could we no longer qualify?" Adam felt his voice shaking. "We're, like, the poorest people on this campus, Amelia, we have nothing to our names."

Amelia was looking down at her hands and was silent.

"Hello? Amelia? Are you listening?" Why did she not get the gravity of this? Then it dawned on Adam what she was thinking. "You don't think it was Roger Fenway, do you?" he said. "Do you think he's blackmailing you to take the job? Oh my God! Do you think that's it?"

"No, Adam. It's not Roger Fenway." Amelia paused. "It's Ted Bristol."

"Ted Bristol? Lisa's—I mean, T.J.'s dad?" He hadn't told Amelia about Lisa yet, and this didn't seem like the time.

Amelia took a deep breath, still looking down at her hands. "Yes. We . . . we had a meeting the other day and I didn't exactly give him the answer he wanted."

"Wait, what? What are you talking about? What meeting?"

"He somehow found out that I hacked into Gibly."

"How? Didn't you conceal your identity?"

"I don't know how, but he found out. And he called me and it sounded like he wanted to fix it, and so I went to University Café to meet him and explain everything. I thought he was going to ask me how to fix the problem. He was so nice on the phone, I was certain he wanted to do the right thing."

Adam felt his face go white. Oh, God. What had she done?

"But then he tried to pay me off, Adam. He didn't want to do what needs to be done to change the monitoring, and he said that the deal just needed to go through."

"How much did he offer you?"

"At first it was ten, then it was twenty-five, then it was a hundred. And a job, nothing specific, kind of like choose your own—"

"Wait," Adam interrupted, feeling his ears turn red. "One hundred . . . thousand?"

"Adam, that is dirty money and you know it."

He couldn't speak. It felt as if there were something lodged in his throat, preventing the expulsion of air.

Amelia glanced away. She knew she had to tell him the last part, but he looked so devastated. "And then I . . ." she said meekly.

"And then you WHAT?"

"When I got home, I e-mailed the editors at TechCrunch with the details of what I'd found. I put a security tag on it so they could only access it during a one-hour window, which they did. They posted about it pretty much immediately. A bigger article came out this morning."

"And you think Ted . . . to get back at you . . . ?"

"He knew about you, Adam. I mean, he knew I had a twin brother and that we were on financial aid. He must have—"

Amelia suddenly realized what she had done. No financial aid meant Stanford was finished. It had been too good to be true, after all, this world where she could spend all her days coding and being around people who were driven by the same pure aim of creation. No, she shouldn't have ever let herself believe four years of this was possible. One year was more than she deserved. Now it would be back to figuring things out, just her and Adam. Just the Dorii.

But when she looked up at Adam's face, painted with anger and betrayal, she felt an even greater panic. Would it be her and Adam—or her alone?

"Adam, say something," she pleaded.

"You," he started, then shook his head as if trying to put it all together. "First you turn down an unbelievable job opportunity. Then you turn down one hundred thousand dollars. Then you knowingly backstab one of the most influential people in Silicon Valley and have our financial aid revoked?" He felt a pit in his stomach, like someone had punched him under the ribs.

"I did what was right. I did what I had to do to keep the Internet free," she said, but, in doing so, felt how weak and naïve that argument sounded against the charges Adam had just lodged.

"Don't you get it, Amelia? We're poor. We're dependents. Taking this high moral ground? Taking risks for an ideal? That's a freedom and a luxury, and it's not one you have."

His use of "you" struck her hard. Everything was always

"we" with them. She understood then just how betrayed he felt.

"Fix this, Amelia. I'm not giving this up. I'm not." He turned and walked out.

Amelia sank back into her chair. This room, this safe place where she felt so at home, suddenly felt foreign.

17

A White Comforter on a Four-poster Bed

Everything was a blur as Adam hopped onto his bike. *This can't be real. How could she?*

The sun was setting and he'd left his bike light at home, but he didn't care. He had to see Lisa. He pedaled hard to Atherton and called Lisa's phone from outside the front gate.

"Hello?"

"I need to see you. I'm outside your front gate."

"What? No, Adam, you can't be here. Dad is—"

"I have to see you, Lisa."

"We're in the middle of dinner. We have guests."

"I'll wait."

"You can't wait out there. They'll see you." He could sense her thinking on the other end, scrambling for a solution.

"Come around to the back gate. The code is eight-nine-two-four. There's a key under the flowerpot next to the side door and a back staircase. Take it to the second floor and go to the third door on the right. That's my room. I'll be there as soon as I can, but it's probably going to be thirty minutes at least."

"I'm on my way."

She hung up. Adam followed her instructions and carefully crept into her room. He wasn't sure at first if he was in the right place. *Could this really be an eighteen-year-old girl's bedroom?* he thought. It was cavernous, with hardwood floors covered by an intricately patterned Turkish rug. A four-poster bed with a draped white canopy was neatly made, a plush white comforter and a dozen or so mint-green and white pillows covering its surface. But the vanity in the corner—a deep cherry wood to match the other furniture in the room, topped with a massive mirror—gave Lisa away. Pictures of high school friends, cheerleading camp (She was a cheerleader? Of course she was a cheerleader.), and Lisa and T.J. in front of the Eiffel Tower were neatly stuck around the edges of the mirror. The vanity drawer was open, and Adam saw it was cluttered with lip glosses and nail polish and metallic eye shadows.

He sat on the stool of the vanity and looked in the mirror. So, this was what it felt like to be a rich girl.

He heard the door crack open and turned, startled.

"Adam, this better be really important."

The temporary calm he'd felt seeing Lisa's things melted, and he felt his purpose and his anger return.

"The university took away Amelia's and my scholarships today. Do you know what that means? I'm out. We're out. No more Stanford. No more California. No more chances. We're back on the street."

Lisa's shoulders sank and her eyes closed in disappointment. "Oh, God," she said.

"Was it your dad?"

She looked down at her hands and then said weakly, "He's a trustee of the university."

"So, he did it?"

"He gives a lot of money to the school. They'd do it if he asked them to."

"Your father's a dirty—"

Her eyes sprung open. "Hey!"

"What kind of a person goes around picking on eighteen-year-old foster kids?"

"Oh, please! Don't you dare play that sympathy card with me. Do you have any idea what that little e-mail of Amelia's did to him? To our family? The deal's probably off, Adam. And, more importantly, he's on the hook for it. He didn't catch it, Adam, and that means his reputation is on the line. Do you have any idea how many people—how many *friends*—invested in Gibly? Do you have any idea how much money could be lost?"

He'd never seen her so animated. "He's breaking the law, Lisa. Doesn't that mean anything?"

"*He's* breaking the law? And what was Amelia doing when she hacked into the system? *She* broke the law, and then brought down this company with speculation based on the confidential information she found."

Now Adam was getting protective. "She did the *right thing*, Lisa. The site was totally corrupt. The deal was totally corrupt."

"That is an assumption that you cannot prove."

"She did! She did prove it; she found the database. She found the rotten money trail."

"She *thinks* that's what she found. Does she have any way of proving it? That that's what it was? That whoever was paying the Aleister Corporation was a bad guy?" Lisa was repeating the lines she'd heard over and over in the house since the news broke.

"If it wasn't true, why would your father have offered her a hundred grand to keep her mouth shut?"

"I don't know, Adam. Maybe he was trying to help you poor, pathetic foster kids?"

Adam felt his teeth clench. He glared at her.

"You little disrespectful, stuck-up . . . How dare you?"

"How dare I?" She laughed. "You, the brother of the girl who is bringing down my family's reputation as we speak, who sneaks into *my* house with *my* father downstairs? How dare you yell at *me*!" Lisa stood up and charged at Adam with every ounce of her anger and frustration. She swung her hand, meaning to slap him hard enough to make him feel what she was feeling. He blocked her arm with his and forced it to her side.

And then Adam pulled her face into his hands and kissed her.

For a moment their lips were pressed hard against each other, then he felt her mouth open against his and her hands slide behind his shoulders. They stood pressed against each other, kissing with passion and force for long enough to forget about Gibly and Ted Bristol. They kissed until all they knew in the world was each other. She finally pulled away and rested her head against his shoulder while he enveloped her slender body in his arms.

"Oh, Adam. I am so, so sorry," she whimpered into his sleeve.

"It'll work out," he said, trying to convince himself as well as her. "And it's better knowing we've got each other."

18

For the Greater Good

Amelia took a deep breath, gathering her strength, and pushed open the glass door. The area was all new, the space to the right still draped in plastic from construction. The receptionist's desk was empty, but there were two workers drilling in a room to the side. Amelia stuck her head in. "Excuse me?" she said. "Excuse me, do you know where Roger Fenway is?"

The men stopped drilling. "Sure thing, kid. Try the office at the end of the hall on the left."

Amelia had tried to focus after Adam left the Gates Building last night, but she hadn't been successful. She'd walked back to her dorm via Stanford's main quad. The quad was empty and silent, save the faint sound of a piano coming from Memorial Church, the majestic centerpiece of the campus, whose tiled mosaic entry glistened in the low moonlight. Without thinking, she followed the music and took a seat in a back pew.

She'd only been in a church once before, when she was very young and their social worker had dragged her and Adam to a Baptist revival. She remembered being terrified and had decided

God wasn't for her. It was nothing like this, though; Memorial Church was a cathedral with a high-crested ceiling of dark wood, the walls covered in sweeping multicolored mosaics. Candles were lit on the altar, creating a glow that bounced off the stained-glass windows and painted the church a beautifully eerie yellow.

A pianist was at the front, seated at a long concert grand piano to the left of the pulpit, practicing a dark and dramatic piece. Beethoven, maybe?

Amelia sat back in the pew and closed her eyes. There was something magical about this scene, and she tried to absorb it as she searched for . . . She didn't know what she was searching for. She also didn't know how long she sat there before the pianist stopped playing and blew out the candles. As he did, she blinked open her eyes and said out loud, "Okay, I'll do it."

She'd tried not to give it any more thought when she woke up; she just got up and went before she could talk herself out of it.

Now the office door was open and Roger was bent over his desk, scribbling something on a notepad.

She knocked gently on the door. "Mr. Fenway?"

Roger looked up, startled, then grinned. "Amelia! Amelia Dory! Hello! What a wonderful surprise!" He stood up and shook her hand, using his other arm to usher her in. "Have a seat. Can I get you coffee or juice or anything?"

She sat down. "Oh no, I'm fine. I just wanted to say I'm in. I mean, I'll do it. I'll join your incubator."

Roger laughed, his eyes bright. "Just like that? Just like that, you're in?"

"Well, it's true you're covering our college expenses, right? And we get a salary?"

"Yes. That's the deal. But who is 'we'? Do you have a partner?"

"Yes. My twin brother, Adam. I want him to be my partner."

"Cool," Roger said. This was a surprise, but if Adam was anything like her, he'd take it. "Sounds great. I can't wait to meet him."

"Okay. That's great, then." She stood up to leave.

Roger laughed at her impatience. "Wait, Amelia, this is what you want to do, right? You seemed pretty adamant about refusing me before. Am I allowed to ask what changed? This isn't something your parents are forcing you into to save tuition money, is it?"

"I don't have parents. They died before I met them. So, no."

"I'm sorry," Roger said.

"It's not your fault." Amelia responded unemotionally, as though she'd given that response several times before. She didn't offer any more explanation.

"Okay, well . . . Let me show you the space at least? Do you have time for that?"

"Yeah," she said. "Okay."

Roger walked Amelia back to the front. "Let's start from the beginning," he said proudly. There were ten offices: his, plus nine for the incubator's companies. Each had floor-to-ceiling windows facing the hall, a sofa, two desks with computers, a printer, and a large white monitor on the wall.

"Have you seen these smartboards?" he asked excitedly, picking up a marker and drawing directly onto the monitor. "They're like whiteboards, but without the chemical markers and the mess. Plus, they take a digital image of everything you write, so you can store all your great ideas."

She had to admit, it was pretty cool.

Next Roger showed her two large conference rooms. "For

investor meetings, when you start having them. Once you've got a good working prototype, I'll make sure you get the right investors. People you can trust, who can add ideas and not just money."

After that, Roger led her to the kitchen. "The office coordinator is on vacation, but you'll meet her soon. Anyway, she went ahead and stocked the kitchen, but just let us know what you like and we'll make sure to have it on hand." He opened the cabinet, which was fully stocked with Clif Bars, bags of fancy potato chips, Haribo gummies, dried fruit and trail mixes, and six full-size-candy dispensers. The fridge made the Gates drink selection look drab; it was filled with sodas in glass bottles, organic juices, and bottles of Starbucks Frappuccino.

Amelia couldn't contain her surprise. "Wow," she said, and smiled at Roger.

He chuckled. "There's the smile! It's always the food that gets you engineers." He patted her playfully on the shoulder.

"And finally," he said, as he led her to one last room behind the kitchen, "the playroom. I think that's what we'll call it. What do you think?"

They stepped into a large, all-glass, enclosed room full of oversized beanbags, a large-screen TV with a Wii hooked up to it, and a low table stacked with puzzles and Rubik's Cubes. "I really want this to be the room where everyone who is part of the incubator gathers and feels safe to share ideas. You can write on all the walls." He took out a marker and drew on one of the glass panes. "And you can take a break or help each other with concepts. I want this to be the energy center of the office, you know? I want you to view this as a community."

Roger's eyes shone with pride for the space, and, as much as she tried to resist it, his energy was contagious.

He smiled at Amelia. He could see her shell starting to crack.

"Listen, Amelia, I know you're hesitant about all this, and I want you to know that you can trust me. I know it's going to take time to prove that to you, but I will. You've got real talent, Amelia, and helping you cultivate it is the most important thing, okay?"

Amelia nodded, not sure what to say. As wonderful as all these perks were, they just felt like reminders of her moral sacrifice, of giving up her ideals for money. As much as she appreciated the interest Roger was taking in her, she still felt like a sellout.

But Adam would love it. She knew that. And she needed his happiness, now. She owed that to him.

"Do you mind if I take a photo?" she asked Roger.

"Of course not."

She took a picture of the room with her iPhone and texted it to Adam. *Welcome 2 our new office. Officially a part of Fenway Ventures.*

Roger took her back to his office, where she signed a contract and a few other legal forms. "I'm guessing you haven't got a name yet? That can wait."

"Doreye," she said. "I want to call it Doreye."

Roger smiled. "Doreye? Like your name plus the device's eye? I like it. We should be able to get the URL for that pretty easily, too. Excellent choice."

19

A Late-night Snack

Patty couldn't sleep. Finals were next week, and she'd temporarily moved back in with her parents to study and avoid the distractions of campus. She glanced at the clock: 2:37 A.M.

She lay in bed, eyes wide open and head spinning with economics theories. Maybe she'd overdone it on the caffeine and Adderall. Suddenly, she remembered the ice cream Felicia had made. She threw off the covers and padded down the stairs to the freezer, where she found the container of ice cream waiting for her.

She sat at the kitchen counter with a spoon and ate straight from the container. Delicious. The full moon was shining through the French doors that led from the kitchen onto the patio, casting enough light for her reflection to show on the stainless-steel refrigerator door. She studied her figure as she spooned the ice cream into her mouth and couldn't help but feel very pretty in the moonlight. She felt natural, her hair twisted back in a simple bun, her cleavage showing in the pink Juicy tank top that matched her pink plaid boxer shorts. She cocked her head to one side and puckered her lips a little, squeezing her cheeks in. Yes, that was a good angle for photos. She needed to remember that one.

She almost jumped out of her skin when a shadow crossed behind her reflection in the fridge. She spun quickly in the chair and found herself facing Chad. "Oh!" she said, but he put his finger to her lip, a grin spreading across his face. How long had he been there? Had he been watching her?

He sat on the stool next to her and reached over to pull a spoon from the dish rack. Then he dipped it into the container and took a bite of the ice cream. He closed his eyes and savored the taste. Patty sat there, spoon suspended in midair. Why was he awake?

Chad was wearing pajama pants and no shirt; his toned chest and shoulders looked like something out of a magazine. He scooped out another spoonful of ice cream, looked at it, and smiled as he directed it toward Patty's open mouth. Their eyes stayed locked as she licked the spoon clean.

Do it again, she thought to herself, her heart racing. And he did, but as he pulled the spoon away, a drop fell onto her bare thigh and began to melt. They both looked down and he let out the tiniest little laugh. He used his forefinger to wipe the spill and place it between her lips. He held his finger against her tongue for a moment, staring deep into her eyes, and then silently withdrew it. And then, without a word, he stood up from the stool and left the room, leaving her, mouth still agape, studying his magnificently chiseled back.

20

The Dorii

It was their first day in the office, and Adam could hardly contain his excitement. Amelia was dreading it but forced a smile as she and Adam pulled their bikes into the Sand Hill Road parking lot, where they met Roger, who was pulling up in his Tesla Roadster.

"The Dorii!" he called out as he walked up to greet them. "You must be Adam," he said, and stuck out his hand.

"Mr. Fenway! It is so excellent to meet you, sir." Adam's face beamed.

"And you as well. Come on in, we'll get you all set up."

Roger gave Adam the same tour he'd given Amelia, smiling proudly as Adam practically drooled in reaction.

"Doreye is the first company in the incubator, so it'll be a little quiet until the other groups join later in the summer. In the meantime, I've hired a recent Stanford grad to run the day-to-day operations, to help keep you on track and make sure you've got what you need. He's on his way over, so you can meet him."

Adam nodded eagerly. Everything Roger said sounded great to him. Amelia had moved to her desk and logged into the computer. Roger glanced over at her. "Open your browser," he instructed.

Amelia clicked the Google Chrome icon and smiled as the home page popped up: www.doreye.com. A simple logo had been constructed, with the text "Adam and Amelia Dory, Cofounders" in bold typeface underneath, plus the address on Sand Hill Road and a phone number.

"I ordered your business cards, too. They're in the desk." Just then he heard someone at the door and shouted, "T.J.? We're in here."

T.J.? Adam glanced nervously at Roger. It couldn't be. But before he had time to absorb what was happening, T.J. Bristol was at Roger's side, tilting his head in confusion at the sight of Adam.

Roger didn't notice. "T.J., meet Adam and Amelia Dory, cofounders of our first company. Adam and Amelia, T.J. is going to be your supervisor and right-hand man."

T.J. almost choked. Did he say Amelia Dory? Was that a joke? T.J. thought quickly. No, Roger didn't know. Obviously he knew about Gibly—it had been headline news for the past week—but Amelia's name had never been released outside the Bristol household.

Oh my fucking God, thought T.J. *I'm their boss.* Despite how much he'd used her name in the past three weeks, he'd never actually seen Amelia. But he knew this girl. Yes! She was that dweeb from University Café that Roger couldn't get enough of. *That* girl was Amelia Dory, the girl who was bringing down Gibly? No fucking way.

"Hey, Adam." T.J. composed himself and gave Adam a half

high-five, half-handshake. "Long time," he said. T.J. hadn't talked to Adam since the night of the graduation party. Adam took his hand, trying to compose himself. T.J. Bristol was his supervisor? Did Roger not know?

T.J. then moved to Amelia. "Amelia Dory," he said slowly. "It is lovely to meet you. I've heard you are quite the computer mastermind."

Roger hadn't mentioned T.J.'s last name, and Amelia hadn't yet pieced together the connection between this guy and Ted. All she knew was he looked like exactly the kind of business jerk she'd been afraid of when this whole thing started, and she sighed disappointedly.

"T.J.," Roger said, "I've got a few other things I want to walk through with you. Why don't you come to my office and leave these two to get acquainted with the new space."

"Sure thing," T.J. said, and the two left the room. T.J. had already adjusted to the situation and was strategizing how he could use this new connection to his advantage.

Adam watched anxiously and, as soon as they were gone, shut the office door. "Amelia, that's T.J.! That's T.J. Bristol! Ted's son!"

"What? No!"

"Yes! Jesus, Amelia, Ted Bristol's son is our new boss."

"What are we going to do?"

Before Adam could answer, the phone rang. Impatiently, he snatched up the receiver. "Listen, whatever you're selling, we're not interested. Just take our name off your list and—"

Amelia watched as Adam's face went pale. He stopped speaking. After a moment, he placed the receiver back in the cradle.

"Adam, what's wrong? You look sick."

"I can't believe this is happening," Adam said. "I never thought I'd hear that voice again."

"Don't tell me—"

Adam stared at the phone as his mouth went dry.

"Amelia, we've got much bigger problems than T.J. and Ted Bristol."

Part II

21

The Secrets We Keep

Three months had passed since that first phone call, and the threats were still coming. They weren't constant or predictable, which made them even more disturbing: Two weeks would go by without a word, just long enough for Adam to think they had given up, and then he'd get a call at two o'clock in the morning. "Get Amelia back on board or we're telling Stanford and your fancy little boss what you did," the all-too-familiar voice would say. In a rage, Adam would yell, "You can't prove anything!" and hang up.

After the first one, Adam told Amelia that The Family had stopped calling. "They wanted to torment us when they found us, but I guess they lost interest," he lied. The calls and e-mails continued, and Adam tried to get his mind off of things.

Students had begun moving back to campus for the new school year. To keep their status on campus as a student residence, the Phi Delta fraternity had to reserve two rooms for nonmembers, and T.J.—now an alumnus—had pulled some strings to get Adam a room there. "Basically, the fraternity picks two cool dudes who they like and want to live with, but who for whatever reason decided not to pledge last spring," T.J. had explained to Adam.

T.J. had also explained that it would be a "great networking opportunity" for Adam. "The relationships you build in the fraternity—and these are influential guys from influential families, Adam—will take you far beyond sorority mixers. It may seem like a get-wasted-and-do-stupid-things party from the outside, but the bonds you form playing beer pong at three A.M. are indestructible, and you'd be surprised how they'll come into play twenty years from now when you're trying to close some deal."

Adam liked that logic and repeated it verbatim when he told Amelia. He didn't need T.J. to convince him to take the room, though. He tried to hide it, but he was excited about moving into a fraternity house. And this wasn't just any fraternity house; Phi Delta was *the* frat—the one Patty and all her friends flocked to—and everyone knew it. In one quarter, Adam had gone from dweeb in the dorm to young entrepreneur in the Phi Delta house. Sophomore year was looking great.

He was in his new room, transferring books from a moving box to the floating bookshelf above the bed, when he heard an e-mail come through on his phone. Ever since he and Amelia had started their company, Adam and his iPhone had been inseparable. Any time he heard an e-mail notification, he dropped everything, interrupted any conversation, to get to it. It could be Amelia with a new development or T.J. with an urgent question, or maybe someone from the press (okay, that hadn't happened yet, but Roger said it would), and Adam had to be prepared to jump into action at any moment.

He opened the e-mail and, as he read, he felt the blood drain from his face.

Adam,

We thought you might not think we were serious, so we figured
we'd share a little something we found in the study after you
left The Family. See attached screenshot. You and Amelia
aren't the only clever ones around here. We need Amelia to do
something for us. You have two weeks to convince her or we're
sending this out. Your company has a blog, right? Maybe we
can post the picture there.

Your Brothers

"Hey stranger."

Adam turned to find Lisa walking through the door. She put
her hands on his shoulders and leaned down to give him a kiss
on the cheek. "Everything okay? You look upset." She furrowed
her pretty brow in concern.

Adam quickly closed the e-mail and swallowed. "Yeah, yeah.
I'm fine. Just—it's nothing. How are you? How is the move
going?"

Lisa had been assigned to a dorm across campus with a
roommate from Nigeria. She was on a coed floor, and Adam had
not been pleased to discover that her neighbor was a starting
player on the men's water polo team.

"Oh, it's great! You know Mom; she had everything unpacked
and in perfect order by lunchtime, but she chipped her nail
when she was putting together an IKEA shoe rack, so we just
went to get manicures." Lisa flashed her hands to show freshly
pink-painted tips.

Adam grabbed them and pulled her close, resting his hands
on her hips. "And your roommate?"

"Seyi? She is soooo sweet. Apparently her family owns a

diamond mine. Can you believe that? She went to school in Switzerland and speaks, like, nine languages. It's crazy."

Great, Adam thought. *Another highly intimidating rich girl.* "I can't wait to meet her," he said.

Lisa scrunched her nose. "You know you can't. I mean, I guess you can meet her, but not as my . . . I mean, you know no one can know that we see each other like this."

Adam let his hands fall from her hips, swiveling back around in his chair to face his laptop. "Yeah, I know." He didn't understand why Lisa still refused to tell anyone they were together or call him her boyfriend. He'd started a company, he'd gotten into a fraternity—kind of—and he had even let her take him shopping with some of the money from Doreye so he could buy a more respectable wardrobe.

"Adam, we've talked about this. I just don't think it's a good idea." She tilted her head to the side and eyed him carefully. "Is that what's behind all this?"

"Behind what?"

"I feel like you've been distant lately, like there's something happening that you're not telling me about."

He turned to face her. She was wearing short white shorts and a tight pink tank top that accentuated her full breasts and small waist. God, she was pretty. He smiled reassuringly. "It's nothing," he lied. "I'm just a little stressed over how busy things are getting with the start-up."

Lisa's cell phone rang and she blushed when she saw who was calling. "I've gotta take this, Adam. I'll text you later, okay? Good luck unpacking." She pecked his cheek and scurried out of the room, answering the phone as she turned down the hallway. "Hey! I'm just leaving somewhere. I'll be out soon, and then I can talk. . . ."

22

Faces

"I'm calling it a day," T.J. said as he popped his head into the Doreye office. "Have you got everything you need?"

"I'm fine." Amelia didn't look up from her computer, where she was deeply engrossed in coding. After a pause, it occurred to her that this might be rude, so she stopped typing and looked up. "But thanks," she offered.

"No prob. See you tomorrow." T.J. waved and was gone.

Amelia didn't care how nice he was or how much Adam adored him; she still didn't trust T.J. Bristol.

The day after their initial meeting at the incubator, T.J. had e-mailed Amelia, asking if they could meet the next morning to "make sure everyone was comfortable with the situation." She responded grudgingly, *I'll be at the incubator at 11.*

T.J. had already been there when she arrived, sitting in the playroom typing away on his laptop. When he saw Amelia go into her office, he got up to join her. "This still a good time?"

"As good as any."

"Listen," he said. "I'm going to be totally straight with you.

What you did was devastating to my family. We lost millions, and I'm not sure my father will ever recover his reputation or his pride. In fact, I think there's a good chance he's going to retire altogether."

Amelia stared straight ahead, her jaw clenched, without a hint of sympathy.

"But despite the fallout to my family, I respect what you did. And it just proved to me how insanely talented you are and how much potential you've got to be a part of the next generation of Silicon Valley. You've got guts *and* brains *and* vision, and that's a rare combination around here. So I want you to know, right from the start, that if I have to pick sides, I'll take yours. I am one hundred percent behind you, Amelia. I want to see you and Doreye succeed."

Amelia squinted. She was studying T.J., trying to figure out what it was he wanted out of this. People like him made decisions on a cost-benefit basis: They calculated what they would have to give up to get what they wanted and, if the latter exceeded the former, they made the sacrifice. So, what was the benefit T.J. had estimated from supporting his father's nemesis? she wondered.

"You can trust me, Amelia." T.J. flashed a smile so charismatic it made her think he should have been a politician. He was so carefully put together that he must have practiced his facial expressions in the mirror—"This is the face that communicates sympathy; this is the face that communicates happiness." Amelia wondered if anything about him was genuine, or if it was all part of a larger calculation.

"Thanks, T.J.," she said. She didn't trust him for a second. "I really appreciate your explaining that. I was a little worried when Adam told me who you were."

"I can imagine," T.J. said. "Which is why I wanted to make

sure it was all on the table from the start. Also, I haven't told Roger, so no need to worry about that."

"Okay," Amelia said. She actually hadn't thought about whether or not Roger knew. She turned to her computer, hoping he'd get the hint that she wanted him to leave.

"Incidentally, I have a lot of confidence in your brother," T.J. said. "I'm looking forward to working closely with Adam this summer. I'm going to turn him into an all-star business guy. I see a lot of myself in him, you know."

She almost laughed. Did T.J. really think it would make her happy that he saw himself in her brother?

"Well I don't really like the business side, so the more you two can take care of it, the better it will be for me." She smiled weakly. "On that note, I'm going to get going on some coding."

"Of course," T.J. said. "Code away!"

That went exceptionally well, he thought as he left the room. Engineers were definitely weird, but he prided himself on being able to get through to anyone.

Burberry Plaid and Something Fruity

Patty could not wait for sophomore year to begin. In preparation, she had started a master cleanse diet, eating only raw fruits and vegetables and drinking a daily mixture of molasses, cayenne pepper, and lemon juice. It was alternately nauseating and boring, but after three weeks, she had lost eleven pounds. To reward herself, she went to Neiman Marcus, the highest-end department store in the high-end Stanford Shopping Center, to pick out a new outfit for the first day of school. She used her mother's account to buy a cute Marc Jacobs floral-print romper and bright blue French Sole ballet flats. Very stylish, but not too over-the-top, and all under five hundred dollars, so her mother wouldn't even notice the purchase when the monthly statement arrived.

She rode the escalator down to the first floor, comforted by the high ceilings, busy makeup counters, and elaborate handbag displays showcasing the newest autumn trends. There was something so pleasing about the place and its promise of fresh starts and pretty new things. It melted away all her stress.

And by "all her stress," she was thinking about Chad. He and Shandi had gone on vacation together in June before he disappeared into an apartment in San Francisco for his summer internship with a private equity firm. Patty didn't really know what "private equity" meant, but her father had been very impressed that he'd landed such a prestigious role. He had explained to Mrs. Hawkins, to her and Patty's (secret) disappointment, that Chad's long working hours would make it impossible for him to come to Sunday dinners anymore. But Patty knew that Chad's internship had ended last week (she'd snuck into Shandi's room and read her day planner) and that he'd be back on campus in a couple of weeks to start his second year of business school.

She couldn't get their last night together out of her head. His finger touching her thigh as he wiped away the drop of ice cream—it was enough to make her want to rip off her clothes right then and there.

Patty closed her eyes, shaking the thought of Chad from her mind as she stepped off the escalator. *Focus on the handbags,* she thought.

She headed toward the Fendi bags, just to look, but on the way, a center display of Burberry watches caught her eye. She gasped. They were so cute! Fifty or so boxes containing the watches were stacked in a circle, with several opened on top to reveal the slender silver chain band and a small square watch face with a pale blue Burberry plaid backdrop and teardrop crystal in the center. She had to have one.

She checked the price: $275.

She glanced around, and then, casually, she picked up one of the display watches and put it on her wrist. After admiring the way it looked on her, she lowered her arm as if to test the weight. Moving around the table, she placed the display between herself and the closest store clerk, a woman at the Kiehl's makeup counter. Then she discreetly slipped the watch off her wrist and into her handbag. She clicked the display box closed and put it back with the others, as though she had decided that the watch didn't suit her after all.

Patty didn't think of herself as a thief, but there was something satisfying about risking it a little. It's not like Neiman Marcus couldn't afford it: The watch was only $275. And she'd just made a purchase anyway. Besides, she knew she'd never get caught. Why would anyone suspect that a well-dressed Atherton girl with a Neiman's account would steal something everyone knew she could afford?

She stopped to sample a new Chanel fragrance, lingering for a second to discuss the floral accents with the woman behind the counter, when she noticed a cute guy in the ties section looking over at her.

"I usually go for something a little fruitier," she told the clerk, glancing over at the man. He smiled at Patty, setting down the Hermès tie he was looking at. "But this is really nice," she continued.

She sniffed her wrist. Oh my God, he was coming this way! He was tall and tanned with shaggy blond hair and dark eyes. She could tell he had a great body under the white button-down he was wearing.

"How do you like the new fragrance?" he asked Patty, making eye contact with the clerk.

Patty was pleased but shocked. She'd never been approached so aggressively. *Hold on,* she thought. Was he going to buy this for her? She blushed. "I love it, actually. It's very fresh."

"What's your name?" he asked.

"Patty. Patty Hawkins." It was a bit weird that he was doing this in front of the clerk, though, wasn't it?

"Patty, I'm Mark. Can I ask you to come with me for a second?"

Whoa. He had just triggered the don't-talk-to-strangers reflex that had been ingrained in Patty since childhood. "Oh, I don't know. . . ."

"It'll be less embarrassing if we step into the back office," he said. "I just need to check your bag." He smiled confidently and held out a police badge.

24

Good Neighbors

Amelia chewed her fingernail as she stared at her instant oatmeal rotating on the microwave plate in the incubator kitchen. She was thinking hard about the radio frequencies on garage door openers and how she might access them so that people could use their iPhones to open their garages. So far she'd found that four different companies operated garage door systems and each had a slightly different pattern. Even though this was less sexy than some of the other Doreye applications she was working on, it was going to take a while to code.

She closed her eyes. "What if I used the—"

Just then the microwave beeped to let her know her breakfast was ready. She didn't pay any attention, engrossed in the algorithm she was thinking through in her head.

"Your breakfast is going to get cold."

She jumped when she heard the voice behind her. She didn't have to turn around to know that the voice belonged to Sundeep, the former Stanford medical student who was working on a medical device start-up. Roger had brought him into the in-cubator five weeks ago.

"Oh," Amelia said, blushing. "I'm sorry, I got distracted." She pulled the bowl of oatmeal out of the microwave, tucked her chin down, and squeezed past Sundeep.

"Wait," he said. "I need to eat breakfast, too. Why don't you take a break from whatever you're doing and we can eat in here together?"

Sundeep was one of those rare people who radiated warmth and kindness. His dark brown eyes always seemed to be smil-ing, and his six-foot-one-inch frame seemed like it was made for hugging. He was originally from Mumbai, but his family had immigrated to the United States when he was eight so his father could go to medical school at the University of Pennsyl-vania. Sundeep had followed in his father's footsteps and been accepted to medical school at Stanford. Last year, however, against his parents' wishes, he had deferred medical school to work on creating a new type of low-power laser that would treat glaucoma. His goal was to find a way to distribute the lasers at a low cost, so that they would be accessible to people in India, where glaucoma was the third leading cause of blind-ness, affecting over twelve million people.

Amelia had learned all of this by reading about Sundeep online. She didn't know why, but he made her horribly self-conscious. It was like his eyes could see straight into her, and she simultaneously wanted to fall into his arms and run away as fast as she could.

"Oh, I should really get back to work," Amelia said.

"What difference will ten minutes make?" Sundeep smiled. "Come on, we've been working next to each other for over a month now, and I don't think we've had a single conversation. I feel like I hardly know you."

Clearly, he wasn't as into Internet stalking as she was.

Amelia blushed and laughed self-consciously. "There's really not much to know."

"Well, then it won't take very long to fill me in." He smiled and pulled out a chair.

Reluctantly, she sat down.

"Where did you grow up?" he asked.

"Indiana."

"That's got 'India' in it. Look how much we already have in common!" Sundeep said.

Amelia smiled. "So how are the lasers coming?"

"How do you know about my lasers?"

"Oh, I . . . Well, I read about them, or about you, online."

"You googled me? I'm flattered. You're supposedly the next Mark Zuckerberg or Larry and Sergey and *you're* googling *me*?"

Amelia blushed, not quite sure what to say.

Just then Roger stuck his head around the corner.

"Amelia!" He was ecstatic. "Amelia, I just got off the phone with TechCrunch. They want to meet you and learn more about Doreye. They're looking for companies to attend their Mobile Conference in Maui this December and are considering you guys. It would be terrific press and a great way to meet other companies for contracts. I told them we'd meet them at University Café. Can you be ready in fifteen?"

Amelia felt her stomach contract with nervousness. Tech-Crunch wanted to meet her? To talk about Doreye? Where was Adam?

"Yeah, of course, Roger. I'll just get my things. Do I need to bring anything?"

"Just your ideas. We'll talk about what to say on the car ride over."

"Adam's not here, though."

"Let's just do this one you and me. We'll get Adam in on the next one."

She looked at Sundeep. "Sorry to rush out."

"No worries," he said, smiling. "It sounds like things are about to heat up around here."

"Oh no, it's just a routine interview, I'm sure," Amelia said.

"Not if Roger's involved," Sundeep said.

The Losing Streak

"Do I only get one phone call?" Patty asked after they had snapped a mug shot, fingerprinted her, and left her in a locked room with white concrete walls and grim fluorescent lighting for nearly an hour.

Officer Mark smiled at her. "No, that's just what they say in the cop TV shows. We'll let you use the phone until you get through to someone who can come pick you up."

She had managed not to cry, which she thought was very grown-up of her, but she knew the minute she saw her parents she would start. How was she *ever* going to explain this to them? They were going to take away her credit card for sure and maybe the car. But they wouldn't . . . they couldn't . . . could they?

She swallowed hard as she dialed her home number from Officer Mark's desk phone. She twirled the cord nervously as she listened to the phone ring once. Twice.

"Hello? Hawkins residence."

Oh my God. Was that—?

"Chad?" Patty breathed into the phone.

"Patty?" He sounded cheerful. "Hey! What's goin' on?"

"Chad! I didn't realize you were—" Patty glanced at Officer Mark, who was giving her a this-is-not-a-catch-up-with-old-friends-call look, and she paused. "Listen, Chad, I'm in . . . Well, I'm in some trouble."

"What is it? What can I do?"

"I'm at the police station. Can you come pick me up?"

"Of course." He didn't hesitate. "I'll leave right now. And don't worry, your parents aren't supposed to be home for another two hours."

She hung up the phone.

Twenty minutes later, Chad smiled politely and shook Officer Mark's hand. "Where do I need to sign?"

How did Chad know he had to sign forms? Had he done this before? Patty wondered about this as she watched him fill out the forms. He was taking responsibility for her release from jail as though he were making a routine bank deposit.

"All set!" He turned to Patty. "Ready to go?"

Patty was silent as she walked to Chad's Land Rover and climbed into the passenger seat. She kept her gaze out the window so she didn't have to look at him.

They drove without speaking. It was the middle of the day, and traffic moved quickly. Patty stared out at the trees lining the side of the road. Sunlight moved through the branches and glanced out at her from among the leafy shadows.

"When I was a freshman in college," Chad said, "there was this huge Carolina-Duke basketball game on a Saturday, and we were drinking aggressively from, like, eight A.M. for it. And around two, right when everyone was starting to filter into the Dean Dome for the game, my suitemates and I decided it was a good time to go streaking." Chad started to laugh. "But we didn't want anyone to know it was us, you know? So we pulled on ski masks and stripped down and ran out of our dorm in this big victory lap. And as we were coming back to the dorm, there was this cop standing, blocking the door, and he hand-cuffed all four of us—not because we were streaking but because, get this—it's against the law in North Carolina to wear a ski mask in public. So we got hauled into the station, wearing nothing but our ski masks, and had to sit there for hours, na-ked, until we sobered up."

Patty gave him a weak smile. She could feel the tears welling up in her eyes.

They pulled into the Hawkinses' driveway. Chad turned off the engine.

"What I'm trying to say, Patty, is that it happens to all of us. We all do stupid things—well, except maybe your sister—and in a few years, I promise you'll be laughing at yourself."

She was looking at him, wanting to believe what he said, but she couldn't keep the tears from trickling down her cheeks.

He reached up with his right hand and wiped a tear from under her eye with his thumb. "And you know what? I think the fact that you push the envelope makes you pretty special. This one's between you and me, so long as you promise not to change yourself to fit their mold, okay?"

26

Can You Hear Me Now?

Roger glanced sideways at Amelia and gave her a reassuring nod. The two journalists from TechCrunch were seated opposite Roger and Amelia at a corner table in University Café, their notebooks and four orange-strawberry-coconut smoothies between them. They had just asked Amelia to explain Doreye's functionality.

Throughout the summer, Roger had encouraged Adam, Amelia, and T.J. to keep quiet about Doreye. The Valley was full of replicators, he'd told them, and if you started talking about your idea too soon, there were leeches who would try to mimic it. Not well enough to replace you, but just well enough to sue you after you got big, claiming it was their idea. Or they'd buy up URLs or patents they anticipated you'd need down the road and then charge you excessively for them. You had to watch out, all the time, especially at places like University Café.

But now, Roger had explained to Amelia in the car on the way over, it was time to start talking. Not too much. Too much hype created unreasonable expectations, or so much demand that you couldn't fulfill all the orders and customers got upset. It was a tricky balance, he explained, but this is where he could be useful.

Amelia took a deep breath. She started slowly. "Well, the basic idea is that Doreye can see other products. It's an application that detects other devices, and then accesses their frequencies so that you can control them through Doreye."

"So, for instance, I could . . . ?" the male reporter, a dark-haired guy in his twenties who looked like the guy from the old "I'm a Mac" commercials, prompted.

"You could turn off the radio with your iPhone. Or open your garage. Or turn on the oven in your kitchen on the drive home from work."

"That's the first phase," Roger interjected. "Tell them about phase two."

"So, that's the basic platform. And it's nice because Doreye is programmed to pick up everything automatically—you don't have to enter any information for each of your appliances, it just detects them and works seamlessly. Phase two, though, takes the core idea of Doreye to a new level. Whereas before we used the phone's antenna to see frequencies of other electronic radio-emitting devices, now we use the phone to see . . . everything. Like how radar works, but with your phone. Doreye will be able to see and remember things like your keys, your wallet, and your car. By activating Doreye you can use your phone to see and find everything."

"And phase three?" the other journalist, who clearly got her style guidance from the Twilight series, dressed in skinny jeans and a Bella-esque plaid shirt, asked. "Is phase three see-ing through walls?"

Roger met her smile. "Might be! We're keeping phases three and four quiet for now, but I assure you, they're big."

The reporters smiled at each other. "This is great stuff," the guy said. "I mean, this brings a whole new level of control to your iPhone. The elimination of three remotes in your living room would be useful enough, but with all the other applications, it feels so . . . futuristic. I love it."

Amelia smiled. Roger beamed.

"And how about you, Amelia? What is your story?"

Amelia blushed; she didn't like talking about herself. "Oh, I'm not that interesting. I mean, I'm just a computer science major at Stanford. I just finished my freshman year."

"And where are you from?"

"Indiana."

"Have you worked on a lot of other stuff before?"

"I've dabbled a lot on my own, but no, nothing public or anything. Roger's the one who convinced me to do something for the public."

Over the summer, her resentment of Roger for dragging her into a business had started to melt. He was so kind and supportive of her that it was hard not to fall under his spell.

"Your parents must be thrilled. Have they been out to see the incubator?"

"Oh, I don't have parents. I never knew them."

"Who'd you grow up with, then?" the girl pressed. It was a leading question to which the journalist already knew the answer. Doreye's technology was fine, but a pretty girl engineer with a pathetic foster kid background was the real thing, a front-page story.

Amelia was taken aback by this question. She wanted to get back to Doreye. "I grew up in foster homes."

The girl scribbled something in her pad. "Great, great." Amelia wasn't sure what that meant.

"Just one more question: Where'd you come up with the name?" the guy asked.

"It's kind of a play on our last name and the 'eye' of the product," Amelia said, a little sheepishly.

"Our?"

"My brother, Adam, and I. Adam's the head of business development. I'm just the engineer," she said.

"So I think that gives you a sense of what Doreye is all about . . ." Roger said.

"Yes, Mr. Fenway. This has been really helpful. We'll definitely get a blurb out about the company over the next week."

"Excellent! Just let us know what else you need." Roger stood up to shake the journalists' hands and Amelia followed suit.

Amelia shot a quick text to Adam: *Just had our first interview with TechCrunch! Doreye's going to be in it this week . . .*"

Roger ushered Amelia toward the door and whispered, "Hold on to your seat, Amelia. Things are about to get big."

27

Songs to Fill the Air

Amelia felt surprisingly light and happy as she rode back to the incubator with Roger.

"See, Amelia?" said Roger. "I told you starting a business with your idea wasn't such a bad thing."

"Maybe you were right," Amelia said.

Roger turned up the radio. "Do you like the Grateful Dead?"

Amelia cocked her head. "Um . . . I don't think I've ever heard them."

Roger almost stopped the car. "You've never heard the Dead?! Oh, Amelia. We've got to get you educated. Let's start with 'Ripple.'"

He flipped through tracks on the dashboard console and started singing along to a song. The sound of the guitar was pretty and mellow; it made Amelia think of floating along a river in a canoe.

Sundeep was outside the office talking on his cell phone when Roger and Amelia pulled into the lot. When he saw them, he hung up and shouted, "How'd it go?"

Roger glowed. "Amelia was perfect. Completely nailed it."

Sundeep held the door for her. "I want to hear all about it."

"So long as you both get some work done today. Remember, I'm paying you kids . . ." Roger joked as he headed in the opposite direction, toward his office.

Sundeep smiled broadly as he walked with Amelia back to her office. "So, it went well?"

"Yeah, I think so. They really seemed to like the idea, and, you know, I'm starting to think this business thing might not be so bad after all. If we get a lot of users on this, it'll actually give me more bandwidth to do more interesting coding. I'd never really thought about how much more complex and exciting the engineering gets when you have a lot of users."

"Totally! That's how I feel about these lasers. If I can get them to market and get a lot of people using them, that gives me a channel to get people other things they need, like food and dental care and access to information. Business gets a bad rap, but really there's a lot of good and exciting stuff that can come out of it."

Amelia bit her lip as she looked at his smiling eyes. Sundeep blushed. They stood like that for a moment, not knowing what to say, when Amelia's phone rang. Startled, she looked down.

"It's Adam, I'd better take this," she said to Sundeep.

"Of course, I'll . . . see you later then."

"Hey, Adam!" Amelia answered cheerfully as she watched Sundeep walk through the playroom to his office.

"You had an interview with TechCrunch?" Adam asked sternly.

"Yeah! Roger and I just got back from University Café."

"You went without me?" His voice was shaking.

Amelia tried to backpedal. "Well, it was super last-minute. Roger gave me fifteen minutes to get ready."

"Why didn't you call me, or text? I could have met you there."

"I didn't realize it was such a big deal."

"Not a big deal? This is our first interview with TechCrunch. How could you not think it was a big deal?"

She was silent.

Adam's hurt started to morph into anger. "Amelia, I'm the head of business development for this company. This is *my* domain. The press is part of the business side, not the engineering side. This should have been *my* interview."

"*Your* interview? And here I thought this was *our* company. I didn't realize you were so interested in splitting things up. Especially since you haven't been to the office in . . . what, three days? Is that what you call contributing?"

Adam was fuming. He hadn't been in the office because he'd been trying to sort out the blackmail. If she only knew how much stress he'd been under for her sake.

"Things are complicated right now, Amelia. Trust me, you're going to feel sorry for saying that."

"You know what I'm sorry for, Adam? I'm sorry I just did something I didn't even want to do to help a company I didn't even want to start so that you could get a little closer to your start-up dream. And you have the nerve to get mad at me. You should be *thanking* me."

Amelia was surprised by her anger.

"I'm going back to coding. I'll see you later."

She hung up the phone.

Adam lay on his bed with his iPhone on his chest, staring at the ceiling. How could Amelia have done the interview without him? Adam wondered again. And why hadn't Roger insisted he be at the interview? He felt a well of anxiety building in his stomach. What if Roger didn't see his value? What if he just wanted Amelia and had only let him join because Amelia insisted on including him?

He looked at his iPhone. After getting off the line with Amelia, he had texted Lisa about coming over. Fifteen minutes had passed and there was no response yet. Great. Now he had two things to stress about: the start-up *and* his girlfriend.

He typed a brief second text—*"Hey u there?"*—and then flung his phone out of reach to keep himself from sending any more messages. He didn't want to come across as desperate. Eyes closed, he listened intently for the bright *ping* of an arriving text. But the minutes crawled by with no such reassurance. Why wasn't Lisa texting him back? And whom had she been talking to when she left his room that morning? He loved her so much. They hadn't had sex yet, hadn't even gotten close, to be honest, but that was okay with him. He'd wait forever if he had to. Of course, he hadn't used the "L" word yet, and neither had she, but he knew she felt the same way. She was just cautious because school was about to start and she didn't want to miss out on the freshman experience because she had a sophomore boyfriend.

Thirty minutes. Still nothing.

It was dark outside when he woke up. Lisa had finally texted, almost an hour and a half after his texts: *"Sorry. Out with the fam. Tomorrow? Sleeping @ house. Will be here in a.m."*

"Sure. B there at 10. Sweet dreams. Miss you," he texted back, feeling his heart sink. Adam had desperately wanted to see her tonight.

He had decided it was finally time to tell her the truth about his and Amelia's past.

28

Mergers and Acquisitions

"I'm considering buying this company. What do you think?" Ted asked T.J. as he slid his iPad across the breakfast table and took a sip of his coffee, watching T.J.'s face.

The iPad was opened to a TechCrunch article on Doreye. T.J. began reading:

An Eye for Success

By now we all know about superstar entrepreneur and investor Roger Fenway's pet-project incubator, and we've all been anxiously awaiting news about what's coming out of the playful tree house on Sand Hill Road. Fear not, dear reader; we've got our first glimpse, and it's looking bright.

The company is called Doreye, and it's setting a new standard for syncing all your devices into a central control panel. Everything, from your television to your cable box, DVD player, garage door, and even your stove, could all be controlled by the Doreye app on your iPhone. If that doesn't make you feel like you've traveled into the future, just wait: Doreye will soon use your antenna like a bat uses sonar. What does that mean? It means Doreye can see and find your keys, your shoes, and even your Uncle Frank. All those easy-to-lose items. Whoa.

Who is behind all this? Amelia Dory, who despite growing up without parents in the Indiana foster care system, got accepted to Stanford on a full scholarship. She's a hard-core nerd; during our interview, she made three *Star Wars* references. But behind her smudged glasses her eyes glowed with an innocent, undeniable passion to change how we interact with the world around us.

Right now Amelia has her twin brother on biz dev (cute, right?), but we figure Fenway will bring in someone legit to run the business soon enough and keep Amelia on the computers cranking out the Next Next Big Thing. Stay tuned.

T.J. put down the iPad. When had TechCrunch interviewed Amelia, and why hadn't Roger told him about it? Wasn't that the sort of thing he was responsible for helping with?

Over the past three months, T.J. had become increasingly worried that his job didn't have the responsibilities it ought to. At first he'd done pages of analysis on Doreye's market potential and constructed a thorough marketing plan that he'd presented to Roger. Roger had barely looked at it before asking if he'd mind sharing it with Adam. Next, he'd tried to get in with Sundeep, the new guy who clearly had no business sense, but Sundeep had politely told T.J. that his customer acquisition strategy model wasn't exactly applicable in rural Southern India. Lately, out of desperation, T.J. had been hanging out at

Facebook and Google headquarters trying to spot engineers who might join the incubator, but he'd had little luck. He was starting to feel like a lackey, not an entrepreneur.

"So, what do you think?" asked T.J.'s father. "I bet Roger would sell it to me, don't you?"

"Why would you want to buy Amelia Dory's company?" T.J. asked morosely.

"Why wouldn't I? Keep your friends close and your enemies closer. Or, if you can, own them."

T.J. didn't disagree with that logic. He took another bite of his Fiber One cereal. As much as he hated to admit it, his father did have good ideas.

"You've been working with them, right?"

"Yeah, sort of," T.J. said.

"Maybe we could put you in as CEO."

T.J. almost choked on his cereal. He could feel his heart beating faster. "Really?"

"Why not? I think you'd make a great CEO."

T.J. blushed. He wasn't sure his dad had ever given him such an important compliment.

"Well, I can definitely find out more for you," T.J. offered, trying to sound nonchalant. "Just let me know what information you need and I'll do some analysis. Roger's pretty tied up with other things, so I've got some bandwidth during the day."

Ted had flicked to another news article on his iPad, but he looked up at his son for a moment. "Sure, T.J. Think you could put together a pitch deck for me by tomorrow?"

"Definitely!" T.J. crowed. Then, aware that he'd sounded too eager, he adopted what felt like a more professional tone. "I'll check my calendar and e-mail you a confirmation this afternoon."

"Great, son. Would be fun to work together on this."

A few hundred feet away, Adam parked his bike behind a tree and crept around the back of the Bristol house. Through the kitchen window, he could see Ted and T.J. eating breakfast. He ducked down and slipped through the back door and up to Lisa's bedroom.

Lisa was seated at the vanity in a pink bathrobe, curling her hair. "Hey, you," she said without taking her eyes off the mirror.

"Hey," Adam said. "How are you?" He walked over and kissed her shoulder from behind. "You look beautiful."

She smiled and held his eyes in the mirror.

"So, look," Adam started, determined not to lose the courage to say what he wanted to say. "I know you think I've been acting funny lately, and you're right: I have. And I want to tell you the reason."

Lisa put down the curling iron and turned on the stool to face him. Half her hair fell in neat curls down her shoulders, and the other half was tied back, sectioned off and waiting to be curled.

Adam loved watching her get ready. There was something very sexy about seeing her natural perfection become even more glamorous with lip gloss and hairpins.

Focus, he told himself. He had her attention now. He had to do it. He grabbed the desk chair and pulled it next to her vanity stool, leaning forward with his elbows on his knees.

"Okay, here goes. Amelia and I grew up in these institutions, sometimes called group homes, that are like modern-day orphanages. To be fair, they weren't terrible places. It's not like in Dickens, with giant creepy buildings full of hundreds of kids eating cold gruel and all that. There were usually no more than a dozen of us, and we spent most of our time at school. But being bounced around from place to place every year or so took its toll. It was hard to feel like we ever belonged anywhere."

Lisa swallowed and nodded her head in sympathy. "I'm sorry," she said. "I was adopted so young that I don't really remember what it was like not to have a family. I can only imagine."

"Well, getting a family is actually where the trouble started," Adam said.

"What do you mean?"

"One day, when we were nine, Amelia and I found out that a foster family wanted to take us in. I guess based on our school records—neither of us ever got in trouble—we were an appealing pair. So, three weeks later, we packed up to go live with the Dawsons. They seemed nice enough. They had three kids of their own, two boys and a girl, ages eleven, thirteen, and fifteen. Instead of calling themselves 'the Dawsons,' they referred to themselves as 'The Family,' and talked constantly about what was expected to be part of 'The Family.' We couldn't even call the father Michael—we had to call him Sir or Mr. Dawson. I guess we should have realized that was weird, but at the time we were so happy to have someone want us, you know, that we didn't think anything of it."

Adam took a deep breath. He was conscious of how much he was talking and worried that Lisa would lose interest. But she was still looking at him intently.

"Anyway, within a few days the niceness stopped and The Family started to ignore Amelia and me. They weren't mean; they just ignored us. They didn't buy us new clothes, didn't offer to help with anything. We found out later that the father, Michael Dawson, was an insurance salesman with a serious online gambling problem. He had lost a lot of money. They had taken us in because it was a huge tax break that essentially offset his gambling debts."

Lisa leaned forward and held his hands. "I'm sorry."

"They didn't actually want us. That first Christmas, the Dawsons bought a used computer. The kids were thrilled but quickly started fighting over it, and so the parents made a schedule that dictated who got to use the computer and when. Naturally, Amelia and I weren't included." Adam felt the bitterness behind his voice and wondered if Lisa could sense it. "Anyway, that enthusiasm lasted for about a month before they got bored and bought an Xbox instead. So, Amelia started using the computer. She loved it. She got totally addicted. She'd come home from school and stay up all night in front of it. No one knew what she was doing, and no one really cared as long as she stayed out of the way."

Adam exhaled, steeling himself for the next part of the story.

"Two years later, the oldest Dawson son got in a big fight with his parents for bombing the SAT. They were screaming at each other in the kitchen, Mrs. Dawson crying that he'd never get into college. They didn't have much money and had pinned all their hopes on their kids. Finally, Mr. Dawson dragged his son to the computer and told him to pull up his score. He thought his son was lying so he wouldn't have to go to college. Amelia was at the computer and they told her to log off. Jacob pulled up the score report and, sure enough, he'd gotten a 1280 out of 2400. They were still screaming at each other and Amelia was standing there, wanting it to stop—she always hated yelling—so she said, quietly, that she could change it, if they wanted."

"She could *change* it? But SAT scores are, like, impossible to access."

"Yeah, well, that's what everyone thought. Mr. Dawson laughed in her face. But the son knew that Amelia was really smart and was always on the computer and he said they should give her a shot. So Amelia hacked into the Web site right then and there and showed them. She changed his score to an 1850."

"That's incredible!" Lisa's eyes were wide. "Did he end up going to college?"

"Yeah. The guidance counselor flipped, she was so excited. His grades still sucked, but he got into Indiana State and left the next year."

"Wow," Lisa said. "All because of Amelia."

"My sister is like a superhero; she can *see* the *matrix*. Firewalls, password locks . . . every type of security setting is just another puzzle for her to solve."

"The Dawsons must have been ecstatic."

"After that, they started paying a lot more attention to Amelia. Amelia was so sweet and innocent—she just wanted to help and be noticed and feel appreciated, you know? One day Mr. Dawson asked her if she could hack into his company's system and increase his sales figures, said he was afraid he was going to lose his job and just needed a little boost. He said he didn't have to be the top salesperson or anything, just needed a higher figure. But he was paid on commission, so he was essentially asking Amelia to help him embezzle money. Then a few months later, he directed Amelia to the bank and had her move money out of the company's bank account into another account. He made up some story about holding accounts for future sales or something."

"Mr. Dawson sounds like a total sketchball. Amelia went along with *everything*?"

"I love my sister, but she's naïve. She only ever sees the good in people. So she helped Mr. Dawson and spent months stealing money for him. Amelia didn't think much about it until a year later when she read an article in the newspaper about a 'mystery hacker.' The Indiana state attorney general was obsessively tracking some mastermind thief who stole money from the State Insurance Bureau. When Amelia realized that *she* was the mastermind, she freaked out. She came to me, unsure about what to do. I told her just to stop, to tell Mr. Dawson that they changed the security codes and she couldn't hack in anymore. But being Amelia, she insisted on telling the authorities the truth."

"Oh my God. What happened?"

"Well, she called the police and told them everything. And the next week, they arrested Michael Dawson and he was sentenced to six years in white-collar prison. They gave Amelia the lightest sentence possible, but she spent three months in a juvenile detention center. That was the only time we've ever been separated."

Adam paused.

"Obviously, we couldn't live with the Dawsons anymore. Part of the deal Amelia struck involved our being placed in another foster home. So I was moved to Michigan and lived there until Amelia could join me. The authorities were really good about keeping our whereabouts a secret from the Dawsons. But at the beginning of this summer, right after we started working at the incubator, we got a phone call from Jacob, the older son. They found us, I guess because of the Doreye Web site. Mr. Dawson is about to be released from prison on good behavior, and they're saying we 'owe' them for ruining The Family. I've been getting e-mails and phone calls all summer trying to blackmail us into embezzling money for them again."

"But how can they blackmail you? What have they got against you?" Lisa asked.

"I don't know," Adam lied, looking down at his hands. "But these people are crazy. They'll do anything."

"Adam, you have to go to the police."

"I can't."

"Why not? You haven't done anything wrong."

"But everything is going so well right now; I don't want to screw things up by getting involved in some investigation. Can you imagine how bad the press would be for Doreye? I just need them to go away, and I don't know how to make them stop calling."

He looked down at his shaking hands. Lisa reached out and clasped them hard between hers. "I know you'll do the right thing, Adam. And I'm really glad you told me. Maybe it'll be better now that you've gotten it off your chest. It's hard keeping secrets."

He looked up at her beautiful smile and warm eyes. "Yeah," he said. "It is." He smiled, then leaned forward and pressed his mouth to hers in a deep kiss. He started to pull her toward the bed, but she stopped him, glancing at the clock on her radio alarm. "I've got to get to a lunch on campus."

"That's okay," Adam said, twirling one of her curls on his finger and smiling at her. "We'll pick this up again later. Thanks for being here for me."

"Of course. I know you'll figure things out."

Adam gave her one last kiss, and then crept out of the room and down the back staircase, feeling like an enormous weight had been lifted off his shoulders.

29

Tea for Two

Amelia was pacing back and forth in the office, biting her fingernails. This was not good, not good at all.

She had just read the article posted on TechCrunch and was freaking out about how Adam would react to the last paragraph. She hadn't talked to him yet today, and he still wasn't in the office. He must have read it, and now he was avoiding her.

She was furious. How could they have written such a thing? Neither she nor Roger had said anything to imply Adam wasn't up for the job. It was total fiction, and it would hurt Adam deeply. Didn't they have any respect for his feelings? Didn't it occur to them how writing something like that would affect her relationship with Adam?

This was just one more reason why she hadn't wanted to get involved in a start-up.

"Is everything okay?"

Amelia jumped. Sundeep was standing in the doorway. He must have seen her pacing.

"No!" she couldn't help exclaiming. "No, it's not okay at all! The TechCrunch article—I just—" She couldn't find the words.

"I know, it was awesome! They practically called you the new star of Silicon Valley. I feel like I should be collecting your autograph."

She stared at him in disbelief. "Did you read what they said about Adam? They said Roger's probably going to kick him out. I never said that!"

"Aw, it wasn't that bad." He stepped forward and touched her arm. "Want to have some tea?"

She stood there for a second and sighed deeply. Then she conceded. "Yeah, okay."

She sat at the table in the incubator kitchen while Sundeep took out two mugs. "Earl Grey? English breakfast? Peppermint?"

"Peppermint," she said. "With two packs of sugar."

He prepared the tea and brought it to her, along with a plate of sugar cookies.

"Thanks." She smiled up at him sheepishly.

"It's nothing."

They sat in silence, sipping their tea.

"You're really close to Adam, huh?"

"Yeah," Amelia said, breaking off a piece of cookie. "We're twins. We've always been together. And without our parents, we were kind of all we ever had."

"No wonder."

"No wonder what?"

"That you feel so protective of him. You're really lucky to have him."

In all her life, she didn't remember anyone ever telling her she was lucky. "You're right," she said, smiling. "I am really lucky."

She took a small bite of the cookie. "Do you have siblings?" she asked, sipping her tea.

"An older sister. She's back in India, married and having babies. Do you want to see?"

He pulled out his iPhone and showed her photos of his nieces and nephews. "This is Sonal and her brother Raj. She's just like her mother: totally bossy. But Raj keeps up with her."

Amelia giggled at their expressions. "They are so cute! Look at his cheeks!"

"Right? Look at this one: Sonal made him play dress-up." He showed her a picture of a little curly-haired Indian boy in an oversized dress and pearl necklace, glaring angrily at the camera.

Sundeep smiled at the iPhone, and then up at Amelia. "Anyway, I'm a very proud uncle, if you couldn't tell."

"Do you visit India often?"

Suddenly, Sundeep's face darkened.

"I should get back to work," he said, clearing his throat.

"What's wrong?" Amelia asked.

He stood up from the table. "Nothing. I just remembered that I have a lot to do today."

Amelia watched in confusion as Sundeep carried his mug over to the sink.

"Sundeep, I'm sorry if I—"

"There's no apology necessary," Sundeep said. He offered up an awkward smile. "Congratulations again on your wonderful article."

30

PowerPoint and Shoot

T.J. arrived at his father's office thirty minutes early, dressed in a suit and tie. He knew it wasn't necessary, but he wanted to demonstrate that he was serious—and should be taken seriously.

He had been up until four o'clock in the morning working on the pitch deck, checking the numbers and making sure that all of the diagrams were properly aligned and up to date. He had put a lot of time into it, but the hours had flown by. Whenever he was working in Excel or PowerPoint, he felt like a machine, and he loved it. He knew so many keyboard shortcuts, and he loved how with five little keystrokes he could launch a major data analysis or create a perfectly aligned org chart.

It was nerdy, he admitted, but there was something gratifying about seeing your ideas communicated in a neat, efficient form that could be presented to investors.

One of his father's assistants, Marie, directed him to the bench outside his father's office, and he flipped through his pitch deck, reviewing his notes.

Doreye, Inc.

The future of a connected world
A presentation by T. J. Bristol

Sales Strategy

- Direct traffic to www.Doreye.com via social-mobile marketing
  - Group coupons, target savvy college students as early adopters
  - Partnerships with major device manufacturers for integration
- Begin a subscription service with ARPU @ $7.00 - $9.50 per month (across different tiers, including premium*)
  - Customer acquisition cost b/w $25 - $35
  - Lifetime Revenue per user over $300 (@ 4%-6% monthly churn)
- Partner with iOS (Apple) and Android (Google)
- Year 1: Focus on core U.S. market
- Year 2: Expand to select countries in EMEA and China
- Year 3: Expand to remaining EMEA and Asia
- Year 4: Rest of World

*Premium service includes 24-hour customer service and "super functionality"

The "Pain Point"

- The average American interacts with 16 devices per day (2011 "State of Electronics" by Nielsen)
- Splitting attention across devices wastes up to 10 minutes per day (61 hours, or 2.5 days per year!)
  - This will increase, not decrease, over time
- Using different devices requires learning different "languages" in order to function.
  - This leads to intellectual fatigue and confusion
  - This is a **significant barrier** to device acquisition

The world is becoming more, not less, complicated

The Market Size

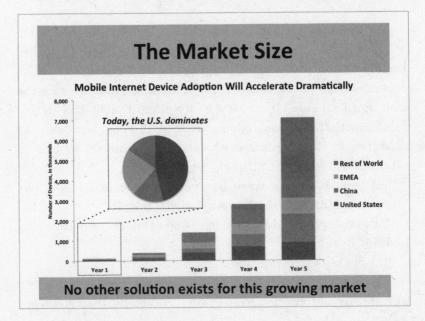

Mobile Internet Device Adoption Will Accelerate Dramatically

Today, the U.S. dominates

Number of Devices, in thousands

- Rest of World
- EMEA
- China
- United States

No other solution exists for this growing market

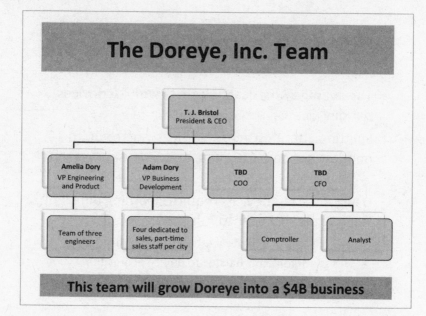

The Doreye, Inc. Team

T. J. Bristol
President & CEO

Amelia Dory
VP Engineering
and Product

Adam Dory
VP Business
Development

TBD
COO

TBD
CFO

Team of three
engineers

Four dedicated to
sales, part-time
sales staff per city

Comptroller

Analyst

This team will grow Doreye into a $4B business

T.J. especially liked the last slide. He thought his name above "President & CEO" just felt . . . right. He knew his father would ask how he intended to fill in all the "TBD" slots, and he was prepared: There were several promising candidates for the COO and CFO roles in his fraternity alumni pool. And he felt confident that, via Amelia's network in the computer science department, they could recruit talented engineers, especially after the nod from TechCrunch.

T.J. heard Marie's voice on speakerphone in Ted's office. "Jay Resnick on line one for you. Can you take it?"

"Sure thing, patch him through," Ted said. "Jay! How are you, buddy?"

T.J. couldn't help but listen in.

"Yeah, it's been a tough couple of months, but we'll recover. The Aleister Corporation hasn't said no officially, they just want to wait until the press dies down and the investigation is settled. I have confidence we'll be back at the deal by quarter two of next year. . . . Of course I know who found the problem. No, if we charged her for hacking they'd discover everything. As it is, they only know about the database. . . . Of course I'm going to take her down; I can't let this go. Listen, can you keep your mouth shut? . . . Okay, good. She's got a new company, thinks she's going to be a hotshot Silicon Valley Zuckerberg type. Frankly, she probably could; she's smart as hell. But I'm going to buy the company and destroy it. Won't ruin my rep, I'm doing it through a shell company. . . . No, I'm putting T.J. in as CEO. . . . Who cares? It'll give him something to do and me a channel to work through. You want in? Guarantee you'll lose your money. . . . Haha, yeah, okay. Gotta run. See you on the course Saturday? . . . Great."

T.J.'s jaw dropped. Had his father really just said what he thought he'd said? He was looking to buy Doreye just to bring it down? And he was putting T.J. in as CEO because he thought he'd be a perfect puppet for its destruction? Didn't he care that T.J.'s reputation would be ruined if he was at the helm when Doreye went down? Didn't he care that Doreye was a good product that could make a lot of money and help a lot of people?

But T.J. didn't have time to dwell on it. His father was calling him into the office.

"Morning, son. You're looking sharp. I can't wait to see what you've got for me."

T.J. forced a smile and began walking Ted through the presentation. He covered the basics on the slides but didn't go into any of the details as he had planned. What was the point? At the end of the presentation, Ted patted him on the shoulder.

"T.J., this is excellent. I think you've got what it takes to be CEO, and after I buy Doreye, it's the first move I'm making."

167

"That's great, Dad. Really exciting."

"I want us to work closely together on this, but I don't want the public to perceive any sort of conflict of interest, you know? I'm worried people might get the wrong idea if they see the investor's son running the business. So I've set up a shell company, Proximate Investments, which will be the investor of record, so that my name stays out of it. But rest assured, you'll still have me for anything you need."

T.J. nodded blankly at his father. He couldn't believe how easily his father was lying to his face.

31

Deal or No Deal

"Is it true?" Adam stormed into Roger's office. "Are you going to kick me out?"

"Of course it isn't true," Roger said. "It's journalism, Adam. They needed something juicy to finish off their piece. Rule number one in press relations: Don't take anything personally."

"But why didn't you bring me to the meeting? I'm the head of business development!"

"You weren't here, Adam, and the meeting came on immediately. And, frankly, as the head of business development, you ought to recognize that Amelia is our star, and her image and her story will draw people to the product."

"What do you mean?"

"I mean that a brilliant female engineer on need-based scholarship at Stanford is a fantastic Cinderella story. You can't pay for that kind of PR. People will latch on to her journey and will want to use the product to support her."

"But I'm a need-based scholarship kid at Stanford, too. Why can't I be the face? Amelia doesn't want it."

Roger looked over the top of his glasses at Adam disapprovingly. "One: That attitude will never make you the face of anything. Being the face can never be the goal. Two: Prove yourself first."

They heard the front door slam, and T.J. rushed by the office door.

"Everything okay, T.J.?" Roger called from his desk.

"Yep. Just fine!" T.J. said.

Roger's phone rang and he answered. "Hello?"

Adam sat down in the chair across from Roger. He wanted to ask him how, exactly, he *could* prove himself.

"Is that so? Just off the article? What's the offer? Uh-huh. And who's the investor? Never heard of them. Well, yes, we'd have to review the terms. If the investor wants to remain anonymous, he can't have voting rights. Okay, send over the sheet and we'll take a look. Thanks, Linda." Roger had a suspicious look on his face as he turned to Adam. "Can you get your sister and meet me in the conference room?"

Adam stood up quickly, suddenly realizing that the call must have had something to do with Doreye. "Sure."

Roger and T.J. joined Adam and Amelia in the conference room. Roger shut the door.

"Well, guys, I've just had a phone call from a lawyer at Winger Partners. You've gotten your first offer."

"Our first offer? You mean someone wants to buy Doreye?" Adam asked excitedly.

"But we haven't even launched the product," Amelia said, cocking her head with suspicion.

"How much are they offering?" Adam asked, leaning forward in his chair.

"Eight and a half million," Roger answered. T.J. clucked his tongue in disgust, but no one noticed.

"Eight and a half *million*?" Adam almost shouted.

"Who is the investor?" Amelia asked.

"A company called Proximate Investments. It's a new fund. The individual investors want to remain anonymous—I imagine they're VCs who are investing as individuals and don't want to have a conflict with their firms. Linda is sending over the terms."

"I can't believe we're going to get eight and a half million dollars!" Adam was practically drooling.

"Well, you have to build in taxes," Roger said.

Adam was exuberant. "Who cares? It's still amazing! Amelia, forget everything I said about the article! This is unbelievable!"

Amelia was silent, staring at her hands in her lap. Roger watched her with a concerned face.

"Well?" Adam said, glancing back and forth between Amelia and Roger. "Isn't it? Isn't it amazing?"

Without lifting his gaze from Amelia, Roger said, "I'd like to hear what Amelia's thinking."

Amelia looked up. Her eyes were heavy. She sighed. "I know it's probably a great deal, and God knows it would make Adam's and my lives a lot easier." She was afraid to look at her brother. She'd already turned down so much money, and she knew he wasn't going to like what she was about to say. "But something about it doesn't feel right."

She swallowed, glancing back down at her hands. "I mean, we've got so much more to do on the programming end, and there are so many more things we've yet to discover or develop. And I guess we could do that under another owner, but I don't know . . . it's just . . . it's our first company, and I guess I'm kind of attached. I'm not ready to give it away to someone else."

Roger's mouth had spread into a closed-lipped smile. Adam's eyes were darting back and forth from Roger to Amelia, trying to understand how the hell this could be happening. Eight and a half million, and they wanted to *turn it down*?

He looked at T.J. for help. "T.J., come on. Weigh in on this, please. It's a killer offer, right?"

Roger glanced nervously at T.J. He knew how much influence T.J. had over Adam and was worried that whatever was about to come out of his mouth would pit Adam even more firmly against his sister.

T.J. cleared his throat. "I think Amelia is right. It's too early to let the company go. You don't know anything about these investors or their motives. Besides, from a purely monetary perspective, if Doreye is worth eight and a half million today, with Amelia still cracking on more code and applications, it'll be worth a whole lot more than that in a year, maybe even in a few months."

Roger turned his head slightly in surprised delight. Adam looked down at the table. "Well, yeah, I guess that's true. I mean, about the increasing value."

"Besides," T.J. said, "you should always keep one offer in your pocket, right? For leverage against the next. Imagine if YouTube or Facebook had settled for their first offers. They'd never have gotten as far as they did."

Amelia looked up at T.J. and smiled. She didn't love his logic, but she was glad to have his support.

"So, we're all okay with telling them no?" Roger looked around the room.

"It isn't time," Amelia said. T.J. and Adam (albeit reluctantly) nodded.

Roger clapped his hands. "Great. I think it's the right decision. It also means we all know that this company is at a new level now. You don't turn down eight and a half million dollars and start sitting on your haunches. Things are about to get exciting, guys."

"Roger, while we're all here, maybe we should start talking about next steps for the team. It feels like we might be ready to hire some help for Amelia. I think Adam and I should start focusing on the sales strategy. I put together a deck for how I think we can approach it." T.J. reached into his satchel and pulled out the pitch deck he'd put together for his father, ripping off the last page with the org chart before sliding it across the table to Roger.

Roger flipped through the document. "Where'd you get these figures? They look really good."

T.J. blushed. "I've been doing some outside research. I wanted to get a handle on the total market size. I've also been researching potential vendor partnerships. If Amelia feels ready, we can start reaching out to vendors to get contracts on board for when the product launches."

Roger looked up from the deck. "Excellent, T.J." He turned to Amelia. "Amelia, do you feel ready to start talking to vendors? And would it be helpful to bring on a developer or two to help you with code?"

Amelia was taken aback: This was really happening. Vendors were going to start seeing her product. She was going to have a programming team.

"Yeah," she said. "Yeah, I think that sounds great. I'll put up a bulletin at Gates to see if I can find any engineers who could work part time with me."

"Great," Roger said. "Let's meet again on Friday for a progress report. Sound good?"

Everyone nodded in agreement. "Okay, then, how about some lunch? My treat."

As they were exiting the conference room, Roger patted T.J. on the back. "Great work, T.J. And good instincts. I'm afraid I underestimated you."

32

Dos Cervezas, Por Favor

At the end of the day, Adam and Amelia biked back to campus, following each other in silence down Sand Hill Road and onto Campus Drive. When they got to Amelia's dorm, Adam stopped and turned to face her.

"We need to talk," he said.

Amelia took a deep breath. "I know."

Ever since they had left the conference room she had been dreading this moment. She knew she owed the conversation to him, but the thought of having to defend herself about turning down all that money made her want to cry. "Dinner at the Treehouse?"

"Sounds good."

They biked to Stanford's student union and ordered burritos at the Treehouse. Adam ordered two beers. Amelia tried to hide her surprise as he showed his ID and the cashier handed him two Coronas.

As they walked outside with their food, Amelia whispered, "Since when do you have a fake ID?"

"T.J. got it for me. Pretty sweet, right?"

They sat at a picnic bench, one of a dozen lined up in the outside courtyard of the student union. The courtyard was bustling with other students laughing and drinking pitchers of beer. Amelia took a sip out of the bottle, trying to be casual about it. At this point, she didn't want to do anything to upset Adam even more. If that meant drinking a beer, so be it.

Adam unwrapped his burrito on the table. "Look," he said. "There's a lot that I have to say and—"

Amelia interrupted him, blurting out, "Adam, I'm sorry, but I just can't take it. I know how much money it is, and I know you think the money will solve all of our problems, but it's just not going to work out if—"

Adam touched her hand. "No, no, this doesn't have anything to do with today. I mean, with selling or not selling."

"It doesn't?" Amelia looked up, holding her breath and looking for confirmation before letting herself feel relieved.

"No. Not that I don't *want* eight and a half million dollars right now, but . . . Well, at the end of the day, I guess I trust your instincts, and Roger's and T.J.'s as well. It's not what I would have done, true. But I'm not the only one in this thing, right?"

Amelia took another sip of her beer, which she surprised herself by actually enjoying. "Oh, that is such good news. Because you know you're more important than any of it. I mean, *we're* more important than any of it."

"I know. That's why I have to tell you what I'm about to tell you," he said. "I haven't been honest with you lately, and, well, here goes . . ."

He took a deep breath.

"Remember the first day in the incubator when we got that call from The Family?"

Amelia nodded.

"Well, they've been calling ever since. And e-mailing. They want you to start embezzling money for them again."

"Tough luck," Amelia said. "We're done with them."

Adam swallowed. "That's what we thought, but the thing is . . . they've got something against me. And they're using it as blackmail."

Amelia put down her burrito. "What have they got against you?"

"After you got caught and went to juvie . . . You know how we had just taken our SATs the week before?"

Amelia nodded, not sure where this was going.

"Well, I didn't do so well." He looked down. "I did okay—I got an 1880—but you got a 2310. And when you left, I sort of freaked out. Because it was awful being away from you, and I started worrying. I knew that with a score like that you'd get into an amazing college and probably get a scholarship, and I wouldn't. And I started freaking out that we'd be separated again. So I . . ." He couldn't look at her. "I used the Dawsons' computer and traced your steps to hack into the College Board Web site and change my score."

He was picking at the corner of his burrito wrapper. "I only increased it to a 2150, and honestly, Amelia, if I'd had all the SAT prep courses most of the kids here had, you know I would easily have gotten that on my own. But . . . somehow the Dawsons found out. They have records of me doing it; they must have had some kind of a keylogger installed. And now they're threatening to tell Stanford I cheated if I don't get you to start embezzling money."

He sat looking down for what felt like an eternity, waiting for Amelia to say something.

Amelia took a sip of her beer. She chewed a bite of her burrito. Then she took another sip of her beer. Adam stared at her anxiously.

"Do you ever think about Mr. Dawson? What he's been doing?"

"He's not doing anything, Amelia. Michael Dawson's in jail. You put him there."

"He put himself there." She bristled at the accusation. "He is a man without scruples, Adam. He didn't care about anyone but himself, and he got a sick thrill out of gaming the system. I never knew people like that could exist—until one became my legal guardian."

"Why are you saying this?"

"Because those people do exist, Adam. Michael Dawson isn't alone, and sometimes I fear that he's not the exception to the rule, either." She closed her eyes and took another bite of her burrito, gathering the courage to say what she'd wanted to say to Adam for months.

"Michael Dawson is the reason I didn't want to start Doreye in the first place. It feels so inauthentic, so impure to create something in order to get rich. Life shouldn't be about winning the lottery as quickly and easily as possible. Life shouldn't be about shortcuts. It shouldn't be about stealing . . . whether you're stealing sales figures like Mr. Dawson, personal information like Ted Bristol, or SAT scores like you . . ."

"Amelia, I didn't do it because I'm a bad person; I did it . . ."

"Adam, I know why you did it. And I know you're not a bad person. But when you came to me a few months ago begging to start a company because it would pull us out of poverty, you sounded just like Mr. Dawson. The way you speak sometimes . . . it scares me, Adam. You're not a bad person, but I think you are capable of becoming one."

They stared at each other in silence. Amelia's words felt like stab wounds in Adam's chest. He closed his eyes in shame, praying that Amelia was wrong but afraid that she was right.

"How long before they tell?" she finally asked.

"Huh?" Adam was startled out of his train of thought.

"How long before the Dawsons tell Stanford?"

"Two weeks."

"Tell them I'll do it," she said.

"But Amelia, you can't! You can't start embezzling again!"

"I didn't say I was going to embezzle money. I said to tell them I would." She took another sip of her beer. The alcohol was making her feel confident.

Adam couldn't believe how calm she seemed. "You're not mad?"

Amelia smiled. "No, I'm not mad. We'll figure it out. I'm glad you told me. I don't want us to have secrets."

He grinned and picked up his burrito again. "Me either."

"So is there anything else?"

He wiped a bit of salsa off the corner of his mouth. "Well, there is one other little thing. Since we're not keeping secrets."

Amelia laughed. "What's that?"

"I've been dating T.J.'s sister, Lisa."

Amelia choked on the beer she was drinking. "You're what? Are you kidding? Are you crazy?"

"Amelia, I think I'm in love with her."

33

Lights! Camera! Action!

"Chad and I are going to watch a movie. Any interest?" Shandi asked Patty after Sunday dinner.

"What are you watching?"

"*Henry and June.* It's about Henry Miller, his marriage to June, and his affair with Anaïs Nin. It's a beautiful film, if you haven't seen it."

"Sure. I'll be right down. I'm just going to throw on some pajamas."

She slipped into a pair of Soffe shorts, slipped off her bra, threw on an oversize sweatshirt, grabbed a blanket, and padded down the stairs. It had been a week and a half since Chad picked her up from jail, and things had been surprisingly un-weird. He hadn't said anything, or even hinted at it in front of the Hawkinses, and she knew she could trust him not to. Plus, the fact that they had this little secret now—in addition to their other little secret—made her feel like they were secret pals, separate from the rest of the world.

Chad and Shandi were seated in two reclining theater chairs

in the middle of the movie room. Patty took the seat next to Chad and laid her blanket on her lap as Shandi started the film.

"Mind if I share your blanket?" Chad whispered a few minutes into the film.

"Sure." Patty smiled.

He lifted the armrest between them and pulled the blanket so that it covered his lap as well as hers.

"Isn't the cinematography beautiful?" Shandi whispered as a shot of Paris panned into Henry Miller's bedroom, where he was lying with a naked Frenchwoman. Shandi's eyes were glued to the screen, totally engrossed.

The actors started having loud, bed-shaking sex. "Did Shandi mention that this film was the first one in the world to get an NC-17 rating?" Chad asked Patty, loudly enough for Shandi to hear.

"Shhh . . . They only rated it that way because they were prudish and focusing on copulation rather than the artistry of presenting the affair. It's not about pornography, it's about Henry Miller's life, which happened to be filled and defined by a great deal of sex."

The film continued, chronicling naïve Anaïs Nin's sexual education by Miller.

Patty was blushing horribly at what was happening onscreen—two naked women were kissing in front of a casually smoking Henry Miller—when she felt Chad's knee press against hers. Her heart jumped. *He just moved in his chair,* she thought. *It's not intentional. It doesn't mean anything.*

But a moment later, she felt his hand settle on her knee under the blanket. Her heart raced, and she focused her gaze forward. *Concentrate,* she thought, *just concentrate on the movie.* Slowly, Chad's elbow pulled back so that his hand was resting on her thigh. His thumb toyed with the edge of her shorts. He let his fingers ever so slightly stroke the skin along her thigh.

She wondered if he could feel her pulse.

"Oh, devastating!" Shandi shouted at the screen as Anaïs tried to capture Henry's attention from his wife, June. "Oh, poor Anaïs!"

34

The Puzzle

"Hey." Amelia stuck her head into Sundeep's office. "Do you have a minute?"

Sundeep looked up from studying a large medical textbook. "Sure," he said. "Come in."

Amelia sat down on the couch and exhaled.

"What's going on?" asked Sundeep from behind his desk.

Amelia shook her head. "I have a problem. It's a puzzle, kind of, that I'm stuck on. And I was hoping a new set of ears might help me think it through."

"Sure. Let's hear it," Sundeep said, leaning back in his chair.

"Well I have a . . . code . . . that I'm working on that's kind of complex. So, start with Node One, which has two options to follow: path A and path B. If I choose path A, the app will run smoothly. The problem with path A is that it requires me to go against my morals—path A steals user data. It's not only immoral, but there is a ten percent chance we are discovered and arrested."

"You shouldn't compromise your morals. Choose the other one."

"But here's the problem: If I choose the righteous path B, no users are compromised, but there is a ninety-five percent chance the entire program malfunctions. So I'm pretty much forced to choose path A."

"Is there any way to put off Node One?"

"No. It's inevitable. And it has to be addressed within two weeks."

"Well, it sounds like you need a path C."

"But there isn't a third option. It's binary."

Sundeep nodded thoughtfully.

"Well, I don't believe in dead ends, and I certainly don't believe in going against what is right. It sounds like you need some new software. Maybe you solved this problem before? Isn't there something you can reuse that might override Node One, and therefore avoid the malfunction caused by path B?"

"You mean, like, create a Node Zero that bypasses Node One?"

"Sure, I guess. Look into some other programs you've written recently. Something that renders the threat of the malfunction moot."

Amelia's eyes darted back and forth as she thought this through in her head. Sundeep watched her with a curious smile. What was it like to be in this girl's brain?

Suddenly Amelia looked up. "Yes! Yes! I've got it. You're absolutely right! Sundeep, you're a genius."

She darted out of the room. Sundeep grinned and shook his head. He hoped she would remember him after she made it big.

———

Back in her dorm room, Amelia opened two windows in her browser. Through one, she hacked into Gibly. Through the other, she hacked into The Family's personal bank account.

With Gibly's eyes on The Family's information, she hacked into Indiana Central Bank and transferred fifty cents from their reserve funds into The Family's account.

Smiling at her work, she took a screenshot of the Gibly report, showing that The Family had just been on Indiana's Central Bank Web site, where they had transferred fifty cents into their personal savings account.

She logged out of all the browsers and attached the screenshot to an e-mail from an anonymous user, which she addressed to The Family.

Dear Family,

Not sure if you've heard of Gibly—it's been in the news a lot lately. Anyway, they've got this smart technology that follows users' Web activity. I wanted to let you know, because it looks like Gibly caught you embezzling some money from the Indiana Central Bank. Looks like they only caught you taking $0.50, so they probably won't notice, but it sure would be annoying if someone caught you stealing more and alerted the authorities. . . .

Don't you just hate these advances in technology?

"Send!" Amelia smiled as she tapped the button.

35

Skintight

Amelia was at University Café, tapping away at her laptop. She and Roger had spent the morning talking to engineers interested in joining the team, and she was full of energy from the interviews.

She'd sent an e-mail to the computer science e-mail list at Stanford and within five hours had received over one hundred responses. She'd had to send another e-mail saying they were no longer taking applications just to stop the deluge.

In the end, they'd interviewed ten engineers. A junior, Ben, had put it best: "Amelia's reputation around the Gates Building is that she's the next Bill Gates. Roger Fenway's name is legendary. And Doreye is already being followed by TechCrunch. You'd have to be crazy not to want to join this team."

Amelia couldn't keep from grinning. She'd had no idea that her peers in the Gates Building even knew who she was, much less admired her.

Roger and Amelia had narrowed the pool down to four candidates: two seniors, a junior, and a sophomore. Roger sent them an e-mail requesting they come to the incubator the following morning to present their "best work."

Amelia couldn't wait. She'd never thought she'd like working on a team, but thinking about how much more they could get done with three people was exhilarating, and she was feeling as confident as she'd ever felt.

"Amelia, you are absolutely glowing today. You must have figured out the problem with Node One."

Amelia looked up at Sundeep, who was standing next to her table. He was dressed in workout clothes, his white iPod earbuds hanging around his neck.

"Sundeep!" She smiled. Could this day get any better? "I did! I figured it out, and I just spent the morning talking to engineer candidates—we're going to hire two new people."

"That's great! It will be awesome to have more people in the incubator."

"Are you getting lunch?" she asked.

"Oh, no. I just finished working out and stopped by to grab a smoothie. Nothing like a peanut butter–banana protein shake to completely undo all the calories I just burned."

She giggled. She couldn't help staring at the definition in his shoulders and biceps, which showed through his skintight Under Armour shirt. He always wore loose button-downs to the incubator, and she'd never realized he was so fit.

They stood for a moment staring at each other. Amelia wasn't sure what to say; all she knew was that she didn't want it to end. She loved the way he looked at her, like he could see right into her soul.

"Well." Sundeep finally broke the silence. "I guess I'd better go order."

"Wait—"

What was she doing? Was she really going to?

Yes, just do it, she told herself.

"Would you . . . I mean, would you ever want to go out sometime? Grab dinner one day after work or something?"

It was the single bravest thing Amelia had ever done, and she could not believe it as the words came out of her mouth. But he was so kind, and so attractive, and she just felt so comfortable with him. And besides, nothing could go wrong today.

Sundeep's mouth opened but no words came out. "Oh, I—" he sputtered. "Amelia, I hope I didn't . . . haven't led you on. I have a girlfriend."

Amelia's heart sank in her chest. She could feel her pulse beating against her temple, and the light in the room suddenly felt painfully bright and harsh.

"Oh," she said. It was all she could muster.

"Hey, I think you're absolutely brilliant. Seriously, you're one of the smartest people I've ever met. And I'm so glad our paths have crossed in the incubator."

"Yeah, glad, sure." Amelia wasn't even conscious of her mouth forming the words. She just needed to get out of there. Now.

"This definitely won't make things weird for me, so don't, you know, don't worry about it at all, okay? I'll see you back on Sand Hill, then?" Sundeep smiled and gave a little wave as he moved to the counter.

"Yep." Amelia shut her computer and threw her water bottle into her backpack. She was out the door before Sundeep had finished his order.

36

The Negotiator

Amelia raced down Palm Drive on her bicycle, ignoring the beautiful view. What had she been thinking? Of course Sundeep had a girlfriend. How could a guy like that not have a girlfriend? He was just being *nice*. God, was she so socially incompetent that a normal guy showing any sign of normal niceness made her think he was interested?

Boys were such a waste of time. Like she could just go off to a dinner anyway: Everything was blowing up at Doreye, and she needed to invest herself in that 110 percent. She couldn't let herself get distracted by stupid . . . crushes.

Oh, God, but she had such a crush on him! The way he looked at her, the way he checked in on her every morning, the way she hoped he'd be in the kitchen when she went out to get tea (she was drinking a lot more tea these days in the hope of those encounters). How could he look at her like that when he had a girlfriend? He did look at her in a special way, Amelia knew it. That wasn't fair to her or to his girlfriend. Maybe she should tell his girlfriend.

Like that would help. That would just make things more awkward at the incubator. Oh, God! The incubator. She would have to see him there, all the time. Maybe she could start working from campus. Now that school was starting, she could say she needed to be at Gates to . . . get advice from more engineers. Yes, that's what she'd do.

She pulled her bike up to her dorm and locked it. Ugh! How could he!

When she got to her dorm room there were six notes push-pinned to the small bulletin board she'd affixed to the door. She'd signed up to be the Residential Computer Coordinator for Alondra, a freshman dorm, because it guaranteed her a single room with her own bathroom and no roommate. But it also meant she had to deal with notes like these, panicked requests from clueless freshmen who didn't know how to set up their e-mail accounts.

Could this day get any worse? she thought as she pushed open the door.

Yes, it could.

Adam was seated on her bed. "Where have you been?"

"Working," she said tersely, throwing down her bag.

"But today's the deadline. They're going to call any minute." As he said it, his iPhone rang. Amelia and Adam stared at the ringing phone with the Indiana area code as if it were an ancient artifact.

"It's them, Amelia. They're going to send the letter to Stanford today if we don't do what they say."

Amelia glanced disgustedly at the phone. "Put it on speaker," she said. He did, fumbling with the buttons in his haste and panic.

"Hello?" Amelia said into the phone, the annoyance resonant in her voice.

"Amelia. Long time." It was Jacob Dawson, the eldest son in The Family.

"Yeah. There's a reason for that," she snapped back. "Listen, I'm assuming you got the e-mail, so there's nothing more for us to talk about."

"What e-mail?"

Adam glanced at his sister. What e-mail?

"The one about Gibly."

"That was from you?"

Amelia rolled her eyes. "Of course it was from me. I sent it from a disguised address."

"But how could you—"

"It's not important, Jake. The point is that I'm not going to embezzle money for you. But I do know how to make it look like you're embezzling money, and use Gibly to get you caught."

"You wouldn't."

"I would," Amelia said sourly into the phone. Adam was watching her, speechless. "Now let's talk about your dad. He gets out of jail when? In a few months? I'm pretty sure the state doesn't look lightly on repeat offenders."

"But that's . . . that's creating false evidence!" the voice on the other end protested.

"And you are blackmailing me to commit a crime!" Amelia retorted. "Who's the worse offender?"

She took a deep breath. "Listen, Jake. If you're going to make me play this stupid game, you'd better believe I'll play it better than you. Leave my brother and me alone. Or I will make sure your father stays in jail for the rest of his life."

With that, she ended the call. It was moments like this when she wished there were still landlines. Throwing down a receiver was far more satisfying than tapping a touch-screen button on an iPhone.

She looked up at Adam, who was staring at her, his mouth agape.

"What?" she snapped.

He guffawed. "That was awesome."

Her irritated scowl melted into a laugh. "I guess it kind of was, huh?" She pushed her bangs out of her face and took off her glasses, rubbing the bridge of her nose. "He caught me on a bad day."

"You should have more bad days. They make you a ferocious negotiator."

She smiled and sighed. "You know that's not what I want to be."

"But it's still good to have in your back pocket," he said, punching her on the arm playfully.

"Listen, I'm going to go over to Gates and bury myself in some code. See you at the incubator tomorrow?"

"Sure thing. I'll be there in the afternoon."

"Great. Let me know if you hear anything more from The Family, but I think they'll be leaving us alone from now on."

37

Cat's Cradle

The Bristols were on the terrace of the Atherton Country Club having drinks with the Morgans, another Atherton family with whom they were dining that night, when Ted excused himself to take a phone call.

T.J. was chatting with Mrs. Morgan—or, rather, he was listening to her go on about her latest personal training session and how it was doing wonders to tone her butt. He'd perfected the art of nodding just enough to indicate engagement, occasionally throwing in an "Oh, really?" or "How interesting" while he thought about something else.

Mrs. Morgan was a piece of work, literally. She could hardly blink she'd had so many face-lifts, and the Botox injections had made her forehead so smooth it was impossible to distinguish happy expressions from sad ones. She was hot, to be sure; a classic cougar who worked out two and a half hours a day to achieve arms like Madonna and used plastic surgery to fix whatever the yoga-Pilates-spinning-kickboxing concoction didn't. Her husband hardly noticed her—everyone knew he had a young model girlfriend in New York, where he took frequent business trips—and, as a result, T.J. knew she sought attention from younger men like him.

T.J. smiled his most flattering smile. "Sounds intense," he said, and stared past her shoulder at Ted, who was listening intently to whoever was on the other end of the line, instinctively nodding at whatever information he was receiving. T.J. wondered whether he'd gotten the news yet that Doreye had turned down the sale.

Finally, the families sat down to dinner. Ted was his normal jovial, charismatic self. *He must have heard by now,* T.J. thought, *but then how could he be in such a good mood?* Why wasn't he saying anything about it? Either way he should tell T.J., right?

By dessert the suspense was killing him.

After dinner, per the club's tradition, the men went to the cigar room for an after-dinner drink and the women went to the ladies' lounge. In the cigar room, Mr. Morgan fell into conversation with another club member, and Ted took T.J. aside, finally addressing him. "So, they turned down the offer. But I guess you already knew that."

"Yeah," T.J. said, shaking his head. "I tried to persuade them, but they just wouldn't budge."

Ted took a sip of his Scotch. "You're a bad liar, son. You should work on that."

T.J. blushed. "What do you mean?"

"I know you advised them not to sell. And I'm very disappointed."

"I—" T.J. scrambled to think of something to say.

"It was a test, T.J. The call with Jay?"

T.J. felt a lump in his throat.

"Did you even bother to look up who Jay Resnick is? Nobody. I was talking to a dead line. Complete fiction." He laughed.

"Come on, did you actually think I hadn't planned for you to overhear that conversation? That I would be so careless? I don't make stupid mistakes like that, son. Jesus, you have a lot to learn."

T.J. was staring at his father. "I don't understand. You mean the whole thing was—"

"A test. To figure out where your loyalties lie." Ted motioned to the waiter for another drink.

T.J. felt his chest rising with every breath. "You mean you never intended to buy Doreye?"

"Oh, I *intend* to buy Doreye. But not yet. It won't hurt enough yet." He grinned as the waiter handed him a new drink. "You see, when you first start a company, it feels like a new baby. You're enthralled by it, fascinated by what it does and the strange and wonderful little strides it makes. But after a year, it's not a baby anymore. Your ego has gotten involved. Slowly you've grown attached to it. Now it feels like it's become a part of you." He sipped his Scotch. "And after another year, it starts to become not just a part of you, but *the most important* part of you. Your identity. And that's when it really hurts to have it taken away."

Ted's eyes were crisp and angry, his jaw set.

"And that, T.J., is when I'll take Doreye from Amelia."

38

Two Thousand Lines of Code and Nothing to Wear

Just opening the doors to the Gates Building made Amelia's heart rate slow to a more relaxed pace. She climbed the stairs and made her way to her favorite cubicle. There weren't many people there, which suited her fine. The pride she had felt this morning about her peers respecting her for the TechCrunch article now made her self-conscious.

She clicked to the latest Doreye code and began typing, but she quickly found herself two hours in with a pattern that wouldn't run. There were over two thousand lines of code, and she had no idea where the error was. Why was she being so sloppy?

But she knew exactly why. Her mind kept drifting back to University Café and Sundeep's words. "I have a girlfriend." Why had he had to show up just then? Right when she was feeling confident enough to do something so stupid? She'd been having such a great day, and then he'd gone and ruined it all. She tried to take herself back to the time before their conversation, to access the elatedness she'd felt after all the interviews. But

Sundeep was like a wall, like this malfunction in her program that blocked everything from working. She hated him.

She took off her glasses and sat back in her chair, closing her eyes and taking a deep breath.

"Amelia!"

She slowly opened her eyes. Was that George?

A strange new version of George stood next to her at the cubicle. Since she had last seen him at the end of spring term, he had lost about forty pounds and cut his hair.

"George?" she said, questioningly, putting her glasses back on.

He laughed awkwardly. "I know, I look a little different. I finally took Google up on their free personal training sessions this summer. How was your summer?" Before she could answer, he stepped in. "Of course, I already know how your summer was. I read the TechCrunch article about you. Man, Amelia, that is just so rad."

Amelia shrugged her narrow shoulders and offered a lifeless "Thanks, George. It is exciting."

She glanced back at her screen, hoping he would take the hint that she wanted to be alone. But he kept going, his eyes shining above his freckled cheeks.

"To think that I was here the night you first made the original Doreye application work! Do you have any idea how cool that is?"

She smiled politely.

"Listen, Amelia." He took a deep breath. "I thought about you this summer—a lot. Not just because of Doreye, but because I think you're a really . . . a really special person, and I'd love to get to know you better. And I thought maybe, if you're up for it, we could hang out . . . sometime."

Instinctively, she began to turn him down. "George, I think you're really—"

But then, abruptly, she stopped herself. Why should she

always decline? Sundeep had a girlfriend, Patty was in her so-rority, Adam was living in a frat house now and, apparently, had a girlfriend. And all she had was two thousand lines of code that weren't working.

"Sure, George. I'd love to hang out sometime."

"Really?" George tried to contain his excitement. "That's great!" He scrambled for an idea, afraid that if he didn't get a plan made now it might never actually happen. "What are you doing tonight?"

Amelia looked at the jumbled code on her screen. It was a lost cause. "Nothing. I'm not doing anything."

"I was going to head over to the LAIR to play ZOSTRA. We have a group that gets together every Wednesday. Do you play?" George was referring to the virtual reality game that had de-veloped a cult following in the computer science community.

"I've never played," Amelia said, watching his face drop. "But I'd love to learn."

"Excellent!"

Who was she kidding? Guys like Sundeep didn't go for her. She was a computer science geek. She might as well act the part.

Meet Me at ZOSTRA

Amelia had heard of the LAIR, but she had never actually been there. Situated across campus from the Gates Building, it was technically a twenty-four-hour study room. Stanford was always updating the equipment in the Gates Building and, whenever they did, they put all the old (meaning six to twelve months outdated) equipment in the LAIR and left the space largely unmonitored.

It had become an upperclass computer science hang, where engineers who wanted to socialize more than code came to "study." They'd start filtering in after dinner and open a problem set. Then they would sign in to Instant Messenger and flirt with people across the room. By ten o'clock at night, everyone was usually huddled around a few monitors watching YouTube clips or two people battling against each other in Angry Birds or Scrabble.

Wednesdays had officially become ZOSTRA nights, starting promptly at midnight.

Amelia followed George through a painted red door and up

two flights of concrete stairs to the LAIR, where two guys she recognized as computer science TAs sat at a table collecting money and handing out player numbers.

"Hey, guys!" George said to the two. "Do you know Amelia? Amelia, meet Jon and T-Bag."

T-Bag, a lean, good-looking blond guy wearing a sports coat with a pocket square, stood up and took Amelia's hand, bowing his head to her in mock formality. "Forgive these imbeciles. Everyone calls me T-Bag, but as you seem rather sophisticated, feel free to refer to me by my Christian name, Theodore."

Amelia smiled with surprise. Who was this guy, with his strange European accent and ornate speech? "Very nice to meet you, Mr. T-Bag," she said, taking his hand and playing along.

Jon, a chubby Asian boy wearing a tie over his t-shirt, khaki shorts, and no shoes, also stood up and shook her hand. "You're not *the* Amelia, are you? The one doing that device-linking thing with Roger Fenway?"

George swept his arms up as though he were a magician presenting his finest act. With these guys, he had an air of confidence and charm she had never witnessed from him in Gates. "Indeed, she is. Gentlemen, you are in the presence of greatness."

"Tickets comped!" T-Bag exclaimed. "May I have the honor of getting you a drink, Madame?"

Amelia wasn't sure if they were mocking her or if they were seriously impressed, but it didn't matter; there was something utterly lovable about these three. T-Bag handed her a plastic cup filled with cheap vodka and cranberry juice. "Our very finest, for the lady," he said, and she felt her heart flutter a little as she happily took it from him.

She and George played ZOSTRA as a team so she could figure out the rules. The game was based on avatars, which each player created and kept from week to week. The avatars challenged one another to different games and tasks—ranging from gladiator-style fencing to who-can-pick-up-a-virtual-girl-in-a-virtual-bar-first competitions—on a large screen in front of the whole room. When you won a competition, you got points that could be used to buy accessories, weapons, and super-powers for your avatar. As the night went on, the crowd got more and more drunk, and more and more into the game.

Three hours and three vodka-cranberries later, Amelia was seated on a beanbag chair between George, T-Bag, Jon, and Jon's girlfriend, Janet, an awkwardly lanky blonde wearing a thrift-store prom dress two sizes too small for her tall frame. They made an astonishingly strange-looking pair, but when-ever she told a joke—which she did often, between swigs of te-quila straight from the bottle—Jon watched her with a loving pride that made Amelia instinctively like them as a couple.

"I think," Janet said drunkenly, reaching out for Amelia's hand, "that you are just delightful."

Amelia grinned into her plastic cup and took another sip. Although she barely knew them, she felt right at home with these people.

"Don't you think so, T-Bag?" asked Janet.

T-Bag raised his glass. "I do, indeed. You simply must join our ZOSTRA nights and get your own avatar. Then you won't have to continue on as that ghastly, unrealistically muscular Italian man," he said, referring to George's avatar.

"Hey!" George protested, mocking T-Bag's accent. "I think he's quite strapping."

"You straight men don't have a clue." T-Bag rolled his eyes, turning back to Amelia and grabbing her hand. "Trust me, dar-ling. We'll design her together, and she will be stunning. I am a second-life fashion genius."

She giggled tipsily. He went on. "Do you have a gay best friend yet? Because I would really love to be that for you."

"Wait," she said. "You're gay?"

"Flaming." He grinned. She grinned back. She'd never met a gay person before, but she liked him. In fact, she liked just about everything right now.

They stayed for another half hour before saying their good-byes. When she tried to stand up, she fell back down, giggling at herself. George put out his hand to help her up. "Let me walk you back to your dorm," he offered.

They walked along the narrow pathways, Amelia chatting animatedly about strategies for next week's ZOSTRA. When they got to her dorm, George waited while she found her keys. "Can you get to your room okay?"

"Yeah, I think so." She smiled.

"Great." He smiled back. "I'm glad you came tonight, Amelia. I had a really good time."

"Me, too," she said.

They paused for a moment, smiling drunkenly at each other.

"Okay, then," he said. "See you tomorrow at Gates?"

"I'll be there!"

40

The Inner Room

Across campus, Adam's lips were clenched around the spigot of a tapped keg, his hands gripping either side of the metal barrel, his legs held above his head by a couple of burly rugby players.

"Sixteen! Seventeen! Eighteen!" a crowd of manically drunk coeds chanted as Adam swallowed the beer rushing out of the spigot. This was his first keg stand, and he was *dominating*, to use a term he'd picked up since moving into Phi Delta. The last guy had only made it to twelve, and here he was on . . .

"Twenty-four! Twenty-five! Twenty-six . . ."

But then something happened. The beer went down the wrong side of his throat and he started coughing into the spigot. The rugby players dropped his legs, and he landed clumsily on the floor.

"Twenty-six!" cried Chris, the Phi Delta social chair, who was standing with a clipboard, recording performances. "Our reigning champion!"

Everyone cheered, and Adam grinned drunkenly, accepting a beer from a cute brunette wearing a tight red dress and five-inch heels. "You were amaaaaazing!" she slurred, pushing her hand into his chest. "What's your name?"

Adam felt on top of the world as he took in the filthy kitchen, strewn with beer cans and red cups. A couple was making out against the wall in the corner. No one seemed to notice, or to care. "I'm Adam," he said as he took a sip of the beer.

"Wait, Adam Dory?" She batted her eyelashes, but the concentration it required caused her to trip on her massive heels. Adam put his arm out to catch her. "Oops!" she giggled. She leaned down and took off her shoes, apparently unconcerned about placing her bare feet on the sticky, beer-drenched floor.

"You don't know who I am, do you?" The brunette pouted.

"Sure I do . . ." Adam lied. He stared at her hard. *Who is this girl?*

"You were the creep who narr . . ." She stopped midsentence, not able to articulate the word through her slurring. "You narr-a-ted my g-chat conversation to Professor Marsh's PoliSci class!"

"Oh! Rebecca?" Despite all that Adam had achieved over the past few months, the feelings of inadequacy resurfaced. "I'm so sorry about that. I really didn't mean to . . ."

"Do you want to dance?" she asked, instantaneously forgetting about the incident and pulling Adam toward the fraternity's common room, where speakers were blasting a Lady Gaga remix.

Adam closed his eyes, letting his body sway with the music in careless abandon, as they moved against each other on the dance floor. He felt her open mouth press against his and let it happen, sinking into the sensation. Then, as if the signal of what was going on finally reached his brain, he pulled away. "I can't . . ."

"Sure you can."

"No, it's not . . . I have a girlfriend."

"Oh." The girl pouted and dipped her chin, her brown curls falling in front of her face. "Wait," she said, her head abruptly popping back up. She glanced around the dance floor. "Is she here?"

"No."

The girl put her hand back on his shoulder. "Then what's the problem?" she asked, leaning in to kiss him.

He pushed her away gently. "Well . . . I love her."

Her red lips spread into a sideways grin and she cocked her head. "Awww . . . that's so cute. She's a very lucky girl." Rebecca turned and walked away, her full hips swinging back and forth in her tight red dress as she headed to the kitchen to find someone else to flirt with.

Adam stood in the middle of the dance floor, surrounded by couples making out or on the verge of it. He felt unbelievably alone. Where was Lisa? He knew she had a dorm meeting and a study group, but that should have ended hours ago.

Suddenly, he panicked. What if she was hanging out with that water polo player who lived next door, that guy with the perfectly toned body and the shaggy blond hair?

He should call her, he decided.

He dialed her number, but there was no answer. Maybe she didn't hear the phone ring. He tried again. Still no answer. This time he left a message, trying his hardest to sound more sober than he was. "Lisa, it's me. Just thinking about you and missing you. Call me."

He waited until the next song was over, and then tried again. Then one more time. Still no answer. What was going on? Where was she?

Maybe she was online. He should go log on to his computer and check.

He stumbled up the stairs to his room. Like all the rooms in the Phi Delta house, his was a two-room double, meaning two guys shared two rooms, but there was only one door in and out. This meant there was an "inner" room and an "outer" room. The outer room was a little bigger, but you had to deal with your roommate walking in and out to get to his room. Adam's roommate, Henry, didn't have any qualms about people walking in and out when he was hooking up with girls, so he'd requested the bigger outer room, and Adam had happily obliged, opting for privacy.

Now he pushed open the door and found Henry sitting on his bed with three girls, all giggling and passing a pipe. The room reeked of pot.

"Adam!" Henry exclaimed, so high he could hardly open his eyes. Henry was English and milked his Britishness for all it was worth. He wasn't bad looking, but he wasn't model-attractive like T.J. or Chris, the Phi Delta social chair. His thick British accent was a golden ticket for getting women, however. Sometimes Adam wondered whether the words he used, like "chap" and "bloody" and "wicked," were even words British people used or just things he threw in to get attention.

"Adam, meet . . ." Henry looked around and realized he didn't know any of the girls' names. "Meet the girls," he said. They giggled and smiled at Henry.

"Want a hit?" one of the girls asked Adam.

"No, thanks," Adam answered, stumbling to the door of his inner room. "I've got to make a phone call."

"Adam!" Henry shouted. "Who are you calling at three-thirty in the morning? Unless it's a pizza boy, I suggest you restrain yourself."

"Ooh, pizza! Can we get pizza?" one of the girls squealed.

Adam shouted from the other room, "It's not pizza!"

"Don't do it, Adam." Henry was standing in the doorway

now, looking at Adam perched on his bed with his phone in hand. "How many times have you called her tonight?"

Adam tried to downplay it. "I only left one message—"

"How many times, Adam?"

"Four."

"Come on, mate. You're embarrassing yourself."

"It's none of your business," Adam said. "Go back to your girls."

"No more calls tonight, Adam. You'll regret it. Mark my words."

Adam motioned for Henry to leave the room. As he shut the door, he dialed Lisa's number.

He heard a sleepy voice pick up on the other end. "Hello?"

"Lisa! Lisa, Lisa. Where are you?"

"I'm in bed, Adam. It's almost four in the morning."

"Do you want to come over?"

"Now? I have class at nine."

"Oh, okay. Well, sweet dreams then."

"Good night, Adam."

"I love you," he said, but she had already hung up.

41

No Simple Highway

Amelia sat across from Roger at Juniper Café, a fancy Greek restaurant in Menlo Park, nibbling at the hummus plate he'd ordered as an appetizer. When she'd googled the restaurant and seen the prices on the menu, she'd realized she probably needed to dress up. She'd stopped by the Gap on the way home from the incubator and bought a simple navy linen dress with spaghetti straps and a pair of gold braided sandals. She paid seventy dollars for the outfit—more than she could remember ever having spent on clothes—but the girl in the dressing room had told her she *had* to get it because it fit her perfectly. Still, she felt like an imposter wearing something other than her normal jeans and plaid shirt.

That morning, they had made the decision to bring Arjun, a shy sophomore from Bangalore, and Ralph, a precocious red-headed junior from Chicago, onto the engineering team. Arjun had worked as a programmer in India throughout high school and was a machine at developing and replicating code; Ralph was an expert on iPhone application software and had interned at Cisco the summer before, giving him exposure to a range of products relevant to Doreye.

They were quirky in their own ways, but Amelia liked them both very much. They would each work fifteen hours a week on tasks that Amelia would assign every Monday.

Roger had taken her to dinner to celebrate the first hires. The restaurant was small and intimate, with only a dozen or so tables covered in white tablecloths. The dining room was dimly lit by candles and stained-glass lanterns mounted on the dark wooden walls.

"Can I tempt you with a glass of champagne?" Roger asked.

"Sure," she said. Since playing ZOSTRA at the LAIR last Wednesday, she had been more open to alcohol. She had never had champagne before; what was the harm in trying it?

"Excellent," he said, motioning over the waiter.

After the waiter delivered the champagne, they toasted. "To expanding your team," Roger said as he clinked her glass. Amelia winced at the sour flavor of the champagne, and Roger noticed. "It's an acquired taste. Talk to me in five years and you'll love it."

Over lamb moussaka and grilled halibut, they chatted about Doreye, the team, their progress, and next steps. After the waiter had cleared their plates, Roger leaned forward and placed his hands on the table.

"So, Amelia, I wanted to bring you to dinner tonight in part to celebrate, and in part to make a suggestion."

She took a sip of her champagne. She was on her second glass and feeling open to ideas, but this still came as a surprise.

"It was a big summer, and you made a lot of decisions. You turned down a lot of money, which shows how committed you are to this product. And now you've hired two new team members, which is going to significantly increase your time commitment. Plus, you've got TechCrunch following Doreye's progress, which means pressure to get a product out sooner rather than later."

She nodded, waiting for the punch line.

"And so, I think you're at the point now where you need to start thinking hard about your priorities. And whether you can really do what you want to do at Doreye while remaining a full-time student. If you want it to succeed in a big way, Doreye needs to be the only road you travel."

Amelia sat up a little straighter in her chair. She adjusted her glasses on her face. "Are you telling me to drop out of school?"

Roger smiled. "I would never tell you what to do, Amelia. It's your decision. But people do take breaks from school. You can always go back later and finish your degree."

"Drop out?" she said softly to herself, looking down at the table. The thought of leaving school had never crossed her mind. That was something people like Steve Jobs did, and, as much press as Doreye was getting, she didn't consider herself Steve Jobs.

Then again, the incubator provided everything she'd ever hoped for: She could code all day long and work on whatever she wanted, just like at the Gates Building, but without having the distraction of English classes and other university requirements. She could move into an apartment and not have to deal with being an RCC or eating dining hall food.

But something in her gut didn't like the idea. As idyllic as it sounded, she . . . What was it? What was holding her back?

She looked up at Roger. "I'm not sure," she said.

He put up his hands. "Absolutely no pressure to decide tonight. I just think you should give it some thought."

The waiter brought out two small plates of baklava.

Amelia cut a piece with her fork, still searching for what it was about leaving Stanford that bothered her so much. It's not like she had to have the degree in order to do what she wanted. The incubator *was* what she wanted.

As she chewed on the flaky, honey-soaked pastry, the memory of last Wednesday flashed in her mind.

ZOSTRA. That's why she didn't want to leave. She had finally found a group of people with whom she felt comfortable, and she wasn't sure she was ready to give that up. But how could she tell Roger she wouldn't commit to Doreye full time because she wanted to play video games with a bunch of computer science nerds?

"Well, look who it is," Roger said, waving at the door behind Amelia.

Amelia turned around to see who had just entered the restaurant.

Her heart sank.

Sundeep was walking toward their table, his hand around the waist of a gorgeous, perfectly dressed and coiffed blonde girl. Amelia felt her cheeks burning with envy. Of course that was the kind of girl he went for. Why had she ever, ever thought he'd like her?

She forced a smile as the couple approached their table. Roger stood to shake Sundeep's hand.

"What a coincidence," Roger said. "We were just celebrating Doreye's most recent expansion. We hired two engineers this morning."

"That's great! Congratulations," Sundeep said, smiling.

Amelia felt the pride of her accomplishment wash away, replaced by embarrassment.

"We're celebrating, too. It's our six-month anniversary." Sundeep squeezed the blonde girl's waist and looked affectionately at her. "Roger, Amelia, this is my girlfriend, Lisa Bristol."

Part III

www.crunchbase.com/company/doreye

Crunch**Base**

Home > Companies > Doreye

Doreye, Inc.

Doreye (pronounced "Door-Eye") is a downloadable device and object recognition application created by Amelia Dory and her brother, Adam Dory. In an interview with TechCrunch, Amelia called Doreye "a remote control for the physical world." The application uses the phone's native antenna and circuitry to receive and broadcast signals across a wider spectrum of frequencies than the manufacturers intended. As a result, Doreye currently allows the user to "see and control" any electronic device with their phone—televisions, garage doors, and even microwaves are accessible via Doreye.

Apple CEO Tim Cook, who tested an early alpha version, called Doreye ". . . scientifically impossible. I'd sooner believe the Loch Ness Monster exists than I would believe Doreye exists. . . . And, yet, here I am using it to unlock my car." The limitations of what is and isn't possible don't seem to prevent Amelia Dory from pushing the horizons of Doreye. Next year, Doreye will be able to recognize and find inanimate objects. "Like how a bat uses sonar," Amelia explains, Doreye will use radio signals and a sleek, lightweight AI (artificial intelligence) to recognize things like your keys, your car, or even your friends.

Amelia Dory holds over a dozen patents related to Doreye. She cofounded the company with her twin brother, Adam Dory, who is the company's COO and head of business development. They started the company six months ago while freshmen at Stanford. Both hail from Indiana.

www.crunchbase.com/financial-organization/fenway-ventures

Crunch**Base**

Home > Financial Organizations > Fenway Ventures

FENWAY VENTURES

Fenway Ventures is a venture fund that focuses on seed and Series A investments to start-up companies. The fund also runs a start-up incubator, which is designed to speed the development of entrepreneurial companies by providing mentorship, as well as business and legal support.

Fenway Ventures is currently incubating two early-stage companies: **WorldSight** and **Doreye**. WorldSight uses advances in laser technology to affordably treat glaucoma in third-world inhabitants. Doreye is a revolutionary software that the Valley has deemed "The next Google"; it transforms anyone's cell phone into both a remote control for electronic devices and an object recognition "radar" for inanimate objects.

Key People

Founder **Roger Fenway** is one of Silicon Valley's most prolific investors and philanthropists. His earliest company, Ultra Effects, revolutionized the postproduction process of filmmaking and invented the motion graphics industry. He continued to focus on the intersection of creativity and technology by founding Micromedia, which created the software behind products that later became Flash and the Final Cut video editing software. A pet project that Roger pursued in his spare time, Kadence, eventually became the music service that formed the backbone of Apple's iTunes. He is particularly known for his laid-back aesthetic, notoriously wearing flip-flops to high-profile meetings.

Analyst **T.J. Bristol** handles supervision as well as business support for Fenway's incubator. He assists the founders in market analysis and fund-raising. Formerly an intern at Goldman Sachs, T.J. is the son of Ted Bristol, one of Silicon Valley's biggest venture investors. T.J. graduated from Stanford, where his father is a trustee and his sister, Lisa, is currently a freshman.

http://www.nytimes.com/pages/fashion/weddings/vows/
Hawkins-Bronson

VOWS

Shandi Marie Hawkins and
Chad Sebastian Bronson

By Margot Langsford

Shandi Marie Hawkins and Chad Sebastian Bronson are to
be married at noon on Saturday at the Hibiscus Grove, on
the island of Maui, Hawaii. The Rev. Frederick Wilton, an
Episcopal priest, will officiate.

The bride, 23, will take her husband's name. She is pursuing
her master of art history degree from Yale University,
where she received a bachelor's degree this past May. She
is the daughter of Ronald and Chloe Hawkins of Atherton,
California. The bride's sister, Patricia Hawkins, a sophomore at
Stanford University, will serve as maid of honor.

The bridegroom, 27, is receiving his master of business
administration degree from Stanford's Graduate School of
Business. He is the son of Bradley Fitzgerald Bronson and
Vivian Wells-Bronson of Darien, Connecticut. Before attending
Stanford, he worked as an associate at Deutsche Bank, and
received his bachelor's degree in economics from University
of North Carolina at Chapel Hill.

The couple met three years ago at the annual Young Patrons of
Lincoln Center charity ball.

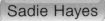

THE WALL STREET JOURNAL | TECHNOLOGY | TOP STORIES

Secrecy Shrouds Gibly Sale and Court Proceedings

BY STEVEN MESSING

In the world of technology, a single blog post can turn success into failure.

Last June, Gibly, Inc. was on the verge of being sold to the Aleister Corporation (TALC.I) for $3.8 billion in what was immediately heralded as the best return on investment in tech to date. Gibly's lead investor and de facto CEO Ted Bristol considered the sale to Aleister his swan song, and Silicon Valley recognized it as the crowning achievement of Bristol's remarkable career.

Days after the announcement and out of the blue, the blog TechCrunch broke the tech story of the decade. Gibly was known for being a remarkable software program that acted as a personal assistant, doing everything from transcribing text messages to managing payments with one's cell phone. The article by TechCrunch revealed Gibly's much more secretive function. A mystery hacker discovered—and leaked to TechCrunch—that Gibly was actually constructed to create a database of users' private information. Over one hundred million users had their passwords, home addresses, credit card information, and more stored in the Gibly server.

The deal was put on hold indefinitely and Gibly was immediately the subject of both a class action suit and a lawsuit by the Federal Trade Commission over privacy concerns. At the time of this writing, Ted Bristol was unavailable for comment.

Rumors abound as to the identity of the mystery hacker who took down Gibly, as well as his motivations. Some claim it's the Internet civil disobedience group Anonymous, while others point toward a covert team at the CIA. Many technology blogs claim it's either a head engineer from within the company or, least likely, a teenager with time on his hands. Regardless, some lone gunman single-handedly cost Silicon Valley's best investors billions of dollars and their reputations.

What Gibly was really up to—or why the sale to Aleister was simply put on hold instead of scrapped altogether—is as much a mystery as the identity of the mystery hacker.

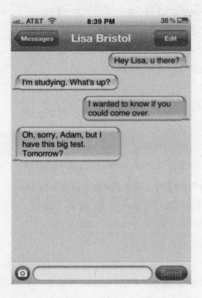

43

Liftoff

"Please remove your shoes, sir," the airport agent said. Adam unlaced his Converse sneakers. He yanked off his socks and tossed them, along with his sneakers, into the gray plastic bin. The security agent rolled his eyes. "*Just* your shoes."

Adam grabbed his socks and fumbled to put them back on. He blushed as he tried to avoid the eyes of the passengers behind him who, like the agent, all seemed to be experts at this airport-security drill. Why hadn't he just followed Amelia to the line without the body scan? Naturally, she had preferred a pat-down to a government-authorized body scan (Who knew what they did with the images? she had insisted), and right now a pat-down sounded far less uncomfortable than the annoyed glare of this security agent.

Adam placed his messenger bag on the conveyor belt. As it slumped against a shopping bag full of wrapped Christmas gifts, Adam felt a tightness in his chest as he remembered that there were rich, happy families who flew to Hawaii to celebrate Christmas. The holidays had always been a dark reminder for

Adam that he and his sister had almost nothing to give or receive, and no family except each other.

"Do you have a laptop?" the agent asked.

"Oh. Yes." Adam had recently inherited a MacBook Air from Amelia, who preferred using Linux over the more polished but less flexible Apple operating systems. Given to Amelia by Roger Fenway as a gift for joining his tech incubator, it was by far the most expensive thing Adam had ever owned. Even weeks after Amelia gave it to him, he kept half expecting someone to come to his door and claim it.

"Please remove it."

"Oh, right."

One day, Adam thought, he'd be a pro at this routine and look back and laugh. But for now, this was only the second flight he'd ever taken, and his embarrassment was mixed with giddy excitement. This wasn't just any flight: Adam and Amelia were going to Maui on a fully paid weekend trip, courtesy of the annual Maui Waves of Disruption tech conference.

Organized by TechCrunch, the leading Silicon Valley blog, the conference showcased thirty promising young companies that would show off their products at the two-day expo. Journalists, investors, and spectators from around the globe paid big money to attend, checking out the new companies by day and networking at huge hotel parties by night.

Adam and Amelia's start-up, Doreye, had been selected for the expo on November 15, exactly a month earlier, and Adam had hardly been able to concentrate on anything since. A free vacation was nice, but even better, Lisa was going to be in Maui the very same weekend for Patty Hawkins's sister's wedding. Adam couldn't believe his good fortune: Finally, fate or God or whatever was starting to make up for the shabby life he and Amelia had had until now.

He was fairly certain he had bombed all his final exams for the term, and he had a glaring "Incomplete" on his transcript from the outstanding essay to Professor Marsh on what he'd rather be doing than paying attention in PoliSci, but he didn't care. Who could think about schoolwork when he was about to be on a Hawaiian beach with the super-hot love of his life?

"I think the gate's that way," Amelia said when he joined her on the other side of security. He couldn't help but be impressed by his sister's calm demeanor. Since the summer, she'd gotten comfortable presenting Doreye and dealing with the press around it, and she seemed to be treating this like just one more interview, as though flying to Maui to stay in a five-star hotel was a normal part of everyday business.

"Aren't you even a little excited?" he asked as he zipped his bag shut.

Amelia looked up. "Honestly?" Her face broke into a huge grin. "I don't think I've ever been so excited for anything." She had been working around the clock for the past three months, struggling to balance Doreye with her schoolwork. The only break she ever took was on Wednesday nights when she went to the LAIR to play ZOSTRA, the virtual reality game her friend George had introduced her to. Otherwise, her autumn term had been a blur of coding, press interviews, meetings with her engineering team, class, and just enough homework not to flunk out. She and Adam hadn't had time for movie nights or anything outside of Doreye, and she was glad they had the flight—just the two of them—to hang out a little.

She laughed as Adam pulled her into a playful hug. This was going to be such an epic weekend.

44

Hawaii 2.0

When they exited the terminal in Maui, they saw a man in a suit holding a sign that read *Adam and Amelia Dory*.

The twins looked at each other. "Our driver," Adam mouthed with a grin. They had a *driver*. And that was after the first class seats and flight attendants who had actually known their names and handed each of them a glass of champagne and real silverware for dinner, along with a little package of socks, mints, and a toothbrush.

The Land Rover pulled into the Ritz-Carlton, a magnificent white fortress surrounded by lavish tropical gardens, fountains, and palm trees. Observing that the trunks of the palm trees were wrapped with Christmas lights, Amelia wondered what it was like to sing holiday carols when it was ninety degrees outside. A beautiful Hawaiian woman wearing a white wrap dress greeted them with leis made of real flowers and led them to their room.

Their suite was airy and bright. Sunlight reflected off the teak wood walls and floor. Two queen beds with plush white comforters faced French windows that opened onto a majestic stone-carved balcony overlooking the whitest sand and bluest water Amelia had ever seen.

Amelia walked out onto the balcony. "Adam, come look at this view!"

But Adam was rummaging through his suitcase for his phone charger. He had forgotten to shut off his phone on the plane and the battery had died; he had been stressed about finding a power outlet since landing more than an hour ago. She looked back and saw him plugging the phone into the wall and furiously tapping a text message.

"Who are you so anxious to get ahold of?"

Adam looked up. "I told Lisa I'd text her when we got here."

Amelia was afraid of that. She knew Lisa was going to be here for the Hawkins-Bronson wedding and was worried she'd be a distraction to Adam. "Are you going to see her?"

"Probably," Adam said. Who was he kidding? He was going to see her even if it killed him. "This place is so romantic, how could we not hang out?"

Amelia swallowed. She also knew that Sundeep was here, and that Lisa had yet to break the news to Adam that she was secretly seeing Sundeep.

Amelia's mind flashed back to that fall's English class. Of all the classes she rarely paid attention in, the freshman Shakespeare seminar she was taking to make up for the English class she'd failed last spring was the one she paid the least attention to. Which was probably why she'd never noticed that Lisa sat a few rows behind her . . . until the day the professor had announced partner assignments for the first project, and she had heard him say, "Amelia Dory and Lisa Bristol, analyzing *Measure for Measure.*" Stunned, she had turned to see Lisa, whose face had gone white. Amelia had put her head in her hands. Seriously? What were the chances?

Amelia had planned to dart out of class and e-mail Lisa, hoping this whole project could be taken care of virtually, but Lisa caught up to her and suggested they meet the following evening to review the text and make an outline. Amelia reluctantly agreed.

All the next day, Amelia was on edge. She felt jealous that Lisa got to date Sundeep, and angry that she was also cheating on her brother. Most of all, though, Amelia felt guilty that she still hadn't told Adam the truth. She couldn't bear the thought of his sadness and disappointment. It was the only secret she had ever kept from him.

Lisa had grabbed a large table at CoHo, the campus coffee shop, and two boys were flirting with her when Amelia arrived. Noticing Amelia, Lisa blushed and shooed them away, motioning for Amelia to take a seat at the table.

"Sorry, didn't mean to interrupt," Amelia said tartly.

"You didn't," Lisa said.

Silence.

"So, I was thinking . . ." Lisa took a deep breath and turned her attention to the text opened in front of her. Her notebook, full of diligent notes in careful handwriting, was also open, and she tapped her purple pen lightly as she spoke. "I was thinking that the analysis of *Measure for Measure* is always around Angelo and Isabella, but maybe it would be interesting to think about the relationship between Mariana and Isabella."

Amelia hadn't actually read the play, but she had skimmed the Wikipedia entry on her iPhone on the way to the meeting, and now she scrambled to remember who Mariana was. "Sure," she said. "That works."

Lisa waited for her to say more and, realizing Amelia wasn't going to, went on. "I think we could set up an interesting dissection of the supporting female characters, and the similarities and differences between Isabella and Mariana, whose moral stances are pretty much antithetical to each other, and yet, working together, the women resolve the central dilemma." Amelia wasn't reacting and Lisa started to realize she hadn't read the play. "And, of course," Lisa continued, "consider the implications of having Mistress Overdone—the prostitute—in the work. Like, is Shakespeare trying to drop a hint that we all prostitute ourselves for something, even a nun like Isabella?"

Amelia nodded absently. "Sure. That sounds good."

"Okay," Lisa said. She was beginning to sound a little frustrated by Amelia's neutrality. "Well, I actually really like this stuff, so what if I take a stab at the outline and I'll e-mail it to you?"

"Great," Amelia said, starting to stand up. If she sat there any longer, she was certain that Sundeep would walk in and join them, and she'd have to pretend not to care.

Lisa looked at her in disbelief. Was Amelia really going to let her do this whole project? Lisa wasn't letting her off *that* easily. "Let's meet again later this week to talk about it," she said.

Amelia stopped and searched for an excuse. There was nothing. She sighed. "Yeah, sure."

By the following week, Lisa had e-mailed Amelia a thorough outline of her proposed thesis. Amelia read it on her laptop during class. It actually made the book sound kind of interesting, which led her to read the play. Well, most of it.

When they met again, Amelia had been a little more animated. Lisa had proposed that they write that Isabella used Mariana for her own gain and, therefore, was no better than Mistress Overdone, the madame in the local brothel. But Amelia insisted Isabella had done what was necessary to stick to her moral ground and that made her strong and respectable. Besides, she said, Mariana didn't have strong morals, she just wanted to get married.

"I think you misunderstand Mariana," Lisa had said.

Amelia looked at Lisa. There was something deliberate and serious in Lisa's tone. Was Lisa talking about Mariana, or about herself? Either way, Amelia respected Lisa's assertiveness and agreed to write the first draft of the paper.

When they met to review the paper the following week, Lisa had basically rewritten Amelia's draft, fixing the broken prose and circular logic. It was a lot better. Amelia was a little embarrassed.

"You did a really good job," Lisa offered. "I love this part." She pointed to the one section of the paper she hadn't changed.

"Shakespeare isn't my thing," Amelia deflected.

"If I had your talent, it wouldn't be my thing, either." Lisa smiled.

They sat in silence for a moment. Amelia hated to admit it, but Lisa was incredibly sweet, and she was actually starting to enjoy their meetings. No one had ever really explained English to her, or forced her to take ownership of her opinions about a character. Even if her attempt at the paper had sucked, it was the first time she had written an essay she hadn't hated, and seeing Lisa's improvements made her respect her partner's ability to understand this stuff.

"I'm sorry I've been a pain of a partner," Amelia finally said.

"It's okay. I wouldn't have wanted to work with me if I were you, either."

More silence.

"For what it's worth, I really care about Adam. A lot," Lisa finally said.

Amelia looked at her over her glasses.

"It's complicated," Lisa said. "I have an obligation to Sundeep."

"I'm not going to break my brother's heart," Amelia said. "It's up to you to tell Adam, but you ought to do it soon."

That had been two months ago, and Adam was still in the dark. Amelia believed it was Lisa's responsibility to come clean to Adam, but keeping this secret from her brother made her nauseous. There were nights when she wanted to blurt out, "Adam! Lisa is cheating on you and I've known all along—please forgive me!" but she couldn't seem to form the words. Now, after two months she made up her mind to do it after the conference. That would give him winter break to recover, she reasoned, and start the new year fresh.

45

Get to Know Me

T.J. saw Adam and Amelia step off the elevator and gave a big wave to them, excusing himself from the tiki table where he was sipping a mojito with two hot, blonde club promoters who had just promised him a VIP table that night at Timba, Maui's hottest celebrity nightclub. The party theme was "Santas and Snowbabes," which was code for hot girls in skimpy fur-trimmed costumes.

"Hey guys!" he said cheerfully, shaking Adam's hand and giving Amelia a kiss on the cheek. "How's the room? Was your flight okay?"

"Yeah, it was cool," Adam said in his best frat-boy, chill tone. Amelia tried not to roll her eyes, embarrassed for her brother. But T.J. didn't seem to notice the way Adam tried so hard to be like him.

"And you, Amelia? Feeling good?"

"Yeah." She smiled. "This place is amazing."

T.J. looked genuinely pleased. "Wonderful! Listen, there's a press conference that starts in about ten minutes. They're all dying to hear from you, but I didn't want to commit you if you weren't feeling up to it." He looked at Amelia questioningly.

"Oh, sure. I feel up to it. Adam, are you okay with it?"

"Great!" T.J. clapped his hands without waiting for Adam to answer. "Let's go get you ready, then."

T.J. led Amelia and Adam to a large meeting room that was set up like a postgame sports conference. There were a hundred or so seats for the press that faced a stage with a long table and three chairs, each accompanied by a bottle of Fiji water. Behind the table was a whiteboard covered in the logos of conference sponsors and, behind that, floor-to-ceiling windows that looked out onto a veranda leading to the white sandy beaches. The press corps was starting to file in to their seats, and T.J. gestured to a man with a headpiece and a clipboard.

"Are these the Dorys? Are they up for joining the panel?" The man smiled at Adam and Amelia.

"Yes! Mike, meet Adam and Amelia Dory. Mike is the press organizer for the conference."

"We're thrilled to have you," Mike said as he shook both their hands. "We're going to get started in a few minutes. Shouldn't be any difficult questions. No one's going to be drilling you on technology or funding or anything. They're just here to get to know the entrepreneurs."

Mike smiled at them both as he snapped his fingers at an assistant, gesturing for her to put two more chairs on the stage for Adam and Amelia. Then, responding to something broadcast in his headpiece, he ran off.

"Wow." Adam turned to Amelia and T.J. "This is so official."

T.J. smiled. Back in Palo Alto, Adam and Amelia had done a lot of one-on-one interviews with tech bloggers, but nothing on this scale. T.J. had spent the last six weeks networking with the press, raising excitement for Doreye and making sure that Adam and Amelia had a seat on every high-profile panel.

T.J. understood that great technology was only part of the formula for a really successful start-up. The other part was about image and perception, making sure users and influential thinkers promoted the brand the way you wanted them to. And this was the part where T.J. really hit his stride. He was determined to guarantee that, when it launched, every cool kid in America would be chomping at the bit to download and own Doreye.

Besides, Amelia had the potential to become an absolute media darling. Sure, at first he'd written her off as awkward and uncool. But then he realized how much America loves a rags-to-riches tale, and what could be better than a foster-kid-turned-successful-entrepreneur story? Not only that, but there weren't many successful female tech geeks. The more time he'd spent with Amelia, the more he'd started to see past her secondhand clothes, unkempt hair, and chunky glasses. She was actually pretty. Her slim waist and long legs were kind of hot, and with contact lenses and a little mascara, her eyes could be stunning.

But it wasn't time for that just yet. People would take to her more now while she was still awkward and poor. Once Doreye started to take off, they'd do a makeover and guys would buy into Doreye because they wanted to sleep with her, while girls would buy into it because they wanted to be her. The only thing people loved more than rags-to-riches, T.J. thought, was ugly-to-hot, and he was planning to accomplish both with Amelia.

Mike's assistant led Adam and Amelia to two seats at the middle of the table and adjusted their microphones. In the other seats were two venture capitalists and the CEO and founder of PocketFun, a mobile gaming company worth $2 billion. They smiled as they introduced themselves to Adam and Amelia.

"You're with Roger Fenway's incubator, right? I've heard such great things about Doreye," said one VC. "I can't wait to see the demo."

Amelia smiled politely. Adam grinned. "We'll be sure you get a front-row seat!"

Mike stood on the side of the stage and coughed into a microphone to get the attention of the press, who started to quiet down. He introduced the panel and opened the floor for questions. The journalists immediately focused on Adam and Amelia, hardly asking any questions to the venture capitalists or the guy from PocketFun.

"Did you come to Stanford expecting to start a business?" a woman in a blue dress asked.

"Not at all!" Adam answered. "We didn't even know what we wanted to major in, much less whether we would start a business."

"But then Roger Fenway found you?"

"That's right. Roger spotted Amelia at University Café and the rest is history." Adam smiled. He was totally in his element with all these people hanging on his every word.

"What is the dynamic like in Roger Fenway's incubator?"

"It's great. We all get along really well, and there's always plenty of free food." The audience laughed, and Adam glowed.

"Amelia, we haven't heard much from you," a young, slender redhead with a foreign accent piped up from the back. "How are you enjoying Hawaii?"

Hearing her name startled Amelia. She had been studying the chandelier hanging from the ceiling—a thousand tiny crystals refracting sunlight into the spectrum of visible light. It was absolutely beautiful. Amelia liked when Adam answered the questions and she could just listen. This was the part he loved, and she was happy for him to take care of it.

She looked at the woman and sat up to speak into the microphone in front of her. "Oh, it's just wonderful," she said, thinking about the beauty of the chandelier. "Then again, I'm happy anywhere I can code." The room laughed lovingly. There was something surreal and comforting about sitting in a room full of people who were so captivated and supportive.

The woman smiled, but her face lacked the warmth of the other journalists; her eyes were piercing. "Does that include juvenile detention?"

Amelia blinked. What had she said? Suddenly the chandelier looked like it was going to fall. How could it be suspended by such a thin little cord? "That . . ." she started, not sure if the word had actually come out. How long had it been since the woman had asked the question? Everyone was staring at her. "That's not . . . public information," Amelia stammered.

No one was smiling anymore. The woman tilted her pretty head and swept her red hair over her shoulder. She glared at Amelia. She was gorgeous and terrifying.

"How did breaking through bank firewalls and embezzling money inform the creation of Doreye?" Every word was perfectly enunciated in the woman's elegant accent.

Amelia felt like the chandelier had crashed down on her, like the gold cord had snapped and the shimmering crystals were shattering around her. She looked over at Adam for help, but he was as dumbstruck as she was.

"They didn't inform it at all, actually. Doreye is the pure creation of a brilliant and promising young entrepreneur." T.J. was leaning over Amelia's shoulder, speaking into the microphone. His hand rested on her back and he smiled charismatically at the audience. "And we, as the Doreye team, are thrilled to give you all the first view of our app at this weekend's expo."

Amelia nervously lifted her eyes back to the crowd. They were nodding and smiling, looking at T.J. with encouragement.

T.J. continued to speak. There wasn't the slightest hint of worry or embarrassment in his voice. "And now we're going to go set up the Doreye demo booth so that we can enjoy this beautiful beach before we show off the technology to you tonight. It's Adam and Amelia's first time in Hawaii, and I want to be sure they catch a few waves while they're here."

The journalists beamed. Adam and Amelia left the panel in stunned silence, grateful for T.J.'s quick save. With a single sentence, he had turned them back into the poor, pathetic foster kids that the journalists loved to write about.

As they filed out of the room, Amelia glanced back for the beautiful redhead who had asked about juvenile detention.

But there was no sign of her.

Is This Seat Taken?

Across the lobby, Mr. Hawkins, Patty, Chad, and Chad's parents and sister were gathered in their hiking gear, waiting for their driver to arrive and take them to a nearby waterfall for a sunset hike.

Shandi and Mrs. Hawkins had opted for the spa over the hike, worried that Shandi would get mosquito bites or some other ailment that might threaten tomorrow's perfect day.

Patty wanted a drink. She'd had to finish three exams and a fifteen-page research paper in two days in order to catch yesterday's flight to Maui. To reward herself, she'd spent the day recovering, lying out on the beach, reading all the gossip magazines she'd neglected during the last two weeks of studying. She couldn't believe how much she'd missed!

She'd made the mistake, though, of coming in at one o'clock in the afternoon to jump in the pool. While she was ordering a pineapple smoothie at the pool bar, she had run into Chad's kid sister, Molly, who hadn't left her alone since. Even when she'd put her headphones in (a clear signal that she didn't want to talk), Molly had poked her to ask what color nail polish she was going to choose for their mani-pedis tomorrow morning. Patty had sucked hard on her smoothie straw, trying to be polite and wishing she'd had the bartender make the smoothie alcoholic.

Now, Molly was going on about which Harry Potter movie was her favorite when the driver pulled up in a Land Rover.

"We ordered a town car," Chad's mother insisted, her tanned arms crossed over her perky, cosmetically enhanced chest. Chad's parents, Mr. and Mrs. Bronson, were Nantucket chic: both ultra tan, blond, and always wearing solid pastel colors, like they'd stepped straight out of a Ralph Lauren advertisement. "There are six of us."

I don't have to go! Patty thought, sensing an opportunity to escape Molly's chatter.

"We can squeeze in," Chad's father insisted. "Molly can sit on Chad's lap."

"Ewww!" Molly squealed. "I am thirteen years old and absolutely not sitting on my brother's lap for the next half hour."

Mrs. Bronson consoled her. "Don't worry, dear. Patty can sit on Chad's lap. Right, guys?"

Chad looked at both of them. Patty wondered if her cheeks were as red as they felt.

"Of course." Chad smiled at Patty as they walked out to the car.

Patty blushed as she crawled onto Chad's lap. She grabbed the headrest behind him for support, but doing so caused her breasts to brush against his face. He pretended not to notice. When she was finally seated, the small of her back pressed into his arm. She tried to balance her weight onto her heels so she wasn't too heavy on his thighs.

"Sarah's cousin's best friend lives in L.A., and she auditioned for that new show *Choir Kids* and said the lead actress Mia Rochelle was totally not that pretty in person," Molly was telling her father with authority.

The car hit a pothole. Patty fell back onto Chad.

"Sorry," she whispered.

"It's okay," he said, and blushed.

"And I *totally* believe it," Molly went on. "I mean, she's got good hair, but everyone would if they spent as much time on it as she does."

They were on a dirt road now, the car bumping and Patty bumping along with it. She tried to stay forward on Chad's knees, tried not to slide back to where his . . . parts . . . were. That was just what she needed: to ram into her future brother-in-law's balls the day before his wedding.

But she kept sliding back. "Here," he said, and he lifted her by the waist, opened his legs, and shifted her weight onto one thigh, pulling her legs between his. "That better?"

"Yeah," she said, noticing that he'd left his hand around her waist, his other arm resting on the top of her thighs.

"Besides, I bet her voice isn't even that good. They can edit everything on TV."

Chad glanced at Patty, who, between Molly's jabbering and the stomach-turning bouncing, looked miserable. He poked her side with his finger and grinned at her in silent commiseration. Patty met his blue eyes—unhappy as she was, she couldn't resist returning his grin.

47

Dinner Table Confessionals

Mr. Bristol had made a reservation at the fanciest seafood restaurant in Maui for a family dinner on Friday night. Between the wedding and the conference, he knew he'd be running around all weekend, and he needed to schedule some family time if he had any hope of not pissing off his wife. Of course, he'd had to book a 5:00 P.M. table to make it to the 8:00 conference demo, so the family was seated at a center table in an empty room, the sun still shining brightly through the restaurant's large, ocean-facing windows and the pianist on the baby grand in the corner playing chipper Christmas carols that sounded totally out of place.

Ted had even been so generous as to invite Lisa's boyfriend, Sundeep, a young Indian guy who was working on some medical device with Roger Fenway's incubator. He wasn't sure what Lisa saw in Sundeep; she was so beautiful that she could have any guy she wanted, especially now that she was in college. Sundeep was a nice guy, sure, but he was a little . . . dull. He didn't play or watch any sports, had no interest in Scotch or cars or cigars, and, frankly, Ted was at a loss for what to talk to him about. But young love was young love, he reasoned, and inviting him along for the weekend had made Mrs. Bristol very happy.

After the waiter took away their entrée plates, Sundeep cleared his throat and lifted his wineglass. "I'd like to make a toast," he said, looking around the table and landing on Lisa. Lisa smiled at him nervously. Her relationship with Sundeep was the biggest stress in her life, and she had no one to talk to about it. Her feelings for Adam had grown so much that every time she smiled at Sundeep, or kissed him, or accepted his affection, she felt like a liar and a cheat. She had tried to get her parents not to invite him to the wedding, but her mother had insisted—she thought she was doing Lisa a favor, and how could Lisa tell her the truth?

T.J. took a large sip of his wine. Oh, God, he wasn't going to propose, was he? He liked Sundeep well enough. He was so friendly that you couldn't dislike the guy, and he thought what Sundeep was doing for India was really impressive. But for his sister? He didn't seem to fit.

"I just wanted to say a big thank you to all of you," Sundeep said. "For welcoming me into your family and letting me be a part of this very special weekend."

Mrs. Bristol was making a pouty, isn't-he-so-sweet face at Ted, squeezing his hand under the table. Ted had stopped counting, but he was pretty sure the glass of wine in her hand was her third, after downing two daiquiris and a glass of champagne before dinner. He'd had his assistant book the presidential suite for the two of them at the Four Seasons and was starting to worry she was going to spend the night hunched over the toilet.

"You see," Sundeep kept going, "I'm not on good terms with

my own family right now." He looked down at the table, nervously wiping the perspiration from his water glass with his thumb. Lisa's eyes got wide: Was he going to tell them? Mrs. Bristol gasped and pressed her hand over her heart in excessive concern. Yes, she was definitely wasted.

"When I decided to pursue WorldSight, I turned down an opportunity to attend Stanford Medical School. It's so competitive there, and they don't let you defer, so I gave up my spot and my fellowship. My father was furious. He's a doctor and always assumed I'd follow in his footsteps to become a cardiac surgeon. My mother was angry, too, but she reasoned that my work on this company was just a phase—something I needed to get out of my system—and I told her I'd consider reapplying to medical school this fall."

Yes, he was telling them. Lisa's mind raced: Was it good or bad for them to know? She took a sip of her wine. Did it matter? He was going for it.

"But I didn't reapply. How could I? The more I work on this, the more I'm certain it's my calling. In response, however, my father officially cut me off. My mother was helpless to do anything, and I haven't had any contact with anyone in my family since."

It was true, and hearing him say it made Lisa's heart heavy all over again. He was such a good person, such a kind soul, and his family was treating him so unfairly. She thought back on the first time he'd told her. She'd just been to see Adam in his dorm room after the Gibly news broke. Her heart was fluttering with her attraction for him and the danger of being involved with the twin of her father's nemesis. She thought about Adam's mismatched socks and the dimple in his left cheek that always appeared when he smiled at his own jokes and the way he didn't even try to contain his excitement at seeing her when she'd come back from her family vacation in France. She thought about all these things and her cheeks got hot and her whole body felt light, and she texted Sundeep to ask him if they could talk, because she knew that she had to break up with him. He'd said yes, and they'd agreed to meet that night. But when they'd met, right as she started to tell him she'd found someone else—that it was her, not him—he'd broken down, put his head on the table, and explained what had happened with his family. He was devastated. She couldn't tell him.

That was last summer, and she still hadn't found the strength to be so cruel. Sundeep didn't have a lot of friends. He spent all his time working on his company or admiring her. What would happen if she broke up with him? She didn't know, and it worried her horribly.

Lisa felt trapped. She loved one guy and felt duty-bound to another. And now he was eliciting the sympathy of her mother, which was going to make this whole thing even more difficult. No, it was not a good thing that he was telling them, she decided.

"So, in conclusion, I'd like to express my gratitude and admiration to the Bristol family for your extraordinary kindness and hospitality."

Everyone clinked glasses and smiled politely at Sundeep. He nodded sheepishly and looked longingly at Lisa. "Thank you," he whispered. She hoped he couldn't pick up on the fakeness in her reassuring smile. She looked around. Some family he'd just gotten himself involved in, she thought. Mrs. Bristol was taking a long swig of her wine, Mr. Bristol was focused on getting the waiter's attention to order dessert and another Scotch, and T.J. was checking his text messages under the table.

48

Waterfalls

"We should let the young athletes go ahead of us old fogies," Chad's father said cheerfully. Chad and Patty had been silent for the half hour the families had been on the trail, and the adults naturally assumed it was because the hiking pace was too dull.

"Oh, it's fine," Patty said, smiling politely.

"Are you afraid I'll beat you?" Chad smiled at her.

Chad's mother laughed. "I'm glad to see the sibling rivalry has already begun!"

Patty glared at them both. She was fiercely competitive, and, especially when it came from Chad, a challenge was too much to resist.

She chuckled coolly. "Please. I could take you any day. I've got nothing to prove."

"I'll believe it when I see it." Chad smirked.

Patty stopped, held his eyes for a minute, and took off, dashing up the hill.

Forty strenuous minutes later, Chad and Patty were both still in a full-on sprint, jumping over roots and dodging branches

until they finally burst into a clearing where an enormous waterfall plunged into a pool of crystal-clear water. A bright red
sun rested on the horizon opposite the waterfall, its light re-
flecting off the water in a brilliant mix of colors.

"Totally beat you!" Chad gasped.

"Did not," Patty panted, looking up at the sunset. "Oh my
God, this is the most gorgeous thing I've ever seen."

They stood for a moment, taking in the beauty. It was the
kind of moment that you know is rare and aren't quite sure how
to take in.

Patty's tanned face dripped with sweat, her clothes wet
from the run. Chad pulled off his sweat-soaked shirt, and Patty
tried not to pay attention to his perfectly chiseled abs. She
wished she were a guy and had the option of taking off her
sweaty top, too.

"I know how we can decide," Chad said. "See that rock in the
middle of the water? First one there wins."

With her hands on her hips and her gaze set on Chad, Patty
used her foot to force one shoe off the other. "You realize I was
recruited to swim for Stanford, right? The best swim team in
the country?"

"Yeah," he said, slipping off his own shoes, "but you're still
a girl."

She slapped him playfully on the stomach and dove into the
water, easily beating him to the rock with her flawless free-
style.

She climbed up and watched the sun slip toward the blue-
green sea. Chad clambered onto the rock beside her and rested
his elbows on his knees, shaking his head to release water from
his shaggy blond tresses. "Okay," he conceded, out of breath.
"You are a goddess and a champion. You win."

Patty laughed. "That will teach you." Her cheeks were flushed from the exercise, and the beads of water made her skin glisten in the dusky light. Her searching eyes were captivated by the setting sun, and she looked like she was deep in her own world, lost in thought about something only she could know.

"You are so, so beautiful," Chad said slowly, his voice honest and raw, born out of a reflex, as though she was so beautiful right then that he couldn't *not* say it.

Patty turned her head toward him, pulling her knees in to her chest and swallowing hard. "You can't say that, Chad," she said with a twinge of anger in her voice. "It isn't fair to me." She glanced back at the horizon, surprised by her own vulnerability. She knew, logically, that it wasn't fair to Shandi, but if she was being honest, she was more upset by how unfair it was to *her*, the way he led her on and made it impossible not to love him.

Chad touched her arm. "I know. I know, Patty." He closed his eyes as if to gather his thoughts. "I know it's crazy, but if you only knew how much I think about you—I can't get past it. Ever since that party when I saw what we might be able to have. I mean, when I felt the *chemistry* between us . . ."

"Don't!" Patty glared at him, trying to look fierce despite the tears. "Don't say these things so you can feel good about yourself. It's not fair to do this to me!"

"Patty, I just don't know what to do."

Patty pulled her shoulder away from his touch. "What you do is *forget about it*! You marry my sister and you stop saying things like that and you stop stroking my arm like this and you stop looking at me with those eyes," she hissed, her heart sinking at how much she didn't really want him to stop any of those things.

The sun was melting and the sound of the waterfall roared behind them.

He leaned into her, their noses barely three inches apart.

She could feel his warm breath hit her lips. His eyes looked into hers, searching, and he whispered, "But what if I'm marrying the wrong sister?"

"Who won?" Mr. Hawkins called out from the shore. Molly splashed into the water as the rest of the hiking crew clambered up the trail to the clearing, *ooh*-ing and *ahh*-ing at its beauty.

The sun slipped below the horizon, and the magical moment was gone.

49

You Can't Stay on Top Forever

The conference expo, where all the start-ups were demonstrating their products, was about to start. Amelia bent over, her hand resting on the table behind the Doreye booth, taking deep breaths with her eyes closed. Adam rubbed her back. "Are you okay?" he asked.

She shook her head, not looking up. "I don't want to do this anymore, Adam," she moaned.

"It's going to be okay." He tried to console her, but he wasn't sure how. She'd been devastated ever since the morning session when the journalist had brought up her time in jail. "Tonight's all about the product. No one's going to be asking you about our past."

"Where's Roger?" Amelia asked.

"His flight got delayed," T.J. said, overhearing her question as he walked into the booth, sliding the cell phone he'd just been talking on into his pocket. "I told him to take the private jet, but he always insists on going commercial. Listen, sorry I'm late. I had a family dinner. I brought you some dessert."

T.J. dropped a white box on the table and looked empatheti-cally at Amelia. "But you don't look very hungry." He pulled her up gently from her keeled-over position and put his hands on her shoulders. He looked straight into her eyes and said seri-ously, "Amelia, you are going to be spectacular tonight. Okay?"

She blinked her eyes. Growing up, she never cried, but she felt tears forming and fought desperately to hold them back.

"I don't care what you did or where you came from. You're here now, and you're the most exciting thing at the expo, and absolutely nothing anyone does or says will change that," T.J. went on.

Amelia nodded her head like a child trying to appease her parent.

"I mean, I'm a total asshole who always looks for the worst in everyone, so if *I'm* saying that . . ." T.J. smiled, and Amelia let out a laugh, wiping a tear from her eye. T.J. was new at the whole self-deprecation thing, but he was pleased that it seemed to be making Amelia feel better.

"T.J.? Do you really not care where Adam and I came from?"

"Not at all. If anything, I think it makes you cooler."

Amelia smiled at the compliment. She might not approve of T.J.'s type, but it did feel good to have him call her "cool." She hesitated, then went on, not quite sure how to articulate what she was trying to say. "I guess . . . I guess I just hadn't realized how much I don't want people to know. Not because I'm afraid of getting in trouble, but because it feels like it diminishes our accomplishment, you know? Like Doreye got here because Adam and I were poor and pathetic and Roger wanted to help, not because the product is remarkable in and of itself."

T.J. smiled. "But the product *is* remarkable in and of itself. And as nice a guy as Roger Fenway is, he is first and foremost an investor: I don't care how much he liked you, he never would have backed you if he didn't think you'd be successful."

Amelia blushed. "I know. Which is why I just want to focus on that, and not on me and Adam or our past."

"I get it. Let's focus on the product then. Not you and Adam."

"Promise me?"

T.J. looked at Amelia in a new way. "Yes, Amelia. I promise. Now come on," he said, "let's go get you back in front of your computer, talking about code." He led her to the front of the booth, where conference participants had already started to gather.

Adam followed them, simultaneously impressed by and jealous of T.J.'s ability to console Amelia. Adam glanced at the box of dessert, computing that if T.J. had just finished dinner with his family, then Lisa was wandering around unoccupied right now somewhere in the hotel. Just then, across the room, he spotted the back of a blond head set on a slender frame. Lisa!

Adam raced across the room and tapped her on the shoulder. "Lisa!"

"I'm sorry?" He heard a British accent as the woman turned toward him. Not Lisa.

"Oh, excuse me. I'm sorry. I thought you were someone else."

"Not to worry, Adam."

Adam blushed and darted back to the Doreye booth, wondering briefly how the woman knew his name.

Thirty people were gathered around the Doreye booth as Amelia started the demo. She was holding an iPhone in her hand and linking it to her laptop, which was hooked up to a forty-eight-inch Alienware LCD monitor suspended above the booth. A television, a radio-controlled toy car, a microwave, and several other devices were arranged on the table.

"I want to be honest about the shortcomings of this alpha version," Amelia said to the crowd. "I haven't yet been able to make Doreye as robust as I want to, which means we can't yet manage multiple devices simultaneously. I set up a queue system, which is a good patch for now, but there's still a slight lag as Doreye switches between devices. The lag is because of the network. I wish we were on 4G. Anyway, in the future this shouldn't be a problem, but for now, fair warning."

The crowd smiled, charmed by the young girl's honesty. They all watched as she proceeded to open the Doreye app on her iPhone and use it to run the other devices on the table. With the swipe of Amelia's finger, the television turned on and changed channels before turning off again. A brief moment later, the toy car moved in a semicircle and stopped next to the microwave, which suddenly turned on. The devices were elegantly operating in concert, and Amelia was the conductor. There was *ooh*-ing and *ahh*-ing as more people huddled around the table.

Just then, though, the microwave shut down. Amelia looked at it quizzically—she hadn't done anything to turn it off. Then the toy car started moving and drove off the table without her touching the Doreye app. She looked at the iPhone in her hand. What was going on?

On the monitor, the devices started flicking off and on, registering as "in use," then "out of use," and going completely haywire. The crowd began to murmur.

"Amelia," Adam whispered. "What are you doing?"

"I'm not doing anything," Amelia whispered back. "I don't know what's going on."

A man in the front row heard her. "Is everything all right?" he asked.

Amelia looked up at the crowd and blushed. "I'm not sure what's going on," she admitted. "Maybe there's an issue with the network here?" She was desperately searching for an answer. "But that's never been a problem before. . . ."

"That's just the carpenter blaming her tools," a British accent called out from the back of the crowd. The group parted, and the blond who looked like Lisa but wasn't sauntered forward. She was glaring at Amelia and smiling menacingly. "It's not the network, it's your program. Not being able to handle multiple devices isn't the only problem. It's entirely flawed software."

Amelia's and Adam's jaws dropped. Who was this woman?

"She stole the idea from us, but she missed a few details. If you want to see the real deal, come with me to the RemoteX booth."

The crowd followed her, leaving the Doreye table empty. Adam, Amelia, and T.J. were stunned.

50

Some Things Champagne Can't Fix

The last thing T.J. wanted to do was to go to Shandi Hawkins's "Moonlight Drinks" reception on the Four Seasons terrace. It would be like every other Atherton party—the same faces, the same what's-the-latest-hot-deal-in-the-Valley chat among the men and how-do-you-keep-your-skin-so-young-looking dialogue among the women—just in a different setting with a few East Coast WASPs interlaced, courtesy of Chad Sebastian Bronson of the Darien, Connecticut, Bronsons.

The demo had been a disaster. T.J. had to figure out who that woman was and what RemoteX was all about. It was peculiar—and suspiciously convenient—for this company to appear out of thin air and make Doreye look like a fraud.

But, in truth, that was secondary. What was really weighing on him now was Amelia, and a deep sense that he'd let her down. He should have stepped in, should have been able to help her recover from the malfunction, should have been able to recapture the audience's attention when that woman interrupted.

He couldn't explain it, except to say that he'd felt so good, so *valuable,* earlier in the day when he'd been able to protect Amelia from the nasty journalist during the panel. And he'd felt exactly the opposite at tonight's demo.

And what if the product did have flaws? The only thing no one on the team ever questioned was Amelia's ability to deliver flawless code. But it's not like he or Adam or Roger could check it. And if the product wasn't flawless, Adam and Amelia's personal story was the only way they were going to sell it.

He rolled his head to stretch his neck and pulled up the sleeves of his pale blue linen button-down so they just covered his elbows. Then he took a deep breath and walked onto the terrace with a forced smile, grabbing a flute of champagne from the tray of a passing waiter as he headed to the bar.

While he waited for the bartender's attention, a cute brunette in a purple maxi dress approached. She was clearly already drunk, the pink cocktail in her hand swirling precariously as she swayed on her heels.

"Are you T.J.?" She giggled.

"I am," he said. She had great breasts and would be an easy score—girls at weddings always were.

She giggled again. "Actually, I already knew that. Everyone has been saying you're the guy to meet." She stuck out her hand. "I'm Lauren. I grew up with Chad."

Good old Shandi, prepping all the single girls for his arrival.

"Very nice to meet you, Lauren. Can I get you a drink?"

"Yes, please! I'll have another one of whatever these pink ones are." Lauren pointed to the menu where specialty cocktails were listed.

He turned back to the bar, motioning to the bartender. Maybe tonight wouldn't be so bad after all.

"Heard about the demo. Tough start for the weekend." T.J.'s father suddenly appeared beside him.

T.J. felt his jaw clench. He tried to sound cool. "We'll get through it. I'm not worried."

He motioned again for the bartender, purposefully keeping his gaze averted from Ted.

"Still, not good news about RemoteX. How'd you miss that there was a competitor?"

T.J. swallowed hard. He was not going to give in to his father's provocations. He focused on the bartender. Why was this guy not coming over?

"I'm looking forward to seeing more about what they've developed. It's hard to tell how many parallels there really are," T.J. answered.

Finally, the bartender approached and took his order. "Jack and Coke and one of those pink cocktails, please."

"I don't want you getting upset over this, T.J." Ted spun around on his seat and lounged against the bar. "Companies at the Doreye level have a *ninety percent* failure rate. So, Doreye didn't work out for you? That's okay. You've learned a lot, and maybe the next one will be huge."

"Doreye isn't a failure. It isn't and it won't be." T.J. could feel his face getting red.

"I guess," Ted continued, "you've got to wonder, given Amelia's background, whether she *did* steal the technology. Poor kid, growing up alone, no moral center. She probably doesn't even realize it's wrong."

This was too much. It was one thing to push T.J.'s buttons about the business, but Ted had no right to pull Amelia into it. He turned to face his father, his brow furrowed and his blue eyes intense. Ted was casually leaning back, both elbows propped on the bar, looking out at the crowd and sipping a Scotch. He was totally at ease as he taunted his son.

"You know what I think?" T.J. said decisively, a mix of anger and total confidence in his voice. "I think Amelia is lucky. It's better to have no father at all than a morally bankrupt, money-grubbing one."

Ted raised his eyebrows and shifted his gaze to his son. "I'm sorry?"

"What you did at Gibly—what you're *doing* at Gibly—is wrong, and you know it. It could threaten *national security*— our safety as a country. You're pleading ignorance for profits, as though that makes you inculpable. But it doesn't. If the person paying for that data is a terrorist and, because of it, we're attacked? That's on you. And that's fucking immoral as hell."

"You don't know what you're talking about," Ted hissed, standing up straight.

T.J. was focused. "Let me tell you what I do know: Amelia was right to tell the press about Gibly. She was right to expose what shady shit you've been up to. You were once respected and admired—you were powerful—and then a little girl took it all away from you. You want your revenge on Amelia? You're going to have to go through me."

"You've always been so full of yourself, son. But what have you ever done without my help? Even this little job that you're so cocky about. Who got you that job? Me."

"You're a shitty father. You tried to compensate for being absent and cold by providing Lisa and me with opportunities. But it's a poor trade. You always put yourself first, always prioritized your business deals and ego over everything that mattered to me. I'd rather have a poor father with no connections—I'd rather have no father at all—than one I disrespect as much as I disrespect you."

T.J. handed a five-dollar tip to the bartender and walked away, leaving Ted looking for the first time in his life like he wasn't sure what to do.

"Did you get my cocktail?" Lauren stumbled away from the group of girls she'd been chatting with and grabbed T.J.'s arm.

"It's on the bar," he snapped, shoving his hands in his pockets and heading for the door.

51

Prove Yourself

Amelia and Adam were back in their hotel room, huddled over her laptop. After the demo fiasco, Amelia had texted George, hoping he was still awake and could gather a few folks from Gates for a Skype conference to figure out what had gone wrong. George had readily obliged.

"I just don't understand what could have happened. The devices have never malfunctioned like that." Amelia was talking to George, T-Bag, and Luke, another engineer who was part of the Wednesday night crew.

"Do you think it was a network issue? Maybe there was too much interference from the other products at the demo," George offered.

"More interference than I've had at Gates? If there's no problem there, with all the computers and iPhones and other programs running, I can't imagine there would be a problem here."

"Unless the broadband is weaker to begin with," T-Bag offered.

"Wouldn't that be a major problem for us, then?" Adam

started, looking a little panicked. "I mean, that would mean Doreye wouldn't work everywhere, right?"

"Yeah, Adam, that's what it would mean," George said in an irritated voice, as though he were talking to a child.

"Or maybe there was just another type of product that interfered. What were the devices around you at the demo?" Luke asked.

"There was the electric car, like, three booths down. That must have taken a ton of energy," Adam piped in.

"An electric car would take electric energy, Adam, not broadband." George was clearly annoyed. "Listen, Adam, maybe you should leave this one to us."

Adam winced. He was just trying to help. Why did this geek George think he had the right to tell him to bug off? He looked at Amelia to stand up for him.

Amelia bit her lower lip and said softly, "I think George is right. Why don't you go find Lisa? This'll probably take a while and be boring for you anyway."

Adam sat for a moment, stunned. Was she serious? Then, realizing she was, he picked up his wallet and notebook. "Yeah, okay."

He'd love to see Lisa, but he had texted her twice and she still hadn't responded.

Adam headed to the hotel bar, his feelings crushed.

"I'll have a beer, please," Adam said to the bartender. The room was dimly lit. Several groups were gathered around low tables with cushioned seats, deep in conversation over the chill house music. Adam took a seat on one of the leather stools and grabbed a handful of nuts from a bowl on the bar, glancing out the window where he watched a party happening on the terrace.

He sipped his beer and tried to think about how he could help with this RemoteX debacle, or at least prove his worth at Doreye. George was right: He didn't understand the technology. But how could he learn? And what else was he supposed to do to prove that he ought to be part of the company? It had been his idea to start the company, and yet he had no idea what he was doing.

"Mind if I join you?" A man in his late fifties took the stool next to Adam's and motioned to the bartender.

"Not at all," Adam said, sitting up a little straighter in his chair. The man looked vaguely familiar, but Adam couldn't place him.

"Macallan twenty-five," the man said to the bartender. The bartender shook his head. "Ah, well then Macallan ten. No ice. What brings you to the hotel bar alone on a Friday night?"

Adam was a little perplexed. He wasn't accustomed to meeting strangers in hotel bars, but this man seemed friendly enough. And it felt rather adult to have a conversation like this—two men exchanging pleasantries over a few drinks.

He shrugged. "Just feeling like a total failure lately."

The man's Scotch had arrived and he clinked his glass against Adam's beer with a laugh. "That makes two of us," he said.

They sat in silence for a moment, each taking long sips of their drinks.

"You know," the man said, "the funny thing about failure is that you never see it coming. You really think you're on the right course and then, out of nowhere, it hits you that you've been fucking things up all along."

Adam wasn't totally sure he understood what the man was saying, but he nodded anyway.

"My problem," Adam said, "is that I'm in unknown territory. Like, I have all these things that I want to accomplish, and this great vision of what it should look like when it's done, but I haven't got a clue what I'm actually supposed to be *doing,* you know? What I'm supposed to be doing day-to-day to get to where I want to be."

The man turned to him and smiled. "Do you drink Scotch?"

"I never have."

"Well, that's the first thing you need to do." He turned to the bartender and motioned for another Macallan. "Act like who you want to be, down to every last little detail, and eventually, you'll become that person. Trust me."

Adam liked this guy. He started to relax and forget about Doreye and contemplate who he wanted to be. James Bond immediately jumped to mind. The man seemed to relax, too, as they drank their Scotch and made small talk.

"I have another problem," Adam confessed.

"What's that? Let's see if I can solve that one, too," the man said jovially. Talking to this kid was making him feel useful.

"There's this girl."

"Uh-oh. Here we go. Tell me about her."

"She's perfect."

The man laughed. "Aren't they all? At first, anyway."

"She's smart and funny and beautiful and . . . I think I love her. But she's holding back, and I think I know why. Well, I *do* know why. It's because she doesn't think her father would approve of me."

"What's not to approve of? You seem perfectly respectable."

"It's just that her father is kind of a big deal, and I'm not . . ."

"Can I tell you a secret?" The man leaned in and whispered to Adam. "I've been told I'm 'kind of a big deal,' and there's nothing about you I wouldn't approve of."

He pulled back and sipped his Scotch. "Especially considering who *my* daughter's dating. Jesus. Nice kid, but no spunk. I can't figure out what she's thinking."

Adam felt his phone vibrate in his pocket and looked down at the text message.

"It's her!" he exclaimed. "She wants to meet at the beach!"

The man chuckled. "Well, what are you waiting for? Get going."

"May I—?" Adam asked as he reached for his wallet.

The man rolled his eyes. "Who are you kidding? This one's on me. It was great chatting with you. Good luck with the girl . . . and her dad."

52

Look, But Don't Touch

Adam dashed through the lobby, past the large Christmas tree display stretching up to the chandelier, past the designer gift shops, around the pool, and down the boardwalk. He didn't slow down until he saw Lisa's moonlit outline in the white gazebo at the beginning of the sand, where they'd agreed to meet. She was looking at the waves, her long dress blowing softly in the breeze. It was like something out of a movie.

"Lisa!" he called out, running the length of the boardwalk and up the gazebo steps.

She turned and smiled. She wore a high-waisted navy chiffon dress with slim crisscross straps that showed off her gently sloping shoulders. Her hair was pulled back in a side twist with a hibiscus flower tucked behind her ear. Her makeup shimmered; her lips glistened in the moonlight.

Adam was suddenly self-conscious about his flip-flops, shorts, and ratty t-shirt, but Lisa didn't seem to notice. He put his hands around her waist and pulled her in for a kiss. "You look absolutely stunning," he whispered.

She returned his kiss, but quickly put her hands on his chest, determinedly. "Wait. We have to talk. I have something I have to tell you."

Adam felt his heart drop. Her eyes were serious and sad. And he knew: She was going to end it. Suddenly, the memories of her never wanting to be called his girlfriend, of how seldom she'd slept over this quarter, of how long it took her to text him back, all hit him like a ton of bricks. He'd been in such denial that he hadn't wanted to accept the truth. The man at the bar was wrong. He wasn't good enough for Lisa or her father.

"Yeah, I know." He pulled away, swallowing hard and turning from her to sit down on the gazebo bench, leaning his elbows forward on his knees and looking down at his feet.

"You do?" She didn't understand. "Did Amelia—?"

"You're not that into me. It's obvious. And you're ending it."

"No! I mean, that's not what I . . ."

But Adam didn't hear her. The Scotch was pulsing through his veins and he was suddenly feeling confident and articulate— and angry.

"You know what bothers me, though?" He stood up and walked back toward her. "You never gave me a real chance. As sweet as you were, I was always the bar boy from your brother's fancy party. I didn't fit into your rich, exclusive world."

"That's not—"

"But you know what, Lisa? You may be embarrassed to stand next to me now, but someday . . . someday I'll fit right into your little moneyed world, and you'll be sorry."

"Adam!" she snapped. "This has nothing to do with money." She was shaking her head in frustration. "My God, Adam. Do you have any idea how much I care about you? How much I love you? But my past is complicated—"

Adam touched his finger to her lips to make her stop talking, a glimmer of hope restored in his voice. "What did you say?"

"I said my past is complicated."

"Before that. Did you say . . . you love me?"

"Yes, Adam. I love you. But—"

Suddenly all his distress transformed to joy. Adam felt like he was going to explode with happiness. He grinned from ear to ear and pulled Lisa into a close hug, kissing her mouth hard, again and again. "No 'buts'!" he exclaimed. "You love me, you love me, you love me. It's the only thing that matters."

Lisa laughed and let her arms fall around his. He looked so happy, and that made her so happy. How could she ruin this moment?

"Whatever it is, it doesn't matter, okay?" he said. "We're together now, and I love you so, so much."

She smiled and leaned her forehead against his. Faint music from the Hawkins party drifted in the air and "All I Want for Christmas Is You" started playing, as if on cue. Lisa pressed her cheek against Adam's and they swayed to the song in the moonlight. Adam listened to the lyrics and wondered whether Santa did exist, after all. And whether (dare he dream it?) maybe from now on he'd be one of those people who flew to Hawaii with his girlfriend's family to celebrate the holidays.

Seconds later, Lisa's phone rang in her purse, but she ignored it. A moment later it rang again. "I better get that," she whispered, breaking their embrace to see who was calling.

"It's my family. I have to go." She pouted.

"No, you don't. Stay."

"Trust me, if I could be two places at once, I would."

"I love you."

"I love you, too," she said as she scurried down the gazebo stairs, her long dress flowing behind her.

As Adam started back, his eye caught the flower she'd been wearing in her hair. *Like Cinderella's slipper,* he thought, as he picked it up. He walked out to the beach and sat in the sand, crossing his ankles and taking deep breaths of the fresh sea air.

He listened to the waves and reflected on the night. Lisa loved him! Could life be any better? He replayed her words and the sight of her lips in the moonlight—those lips that loved him, that he was allowed to kiss and admire, that belonged to him.

Then he thought about her good-bye. "If I could be two places at once, I would." If only!

Wait, two places at once? With a start, his mind snapped to the airport gate that morning. All the expo participants had been on the same flight. He never would have missed seeing a woman who resembled Lisa. Was she not a passenger? TechCrunch had purchased the tickets and made sure they would all be on that plane. Why would they have made an exception for her?

Adam's mind suddenly felt alert. He stood up, brushed the sand from his shorts, and walked, deliberately, back toward the hotel. He thought about his conversation with the man in the bar that night: Choose who you want to be and start to act like it. He could feel his heart pounding in his chest, but he pictured himself as James Bond—the bad-ass blond 007 who took out guys left and right—and let the thought motivate him as he glanced around to make sure no one was looking. Then he carefully slipped through the door to the conference room where the booths were still displayed.

The lights were out and the room was silent, save the buzz of the electronics in place. *Okay,* he thought, *what would Bond do?* Adam tiptoed toward the RemoteX booth. A laser-thin ray of blue light shot out from the corner. An alarm! He jumped to avoid it, then realized it was just the glare from a computer at another booth. *Calm down,* he told himself.

He reached RemoteX and slowly wiggled open the drawer under the booth, covering his hand with his shirt as he did so, so there wouldn't be any fingerprints. He used the light from his iPhone as a flashlight, glancing into the corners of the room to be sure there weren't any security cameras.

In the top drawer were a pair of scissors, some wire, a garage-door opener, a television remote, and an MP3 player. He shut the drawer carefully and squatted to open the bottom drawer. It was empty, except for a small shoebox in the back corner. Adam pulled it out and took the lid off.

"Bingo," he whispered.

A pile of magazine clippings and online article printouts about Doreye were stapled together and folded neatly on top. Below it was a shoddy device, opened, with switches and wires sticking in and out like someone didn't know what they were doing. It resembled a control panel. At the bottom of the box he found a slim plastic container filled with little metal chips that looked like the SIM card in the back of a cell phone. Adam wrinkled his brow. What were these? There must have been fifty of the chips in the box. He used his fingernail to pull one out and slipped it into his pocket.

Adam discreetly replaced the contents of the shoebox and slid the bottom drawer closed. He tiptoed back to the Doreye booth and checked the drawers: nothing unusual. What could the chip be for? And why was it in the RemoteX shoebox?

Adam closed his eyes. *Think! What would James Bond do?* All he could think about were images of beautiful women and fast cars.

His eyes snapped open: the toy car!

He looked across the devices at the Doreye booth until he found the radio-controlled toy car. He picked it up and drunkenly snapped open the chassis to where the rechargeable battery was inserted. He slowly pulled out the battery and squinted to see . . . yes! A small metal chip, just like the one in his pocket, was tucked behind the battery, preventing two wires from meeting. He wasn't sure what the wires were for, but he was pretty sure the chip was not supposed to be there.

Adam looked across the other devices on the table. He didn't have to disassemble each one to know that the blonde British girl had sabotaged those, too. "RemoteX, I'm on to you," he said with a satisfied smile.

Just then he heard a noise and a swath of yellow light streamed in from the conference room door. Adam froze.

Instinctively, he ducked behind the Doreye table and peered toward the door, trying to figure out who it was. His mind raced. If he got caught, what would people think? They'd probably think *he* was sabotaging RemoteX. Or, at the very least, he'd get kicked out of the conference and everyone would think he was the fucked-up, add-nothing leech to his sister they'd suspected all along. He had to get out of there now . . . but how?

Adam heard someone whistling as he crawled behind one booth, then the next. Suddenly, the overhead lights snapped on and he peered out from behind the booth where he was crouched. A man in a cleaning uniform was pushing an industrial vacuum on the far side of the room. He was wearing headphones and looking away from Adam, going about his business. Adam felt his chest empty the breath he'd been holding. He quickly stood up and raced out the door.

53

Footprints

After three hours of trying to find a solution, Amelia told her friends back in Palo Alto to go to bed. She sat staring out the window for a while, searching the Hawaiian stars for an answer and, finding none, took a deep breath and went to locate Adam. She knew he was upset, and she felt bad. He'd only been trying to help. But she'd also been relieved that George had had the guts to tell him he was slowing them down.

She wasn't sure where he'd gone, but she guessed he'd wandered down to the "Ugly Sweater" party a group of conference participants were unofficially throwing in one of the ballrooms downstairs. The last thing she wanted was to be social with a bunch of dressed-up, drunk conference-goers, but she hoped it was late enough that they'd all be on the prowl for someone to hook up with and not bother her with questions about Doreye.

Amelia arrived in the lobby and followed the cheesy Christmas music down the hall, gulping anxiously before opening the door.

The room was enormous, with another crystal chandelier

hanging from the center and floor-to-ceiling windows across the back, which overlooked the beach and the crashing waves illuminated by the full moon. A huge palm tree decorated with lights and Christmas ornaments towered over a garland-trimmed tiki bar, and poinsettia blossoms were mounted on tiki torches. A wooden dance floor had been constructed in the middle of the room, and it was packed with drunk twenty- to fifty-somethings, all looking equally ridiculous in red and green turtlenecks, checkered suits, and oversized crocheted holiday sweaters.

"Amelia?"

She turned around to find Sundeep, clad in a two-sizes-too-small bright green turtleneck and red chino pants, an oversized reindeer pin clipped to his shirt, and a Santa hat in hand.

"Sundeep!" She tried not to gawk at how ridiculous he looked. "I was just looking for—"

"Adam?" he interrupted. "I haven't seen him, and I've been here for a while."

Amelia's shoulders dropped in disappointment. Why did everything about this day have to be a challenge?

"Do you want to get some fresh air?" Sundeep asked.

"Yeah," she said, and followed him outside onto the beach. Fresh air was exactly what she wanted: lots and lots and lots of fresh air to make everything else evaporate.

They strolled along the warm sand in silence, until Sundeep finally said, "What's wrong?"

Amelia pursed her lips and took a deep breath. "It was the expo today. Doreye didn't work." She tried to stop them, but tears filled her eyes. "And I just spent three hours trying to fix it, and I've done everything right, Sundeep! It should be working." She was sobbing now.

He stopped her, gently holding her shoulders to steady her.

"I heard about the other company," he confessed. "And you know what else I heard? That you're the smartest person in Silicon Valley. The next hotshot engineer. The next big thing. You *will* figure it out, Amelia. Of that I'm absolutely certain."

She shook her head and broke free of his grip. They continued walking.

"You know what I think?" he asked.

"What?" she asked, sniffling.

"I think women as strong as you don't cry over iPhone applications."

She swallowed.

"Do you want to talk about the press conference?" he asked.

"No." She kicked a conch shell and kept walking. "What is there to talk about? I did it. I'm guilty. I hacked in and embezzled money and knew what I was doing wasn't right. I spent three months in juvie and it was completely and utterly horrible. And now everyone knows and they're going to bring it up and I'll never escape it."

"You can't change your past," Sundeep said. "But you can decide how you're going to use what's happened to you."

She didn't respond. He tried another angle. "What happened to you, Amelia . . . it's part of you, and you may not want to do it again, but it made you a stronger person, a more honest person."

"I wish I could be as honest as you," she said. "I mean, you don't have a flawed bone in your body. You're smart and caring and totally . . . perfect. Your life is perfect."

Sundeep was silent. Finally, he said quietly, "That's not true."

"I don't believe you."

"I haven't been entirely honest with you." He turned to look at her, the corners of his mouth pinched tight. "My family disowned me, Amelia. Last spring. And now I've got nothing."

They had walked back up to the hotel entrance, and she

stopped before opening the door. So that's what Lisa had been talking about. "Oh, Sundeep." Her heart genuinely ached for him. "I am so, so sorry."

Sundeep was looking at the stars, as if trying to fight back tears of his own, but he forced a smile. "It's okay. It'll work out. Sometimes other people don't understand why we do what we do, but we can't let that keep us from fighting for what we believe in."

If Amelia had been a hugger, she would have given him a hug. But she was still attracted to him and was embarrassed that he might know that.

A drunk man in a crocheted reindeer vest stumbled up off the beach beside them. "Ooooooh!" He yelled at the pair, lifting the eggnog in his right hand and spilling it onto the patio. "Somebody's under the mistletoe!"

Amelia and Sundeep glanced up, and sure enough, they were standing directly under a thick tuft of mistletoe suspended from a light fixture on the wall. "That means you have to *make out*," the drunk guy hollered as he stumbled through the door to the bathroom, leaving Amelia and Sundeep both blushing furiously. They paused, caught in the moment and the embarrassment and the comfort of each other's presence.

"Amelia!" Adam's voice called from inside. He was running down the hall toward them. "I've been looking everywhere for you. I figured it out! I figured out how RemoteX sabotaged us. There is nothing wrong with Doreye!"

54

Yours, Virtually

Amelia pretended to go to sleep when Adam did. He was in a great mood, and she didn't want to upset him with her nerves. She lay staring at the ceiling, heart beating and mind racing as she listened to her brother's slow, steady breathing.

She kept thinking about the chips Adam had found in the Doreye devices. T.J. had shipped their presentation to Maui days ahead of time; someone could have easily added an override switch to the terminals in each device's radio receiver. It was an easy hack to do for an engineer with time and a wire wrap tool. But why would anyone want to sabotage their demo?

Unable to sleep, she slipped out of the bed, picked up her laptop, and quietly opened the sliding door onto the balcony of their room.

The air was thick and heavy, but a cool breeze blew from the ocean, bringing with it the scent of salt and tropical flowers. She closed her eyes, listened to the gentle melody of the bugs buzzing below, inhaled deeply. She looked up at the full moon overhead and wondered for a minute how life had led her here, to this balcony in Hawaii at a TechCrunch conference where her start-up company was on display.

Then she sat down in one of the rocking chairs, opened her laptop, and logged into ZOSTRA, the virtual world she'd joined with George, T-Bag, Janet, and Jon. Wednesday nights were when everyone met at the LAIR to get together in the virtual world, but individual players could log on anytime to work on his or her avatar. As players completed tasks and challenges, they got points they could use to buy virtual goods.

Amelia had created an avatar that wasn't much different from herself. Her avatar had more voluminous hair and bigger breasts, and she wore contacts, but Amelia didn't spend any money on clothes or handbags like a lot of the other girl avatars. One Wednesday, virtual T-Bag (a stunningly buff and attractive blond) had taken virtual Amelia on his virtual private jet to virtual Rodeo Drive to model Gucci and Prada. Everyone had laughed and Amelia had blushed, but she'd quickly stuffed her virtual Jimmy Choos in her virtual closet.

Instead, she used points to buy more and more complicated weapons to fight bad guys. She'd quickly mastered nunchakus and daggers. She was saving up for a master sword, like the one Uma Thurman used in *Kill Bill*, to fight a Russian terrorist named Boris, the virtual creation of a small and timid red-headed girl from Minnesota who had been playing ZOSTRA for four years and had serious skills.

Amelia was shooting virtual clay pigeons when another avatar appeared on the right side of her screen. It was George. He didn't say anything, just started shooting clay pigeons next to her. He was better than she was, and when they'd finished the round, she sent him an instant message to tell him so. The IM popped up in a speech bubble above her avatar. In the bubble above his, he said, "You're quickly surpassing me, young grass-hopper."

"There are too many pigeons to shoot. It's getting more difficult to see them all."

"That's what happens as you get better."

"Maybe I don't want to get better."

"Then how will you beat Boris?"

"Maybe beating Boris isn't the only point of the game."

There was a pause. Amelia anxiously watched the speech bubble above George's head. Finally, he responded. "I think some players have talents that are so exceptional they have a responsibility to use them, even if it's hard."

"Then I'll stop getting better."

"You can't. It's not in your nature."

Amelia felt tears welling up in her eyes again. "I don't like this, George," she typed.

"You're the strongest woman I know, Amelia. In addition to being the smartest and the most beautiful. You can do this, I know you can."

Her eyes hung on the word "beautiful," and she felt a single hot tear roll down her cheek.

She waited, feeling her heartbeat slow down. She wasn't sure why, but she suddenly, desperately, wished George were there.

She typed "I wish you were here," and stared at the blinking cursor at the end of the phrase, without clicking "Send."

Just send it, she thought, her finger resting on the "Enter" key. But just then another message popped up in the speech bubble above virtual George's head. "Have to sign off. Good luck tomorrow. Let me know how it goes."

Just as well, Amelia thought, as she backspaced the line and instead sent, "I will. Thanks, George. For everything."

55

Tell Me Your Secrets, I'll Tell You Mine

T.J.'s alarm went off at 5:30 A.M., but he was already awake, feeling guilty about what he'd said to his father the night before. It was unnecessarily harsh and dramatic. Ted hadn't been trying to egg T.J. on. Probably he had only wanted to hear what had happened. Shit, he was probably even trying to have a civil conversation with T.J. and just didn't know how to go about it in an uncompetitive way.

T.J. pulled on a pair of shorts, laced up his tennis shoes, and headed to the hotel gym.

He was surprised to hear someone already there, running hard on the treadmill, and even more surprised when he saw that it was Patty.

He stepped on the treadmill next to her and started upping the speed on the belt. "Couldn't sleep either?"

"Nope!" she said, pulling an earbud out of her right ear, then replacing it, politely indicating that she didn't want to talk.

A large mirror faced the treadmills, and as T.J. started his run, he couldn't help but notice their impeccable form. Patty's legs were all long, lean muscle as she pounded away at a seven-minute-mile clip, and T.J.'s chest and ab muscles glimmered—not an ounce of fat anywhere—as he ran at a slightly more reasonable eight-minute-mile pace. Say all you will about rich Atherton kids, he thought, but they had phenomenal figures. Like modern-day Greek gods.

They were both panting heavily, staring into the mirror but not looking at anything in particular, as they contemplated their own concerns. When Patty's machine hit nine miles, she slowed the belt down to a quick walk. T.J. followed suit.

"Don't stop on my accord." She smiled, out of breath.

"I happen to be finished, too," he said. He wasn't about to admit that he'd just forced himself to run two miles farther than he'd intended because he had too much pride to start after and finish before a girl.

"I was going to grab a smoothie at the juice bar after this. Want to join?" T.J. asked.

"Sure," Patty said. "Just going to stretch a little. Meet you there."

T.J. was sitting at the tiki-themed juice bar watching CNN on the television screen when Patty joined him, a wet towel hanging around her neck. He pushed a tall glass of white foam toward her. "I ordered you a coconut-lime smoothie. It's the best one."

"Thanks." Patty took a long sip through the straw and climbed into the high chair beside him. It was delicious.

"So, what were you running so hard about?" she asked T.J.

"I was kind of an asshole last night. Felt bad about it. Punishing myself, I guess. You?"

"Too long a story to tell over smoothies."

"We could ask the bartender to put some booze in them, if that would help?"

Patty laughed. That actually didn't sound like such a bad idea. "Nah. I'm getting my nails done with the bridesmaids in an hour. My mother would disown me if I showed up drunk."

"Fair."

They sat for a few moments in silence before T.J. finally said, "So, you're really not going to tell me?"

Patty studied T.J. for a moment. She desperately wanted to tell someone. It was so difficult to hold it all in. T.J. already knew the beginning parts of it. The first night something happened between her and Chad was last spring at T.J.'s graduation party. The security cameras caught them in his father's garage . . . together in the Lamborghini's backseat. When it happened, T.J. had been a jerk about it, trying to blackmail her. Despite that, it seemed like he had grown up a lot since then. For some reason, she felt like she could trust him.

"It's Chad," she said softly, looking down at her bare feet. She desperately needed that pedicure.

T.J. sat up in his chair, his curiosity piqued. He tried not to seem too interested. "Oh?" he said.

"It's so wrong, T.J. I know it is. But I like him. I really, really do. And . . ." She couldn't say it. She'd never said it out loud.

"And?"

"And I think he likes me, too."

"Why do you think that?"

"We went on a hike yesterday. To a waterfall. And he told me so. He said he thinks about me all the time." Patty's face reddened. "He said he thought maybe he was marrying the wrong sister."

T.J. almost choked on his smoothie. "Wow."

Patty shook her head, as if trying to get the whole thing out of her mind. "It's so stupid. It'll all be over tonight, no matter what. I just have to stop thinking about it."

"Maybe it won't all be over tomorrow. Maybe it's just beginning." T.J. smiled coyly.

56

Panic

Adam slept deeply until ten o'clock in the morning. The sun was streaming through the flowing white drapes at the balcony windows, and he was full of the euphoria that only comes after a night of dreaming about your true love. Yesterday had been an emotional roller coaster, but everything felt right now that he knew Lisa loved him.

Not to mention that he'd discovered the problem with their presentation yesterday. RemoteX was trying to sabotage Dor-eye with that chip. They had decided not to say anything until they'd had a chance to tell T.J. and Roger. Roger's flight was rescheduled to land this morning, and T.J. would be at the Hawkins wedding all day, though he said he'd slip out after the ceremony to check in on them.

Adam stretched his arms over his head and rolled out of bed, careful not to wake Amelia. Someone had slid an envelope under the door to the room, and he picked it up along with the free copy of *The New York Times*.

Inside the envelope was a handwritten note from Mike, the conference organizer:

Wanted to get you the questions for today's Q&A in advance of the session. Good luck.   —Mike

Behind it was a typed list of questions submitted by the press, which they planned to ask Adam and Amelia at the Q&A. Adam felt the blood drain from his face as he read the list:

What is your current relationship with the Dawson family? When was the last time you were in contact with them?

Are you aware of Mr. Dawson's upcoming release from prison? Will you reach out to him?

Is Stanford aware of your criminal past? Do you worry about what will happen now that it's public?

You're on fellowship, meaning individual philanthropists fund much of your education. Do you feel a responsibility to tell them what you did?

How has Roger Fenway handled knowledge of your crime? Is he concerned about potential legal fallout?

When did you learn to hack through security walls? Have you ever done it since, for any purpose?

You know how to hack into very sophisticated systems. Is that how you infiltrated RemoteX and stole their technology?

Your peers have noticed that you are both wearing much more expensive clothes than you did a year ago. How have you funded your new wardrobes? Can you honestly say that your income is "clean"?

Every single question involved some aspect of Amelia's past. And each was worded deceitfully. Even if Amelia's answers to the questions were fair and honest, the way the questions were phrased made her sound like a criminal. Like the one about the fellowship: They weren't even on fellowships anymore, but if someone in the public heard that question, all they'd focus on was this idea that Adam and Amelia were thieves taking advantage of naïve benefactors. It was appalling.

Adam felt his heart race. He looked at Amelia, still sleeping in the plush white bed. They'd gone to bed at 3:00 A.M., but he'd heard her get up in the middle of the night and was worried she wouldn't sleep. He was relieved to see her sleeping so peacefully now and dreaded having to wake her. These questions were going to devastate her all over again. But they had to figure out what to do, and fast. The panel started in an hour.

Adam shook her gently. "Amelia?"

She rolled over and sighed with her eyes still closed. "I think I could get used to this bed," she said, and smiled. She couldn't remember them, but she knew that she'd had really nice dreams. Her smile turned into a grimace, though, when she saw Adam's worried expression. "Oh God," she moaned. "What's wrong?"

"Don't freak out."

But she could already feel serious anxiety setting in. She just couldn't handle any more right now. She pulled her legs out from under the covers and put on her glasses. "What is it?"

"We got the questions for today's Q&A. The journalists submitted them to Mike, and he slipped them under the door so we had time to prepare."

"And?"

"And they're all about your time in juvie and your hacking abilities."

It felt like a nightmare. She fell into her pillow, shaking her head. "Why won't they stop? Oh God, Adam, I hate this all so, so much."

He didn't know what to do. Amelia had always been the strong one, the one who could take a bad situation and rationally develop a plan of action. But she was in no state to solve this problem.

His mind raced. "We have to get them to cancel the Q&A."

"How?" Amelia moaned from the pillow. "It's why they all came. Adam, why did we ever do this? I just want to go home."

"T.J. knows Mike, right?" Adam's mind was suddenly lucid. "And, for that matter, everyone in the press. He can convince them not to ask those questions."

"But he's at the wedding, remember?"

"You have to go get him. No," he reconsidered. "I'll go get him. You might run into Ted Bristol."

Adam scrambled to pull on a pair of shorts and a polo shirt—one that Lisa had helped him pick out—and dashed out the door. "Don't worry about anything, Amelia. Order some room service and take a shower and I'll figure this out, okay? Everything's going to be fine."

This was all going to work out. It had to.

57

Prepping and Primping

"Oh my God, you must be so nervous."

Patty glanced up from the *InStyle* magazine in her lap and into the mirror at the very gay hairdresser wielding a hot curling iron and a coy grin. He was a super-thin, bald Asian guy, dressed completely in black, including thick plastic glasses, and he'd clearly had at least six cups of coffee already this morning, or a lot of something else. "Marc, with a *C,*" he'd introduced himself. Patty didn't trust hairdressers who had no hair of their own.

She smiled politely. "Why would I be nervous?"

"Well, it's your sister's big day. I mean, I'd be totally nervous that I'd ruin it."

Patty felt her cheeks burn. What did he know? She lifted her eyebrows and he quickly backtracked. "I mean, that I'd step on her dress or forget to grab her flowers or whatever."

Whew, she thought. "No, I guess I'm not really that nervous." She went back to the article about finding the right-fitting pair of skinny jeans.

"Ahhhh!!!!" Marc with a *C* squealed, dropping the curling iron in order to clap as he turned from Patty to Shandi, who had come out of her private room and was twirling in the middle of the Four Seasons salon for all to see, her veil perfectly affixed atop a knot of careful curls. Her bangs were swept gently across her forehead, and her makeup was flawless. Even in the tank top and shorts she was wearing, she looked like a princess.

The four other bridesmaids, two from college and two from Atherton, turned in their salon swivel chairs and chirped gleefully along with their respective stylists. Patty swallowed hard, took a deep breath, and called out, hoping she didn't sound fake. "Oh, Shandi, you look so pretty."

Not like Shandi heard, anyway. She was already at the mirror, examining each individual curl. "Are you sure?" she asked, pointlessly. Of course, everyone insisted she was absolutely mad if she thought she looked anything less than perfect.

Patty couldn't wait for all this to be over. She'd gotten good enough at swimming to prove to herself that her athleticism matched that of her nationally ranked tennis-playing sister; getting into Stanford had validated that she could match Shandi academically. But when it came to looks, Patty still felt totally, utterly inferior. She felt okay when Shandi wasn't around. She could see that her legs were shapely, her stomach flat, her skin smooth, her face not so unattractive. But the minute Shandi came back into the picture, Patty felt like a fat cow. She looked at her sister's thin frame and high cheekbones and knew that, even if she stopped eating for a month, she'd never be as pretty.

And all she could think about now, sitting here with her hair actually looking really amazing (maybe Marc with a *C* wasn't such an idiot), was that she'd never get to feel the way Shandi felt right now, with everyone *ooh*-ing and *ahh*-ing around her. That on her own wedding day, when she ought to feel like the most beautiful woman in the world, Patty would come out of her private room, and Shandi would be sitting where Patty was sitting now, and, even in her veil, Patty would feel less beautiful than her effortlessly perfect matron-of-honor sister.

She put down the magazine. Now was not the time to be reading about skinny jeans.

When they were finished, the bridesmaids went up to their rooms to get dressed. Patty was following their lead when the photographer, who had been capturing the morning, asked her to stay behind. "I want to get a few shots of you helping your sister get ready. These are always fantastic." She winked.

Patty grimaced, looking down at the workout suit she was wearing (why hadn't anyone warned her the photographer would be on hand?) and reluctantly followed her sister to the bridal suite, where her $7,500 ivory-lace-with-buttons-down-the-back Vera Wang dress hung from a three-panel mirror.

The photographer instructed Patty quickly to put on her own dress while she sat Shandi on the chair at the vanity and directed her to peer into the gold oval mirror. "Just beautiful!" she kept saying.

Patty watched miserably as she slipped on the pale pink, empire-waist, floor-length strapless chiffon bridesmaid dress she assumed Shandi had picked out because it made her look especially like a blimp.

"Ready?" the photographer asked Patty, who nodded. "Okay, come help your sister put on her gown."

Shandi slipped off her shorts and shirt, revealing the pristine white lace La Perla bra and underwear she'd saved for today. She looked like a lingerie model, her thin hips and shoulders balanced by round, firm breasts and butt. "Here, help me climb into this before Diane snaps one of me naked." She motioned for Patty to come over.

Patty slipped the heavy gown off the hanger and, careful to avoid stepping on the fabric, knelt down so Shandi could support herself on Patty's shoulder while she stepped into the dress. Patty stood behind her, carefully pulling shut the hook-and-eye clasps that lined the back, as the photographer snapped away.

When Patty was finished, she looked over her sister's shoulder into the mirror, scanning the dress from the bottom all the way up to her sister's face. But when she got to Shandi's eyes, they were directed at Patty's reflection, not her own. Shandi's face was still and looked . . . sad.

She was silent for a moment, then said quietly, "You are so beautiful, Patty."

Patty felt her skin tingle, but didn't know what to say, and so said nothing. Shandi turned to face her, just a tiny glimmer of wetness in her blue eyes.

"I don't know when you went from being my kid sister to such a gorgeous, strong woman, but I'm really, really sorry I wasn't there—or wasn't paying enough attention—to witness it."

Patty shook her head and looked down at her feet, not knowing what else to do, but Shandi kept going. She reached her hands up and held her little sister's cheeks in her hands. "Listen, you have something really special, Patty. Something I never had. You have fearlessness and decisiveness and a lust for life. And I don't think I've ever told you, but I admire you so, so much for that."

Normally, Patty would write off any affirmative thing her sister said as a backhanded compliment, a patronizing "Oh, you're so lucky you have such a good appetite; I wish I could eat like you do!" kind of thing. But Shandi was actually being genuine.

Shandi took a deep breath and turned back to the mirror.

"Do I look okay?" she asked, really seeming to mean it.

This Patty could answer, honestly. She whispered, "You look absolutely stunning, Shandi. Completely, completely beautiful."

"I'm so nervous, Patty," Shandi confessed, swallowing hard.

"Don't be!" Patty said, suddenly jumping at the opportunity to be her sister's cheerleader. "You're going to do everything just right. And even if you don't, no one will notice. They'll be too busy admiring how perfect you look."

"Not about getting things right," Shandi said slowly. "I mean, about the whole thing. About whether I'm doing the right thing. But I guess it's too late." She tried to laugh.

Patty felt her heart clench. Did "about the whole thing" mean "about Chad"?

"No!" Patty exclaimed. "I mean, I feel like it must be totally normal to have doubts right before the big moment, but seriously, Shandi, you shouldn't. Chad is unbelievable. Totally unbelievable. He's smart and funny and gorgeous and . . . you are going to have an amazing life together."

"You're the lucky one, Patty." Shandi neither agreed nor disagreed with what Patty had just said. "You've got your whole life in front of you. Can do whatever you want, nothing to tie you down. And you've got the personality and courage to do it, you know? Even if I still had your freedom, I'm not sure I'd have your courage to take advantage of it."

"You're twenty-three!" Patty laughed. "You're not exactly old! And you've got everything in front of you, plus you've got a partner to do it all with!"

Shandi gave her a thanks-but-you-couldn't-possibly-understand smile. It wasn't condescending, just . . . sad.

The photographer coughed softly from the corner. Both sisters had forgotten she was there.

"Sorry to interrupt, ladies, but your mother wants to take a few private pictures with the bride."

"Of course!" Shandi quickly snapped herself back into wedding mode, her eyes shining brightly in fully confident, self-absorbed, happy-bride fashion.

"Thanks so much for your help, Patty," she chirped as she followed the photographer out to meet their mother.

58

You Can't Win All the Time

Adam punched the elevator call button furiously. "Come on!" he yelled at the button. Now was the chance to be a hero, and he wasn't going to miss it. The doors finally opened and he rode the elevator to the lobby, dashing to the front desk.

"Where's the Hawkins-Bronson wedding?" he belted.

"It's in the Hibiscus Grove, down the street. The next shuttle should be leaving in about five minutes."

Adam didn't have five minutes. He rushed outside and stopped under the porte cochere, desperate for a solution. The doorman was helping a woman out of a red Porsche Carrera GT while her husband stood with the bags waiting for the valet. Adam rushed to the valet stand and grabbed a blank ticket. He ripped the ticket in half and gave the bottom portion to the man, who looked at Adam's khaki shorts and flip-flops suspiciously.

"Our valet had an emergency phone call," Adam said calmly. "I'm an office intern, and they asked me to stand in until he's back."

Adam glanced nervously over the man's shoulder, spotting

the real valet coming back. But the man seemed satisfied and handed Adam the key. Adam grabbed it, skipped quickly to the driver's side, and sped off toward the Hibiscus Grove, his adrenaline pumping with the $450,000 accelerator under his foot.

He left the car outside the small villa nestled next to the Hibiscus Grove and dashed through the door onto the terrace. Elegantly dressed, beautiful people were milling around, sipping champagne, all smiles for the half-dozen photographers swarming the crowd. Adam's eyes darted around, looking for T.J. Where was he?

He ran to one wall of the terrace. If he stood on it, he could get a better view of the crowd. He climbed up and peered out, his heart racing with adrenaline. "T.J., where are you?" he muttered under his breath.

He scanned the crowd. But his eyes darted back to the corner. Did he just see what he thought he saw? Who was that standing under the palm tree? It couldn't be . . .

Adam's heart sank. No, it didn't sink; it collapsed, crashed, plummeted to the center of the Earth. All the blood in his head rushed to support it and he felt like he was going to faint. Lisa—*his Lisa*—was in the gazebo. And she was kissing—it couldn't be!—the Indian guy from the incubator.

He shuddered. He didn't know how to process this. What the hell was going on? He climbed off the wall and sat down. He needed a drink. A waiter passed by with a tray of mimosas, and he grabbed one. He had to see it again, to confirm. He walked closer to the gazebo. There was no doubt: Lisa and Sundeep were holding hands. He was smiling and whispering in her ear and she was laughing, tossing her head, her perfectly sculpted golden curls falling down her back. Adam downed the mimosa and grabbed another.

"Did you decide to crash the wedding?"

Adam turned his head toward the voice. The man with the Scotch from last night stood next to him, one hand in his pocket and the other holding a glass of champagne.

"Are you okay?" the man asked, noticing Adam's distraught expression.

Adam took a deep breath and tried to refocus on why he had come. "I have to find T.J.," he stammered. "T.J. Bristol. Do you know him?"

The man chuckled. "Sure, he's my son. He's right over here."

Ted turned to motion for T.J., who was standing close by, chatting with an older woman, and so didn't see the stunned expression on Adam's face. Holy shit. *That's* where he'd seen this guy before; at the party last June, giving the toast for T.J. His brain couldn't handle all of this.

Ted turned back before Adam had time to recover his expression. He lifted his eyebrows in a what-the-hell-is-wrong-with-this-kid grimace as T.J. broke away from his conversation and joined them.

T.J. noticed Adam's dumbfounded face, too. "I see you two have finally met."

"Actually, I don't think we ever officially have." Ted stuck out his hand jovially. "I'm Ted Bristol. What's your name?"

"Adam," Adam stammered, taking Ted's hand.

T.J. rolled his eyes. "Adam *Dory*," he said. "Amelia's brother."

Ted clucked his tongue. "Well! Adam Dory!"

Adam blinked his eyes closed, half expecting Ted to punch him.

But instead Ted smiled. "It appears there are two extremely impressive Dorys."

Ted's smile was genuine and warm, not conniving, and Adam blushed. There was always talk about Amelia, but it was the first time Adam could remember anyone ever saying he was impressive. He knew it was wrong, but he felt a weird connection with Ted.

"So, what's up?" T.J. asked. "Why on earth would you come to this wedding if you didn't have to?"

Adam's mind was racing. If this guy was Ted, that meant Lisa was his daughter, and hadn't he said last night that he didn't like her boyfriend? And her boyfriend was Sundeep? Unless she was a total slut and she was kissing all sorts of boys in the gazebo. No, that couldn't be. Lisa wasn't a slut. She was perfect—she *loved* him!

Focus!

"It's Amelia. The panel, I mean. You have to stop the Q&A," Adam stammered.

"Too late," Ted said, showing T.J. and Adam his Android phone, where he was live streaming the conference.

"What do you mean?" Adam grabbed the phone and stared in horror at its screen. Amelia was standing at the side of the stage, about to make her presentation. Adam glanced at his iPhone. It was 10:55 A.M., and he had three frantic texts from Amelia: *"Where are you???"*

Had he been watching Lisa and Sundeep for that long? How many mimosas did he drink?

"No! We have to stop the Q&A. They're going to drill her on questions about juvie!" Adam rushed out. T.J. followed.

"The ceremony starts in one hour," Ted called. "Your mother's going to kill you if you miss it."

But neither Adam nor T.J. heard as they dashed back to the stolen Porsche.

59

Or Can You?

Adam raced to the side of the stage just as Amelia walked out, taking the microphone from the previous presenter. T.J. left to find Mike. Amelia was scheduled for a ten-minute presentation and a fifteen-minute Q&A. If T.J. could get to Mike fast enough, there was still a chance he could derail the Q&A.

"Found you!" Adam turned at the sound of a familiar voice. Roger Fenway was next to him, one hand on the handle of a rolling suitcase, his face flushed. He'd obviously just come from the airport.

"This is not going to be good," Adam moaned. But Roger didn't hear. He was smiling brightly at Amelia, his gem. He obviously hadn't heard about yesterday's disaster, Adam thought.

Amelia took a deep breath and began to speak into the microphone. The PowerPoint presentation she'd prepared with Roger and T.J. back in Palo Alto was projected on the screen behind her, and her iPhone and all of the devices controllable by Doreye were on a table in front.

"My very savvy business team helped me prepare a presentation," she said. Her voice was calm and clear. "It goes through the numbers on our business, the market potential, and lots of other things I'm sure you all are interested in."

She used the monitor control to click quickly through all the slides, so fast no one could read them. "But I'm going to disappoint you, because I don't want to talk about any of that today." She clicked one more time, and the monitor went black.

Adam glanced at Roger. What was she doing? But Roger was still focused on Amelia, beaming like a father proudly watching his son's first Little League game. The audience was silent, and the room was thick with anticipation.

"Instead," she said, "I'm going to talk about honesty."

She paused, letting that sink in. "When I was fifteen, I did something very dishonest. First I hacked into the College Board Web site and adjusted the SAT scores of my foster brother. Then I hacked into an insurance company's database and adjusted the sales figures of my foster father. And then I hacked into a bank and embezzled money into his account.

"And then one day I woke up and realized that what I believed was helping the only family I ever had"—Amelia swallowed—"was actually causing innocent people to suffer. That people worthy of recognition for good test scores, worthy of commissions for high sales figures, worthy of the money they worked hard to earn, were being penalized because of what I was doing. And so I confessed, and I stopped, and I accepted my punishment and spent three months in jail."

No one in the audience dared to even blink in case they might miss something.

"And I wouldn't do it again," Amelia said. She shook her head and laughed. "Absolutely not. But I will take what lessons I can from it, and that's what I'd like to talk about today. You see, through that experience, I met honest people and I met dishonest people, and I learned the difference. I made a vow always to be honest, but I've unfortunately learned that there are still a lot of dishonest people in the world, and they don't always get caught."

Amelia walked over to the microwave and opened the back panel, pulling out the chip.

"This little chip here"—she held it up—"is the reason Doreye didn't work during yesterday's demo."

She set it aside. "It overrides radio frequencies. The person who put it there is a *dis*honest person. I won't slander anyone, but given all you were able to dig up about me, I'm sure you can figure this one out, too."

Amelia proceeded with a flawless demo, using the iPhone to work all the devices on the table. The audience relaxed, smiling excitedly in anticipation of this stunning new product, which was working just as well as the hype had promised.

When she was finished with the demo, Amelia turned back to the press. "I believe that, if we work together, and if we're honest, we can take computer technology to a level none of us has yet conceived. This is just the start."

Thunderous applause erupted. One by one, the audience started to stand, cheering loudly. Amelia closed her eyes and let out a deep exhale. Adam could see her hands shaking.

Then she added, "I believe there were a few questions you'd prepared. I hope I've addressed them adequately." With that, Amelia walked off the stage, the crowd still applauding.

Roger Fenway opened his arms, and Amelia fell into them. "You were absolutely brilliant," he whispered, planting a grandfatherly kiss on the top of her head. Cameras snapped all around them, the journalists delighting in the perfectly captured moment of mentor-mentee affection.

She stood back and smiled at Roger, her eyes bright. "Thank you so much," she said quietly.

T.J. ran up to her. "Jesus, Amelia! Where did that come from? You were unbelievable!" He pulled her into a hug, his face radiant with astonishment and adrenaline. "You just catapulted this thing onto a whole new level. Do you have any idea how much you owned that crowd?"

She laughed modestly. "Thank Roger," she said. "He gives a hell of a pep talk."

Amelia and Roger exchanged a knowing glance. Right after Adam had left this morning, Roger had called her to check in. After she'd babbled into the phone, he'd calmly told her she needed to wait exactly three hours to have a breakdown. For now, she had to bolster herself. "Act like it's not you. Pretend like you're playing the part of someone else, a fierce and intimidating woman who doesn't take shit from anyone." Together, they'd written what she would say and he'd instructed her to stand in front of the mirror as she practiced the speech into her phone.

Amelia finally turned to Adam. Adam didn't know what to say. He'd failed her, and he knew that she knew it. He'd gotten distracted worrying over Lisa, and somehow while he was gone, his sister had become . . . awesome.

"You were amazing," he finally offered.

"Thanks." She nodded.

Adam turned to Roger. "Answering their questions before they asked them was a pretty bold strategy."

Roger smiled. "Well, I ain't often right, but I've never been wrong."

Amelia laughed. "Can we please go get lunch now? I'm starving."

As they walked toward the dining room, Adam dug his hands into his pockets. His fingers landed on something: the flower from Lisa's hair. He held it up and contemplated it for a moment before tossing it into the garbage can in disgust.

60

Here She Comes

Patty was standing in the upstairs sitting room of the villa next to the Hibiscus Grove, looking out at the wedding guests below. Shandi was posing for pictures somewhere, and the other bridesmaids were happily drinking champagne and putting the finishing touches on their makeup.

From here, she could see all the guests milling around on the terrace outside. She admired Lisa Bristol's silky, gold one-shoulder dress and the little Judith Leiber clutch she carried effortlessly. She looked like a little goddess. What was she doing with that boring Indian guy? Nevertheless, Patty was jealous of Lisa. Not in a malicious way (How could you not like someone so sweet?), but in a wish-I-was-her kind of way.

She took a sip of champagne and scanned the crowd for T.J., but she couldn't find him. He was probably off with some newly found hot girl, she thought. She heard her phone signal a text message.

"I need to see you immediately. Can you come to my suite downstairs? And come alone!"

Patty almost coughed up her drink. Was Chad serious? In less than an hour he would be married to her sister. What kind of horrible person was he? She felt any lingering attraction melt. This guy was bad news.

She was in the middle of typing an angry response when another text came through.

"URGENT!! PLEASE!!"

She sighed. Fine. One more meeting; but if he thought she was going to sleep with him he had another think coming. She erased what she had started to type and tapped, *"On my way."*

She crept out the side door and back through the lobby to the east wing groom's quarters, prepping what she was going to say. She wouldn't even enter the room, just stand outside and tell Chad, defiantly, that it was over and he needed to leave her alone.

Before she could knock on the door, however, it swung open and Chad pulled her by the wrist into the room.

"Chad, I cannot do this anymore," she said, just as she'd rehearsed on the walk. "You are marrying my sister and—"

"No, I'm not!" Chad shouted, panicking. She'd never seen him so flustered. He was freaking out.

"What are you talking about?"

"She's gone, Patty! She's gone!"

Patty looked at him like he was an idiot. "What is wrong with you? She's taking photos. I was with her an hour ago."

"No, she's not!" Chad was pacing back and forth in the room, pressing his hand to his temple, trying to think. "The photographer came in here forty minutes ago looking for her. She said Shandi had asked if she could leave her alone for a few minutes, and when she came back ten minutes later, Shandi was gone. The photographer thought we were having some romantic prewedding tryst. I've called Shandi a dozen times. I ran around the entire grounds. She's nowhere."

Patty looked at the clock. It was 11:42 A.M. The processional started at noon.

"Nothing's wrong, Chad," she said calmly. "She's upstairs in the bridal suite. I just walked past her to come up here," she lied, wondering whether Shandi actually had been in the bridal suite. "You need to go to the altar and get in place, okay? You'll see her in, like, twenty minutes, and then you'll be married and you'll laugh about this."

Chad grabbed a bottle of water off the minibar and took a long swig. "You're right. She probably just got distracted with all the getting ready."

"Exactly."

Chad put down the water bottle and gave Patty a hug. "You're the best," he said, and ran out the door.

Patty waited thirty seconds, and then ran upstairs as fast as she could to figure out what was going on.

61

Competitive Advantage

"I wanted to thank you for today." Amelia was washing her hands in the bathroom when she heard a thick British accent perfectly articulate each word.

The bathroom was otherwise empty. The blonde woman looked Amelia in the eyes and smirked tightly. A moment passed before she took a lipstick tube out of her oversized purse and leaned toward the gold-rimmed mirror to apply it.

Amelia looked at the woman's reflection in the mirror, her hands still under the running water. "What for?" she asked cautiously.

"For putting us on the map," the woman said, her eyes focused on her mouth in the mirror, carefully drawing the deep red to the edge of her top lip. She puckered a few times to settle the lipstick, and then she turned to face Amelia and stuck out her hand. "I'm Violet."

Amelia studied the woman. She couldn't tell how old she was. She could have been twenty or thirty-five. Her wardrobe was too sophisticated for college, but her skin had the flawless glow of a teenager. Amelia shook her hand but didn't introduce herself. Violet obviously knew who she was.

"What do you mean?" she asked instead.

"I mean, before this, no one knew a thing about RemoteX. We weren't even invited to the conference. We snuck inside the day before, pretending to be hotel staff, and added our booth to the expo floor. Now, though, when people leave, all they're going to be talking about is RemoteX. Doreye and RemoteX. Money can't buy the kind of publicity you just got us."

"But they think you're dishonest. My brother figured out how you cheated. We exposed you."

Violet smiled. "They think RemoteX is dishonest for *now*. But give me a week, maybe two, and the story will change. Besides, any press is good press."

Amelia was looking at her suspiciously.

"I knew you'd never figure it out in time," Violet said. "Your *brother*, however, I underestimated. He's not as naïve as you. There's real potential in Adam Dory." She smiled at Amelia, but Amelia didn't seem to register it.

"You see, your problem is that you assume people are good. Despite all that you've been through, in your happy world people are incapable of acting selfishly or maliciously. You never even thought to consider that I might have done something to mess up your presentation. Instead, you worried that *you'd* messed up something."

Amelia stared at Violet in silence, studying her warily. Violet shrugged it off with a laugh.

"Look at me like that all you want." She turned back to the mirror and touched her hair to pull it into place. Amelia, intimidated, glanced down at Violet's purse and saw a mess of red hair tangled underneath a wallet, a brush, and eyeliner. Each strand of hair looked like an overgrown tendril.

"Not all of us are cute little orphans with Roger Fenway in our back pocket. Some of us have to make things happen."

"Were you . . ." Amelia's mouth was dry and her hands still a little wet. "Why did you pretend to be a reporter at the press conference? Why did you ask me those questions about my past?" Violet dropped her lipstick into her purse and snapped it shut, hiding evidence of the wig with the red hair.

"Why did you try to sabotage me? Who are you?"

"See you around, Amelia." She waved as she walked out the door. Amelia watched her leave in the reflection in the mirror.

62

Speech!

Chad's hands were clammy and his cheeks were a deep crimson. He'd been standing at the altar for fifteen minutes. The string quartet had repeated Bach's "Air on the G String" three times, waiting for the cue to switch to the processional music so the wedding could begin.

Chad felt everyone staring at him, looking for his expression. People were discreetly checking their watches and iPhones. The wedding was supposed to have started already. Why wasn't anyone making an announcement?

Chad tried to push away his worry and focus on how beautiful everything was. The guests were assembled on the lawn at the Hibiscus Grove, under a white canopy tent. The grass had been trimmed to the length of a putting green so as not to catch on women's heels. The curved dark redwood altar was covered in white lilies—Shandi's favorite—and looked out onto the ocean, where the high sun was gleaming over the water. Quiet bamboo fans whirred over the three hundred guests, all seated in cushioned white folding chairs. The aisle between his family's side and hers was sprinkled with white rose petals. His eyes followed the aisle down to the French doors of the hotel's side terrace, through which, he was sure, the ushers would soon be guiding his mother to the front row so that the ceremony could start and he could marry Shandi.

His eyes strained to see past the doors. Where was Patty? Where was *anyone*? Craig, his best man, leaned over to him. "Don't worry, man," he said. "The longer you have to wait, the better the sex will be tonight." Chad forced a smile, appreciating Craig's clumsy effort to cheer him up.

The crowd turned at the sound of the doors pushing open. *Finally!* Chad jumped, looking anxious.

But it wasn't Patty, or Shandi, or the ushers. It was . . . T.J. Bristol.

Chad hadn't known T.J. that long, but in all their encounters he'd never seen him at all discomposed. Yet here was T.J., his clothes a mess, his hair disheveled, with a distraught look on his face. From his spot at the altar, he saw T.J.'s chest rising and falling in deep breaths, like he'd just finished a sprint.

T.J. ran midway down the aisle and stopped, looking up at Chad with eyes full of concern, and opened his mouth to speak.

From: **Ted Bristol <ted@gibly.com>**
To: **Adam Dory <adam@Doreye.com>**
Subject: **Great Meeting You**

Hi Adam,

I hope you enjoyed crashing the wedding! Did you stick around long enough for all the drama? Poor Ron Hawkins had about five heart attacks.

Am leaving Maui tomorrow, but would love to grab another Scotch with you when we're back in the Bay Area. Don't worry—it's on me. I'm impressed with what you're doing with Doreye and can tell you're very driven. I'm an excellent judge of character.

Shoot me an e-mail. I'm looking forward to it.

Ted

"Sir, I don't want to tell you again. Turn off all electronic devices." The stewardess's aggravated tone startled Adam, who was glued to his iPhone. He glanced up, gave a slight smile, and apologized.

"Adam, it's a real threat." Amelia sighed. "The signals that the network gives off can interfere with communication and flight-control devices in the cockpit. Your phone could endanger everyone on this flight!"

She brushed her hair away from her glasses as she glared at Adam. It had been a rough couple of days, and she was exhausted, ready to head back to Palo Alto.

"What's the e-mail, anyway? Good news? You're smiling."

With a swipe, Adam saved the e-mail message before shutting down his phone.

"It was nobody, Amelia. Just spam."